The Scorns of Time

The Scorns of Time

A Novel

Ardythe Ashley

warbler press

First Warbler Press Edition 2025

warblerpress.com

ISBN 978-1-965684-96-2 (paperback)
ISBN 978-1-965684-97-9 (e-book)

In loving memory of my sister, Doreen.

CONTENTS

I. So long a life.

"**W**HO'S THERE?" CRIED out Elsinora fearfully into the darkness upon the approach of unfamiliar footsteps. Sword held tightly in her hand she turned to face the intruder whose menacing presence she could only faintly distinguish from the looming shadows. She thrust the sword at the instant he lunged, and she felt it's blade penetrate yielding flesh, striking hard against bone, and then his crushing weight fell against her, pushing her out of bed onto the floor with a thud that abruptly returned her to wakefulness.

"Oh for God's sake," she muttered. "Not again!"

Lying flat on the floor next to her bed, she felt both the relief of knowing the intruder had been prowling only the battlements of her sleeping mind, and annoyed that she had once again been thrashing at ghosts in the night.

She felt jolted, but unhurt. The thick padding which was installed under the Oriental carpeting had done its job, cushioning her fall, though she would probably need to call Hesper for some assistance in getting her old framework up, and back into place. Sometimes she was she nimble. Often, not.

From this prone position, the copper glow of the nightlight melding into the silver light of a waxing moon changed the known world into an other-world.

Her bedroom was spacious, with comfortable chairs and

solid furniture handcrafted of oak and mahogany, now out of fashion, but with the strength to endure until fashion returned. Small artworks were displayed here and there, treasures she had collected over the years, sometimes to encourage a developing artist, but often purely for the pleasure they brought to her eye. She found it interesting to view her possessions from this curious angle and in this ghostly light.

Her assortment of perfectly cast bronze animals had thrown moon-shadows onto the walls large enough to scare little children; the running dog turned into a menacing, wolf-like creature; the tiny cat with the raised paws enlarged into a pouncing mountain lion.

Her eyes roamed the bright, realistic paintings that she enjoyed by daylight. Now they had blended into gray abstracts. Her glazed ceramic pots appeared to hold flowers that were sleeping under a spell.

It amused her to lay in the posture of the grave, her arms crossed over her chest like a marble sculpture on a sepulcher, and for a few peaceful moments she gazed at the ceiling which seemed far away, farther than a night sky. If she could fall upwards she would disappear into its vast darkness, as she had once plunged downwards and vanished into bottomless blackness. She remembered this event all too well.

Years ago, shortly after the death of her husband, Oliver-Paul, she was playing the thankless role of Gertrude in a Broadway production of *Hamlet*. Upon her entrance she had plunged from the top of a staircase placed stage-left in the Mark Hellinger Theater. The steps were designed to represent the upper reaches of Elsinore Castle, but the stagehands, after rolling the stairs into place, had not secured the construction to the floorboards properly, and when she had taken a step forward, as she said the words "...our o'er hasty marriage"...the structure had unexpectedly skidded and she pitched down head first from the topmost tier, missing the edge of the stage by inches and on into the cavernous orchestra pit.

The collision with the floor was extreme. Elsinora, like everyone, was accustomed to soft landings onto a bed, or the grace of an airplane touching down, or the sinking of feet into the warm sand on a beach, not the sudden shock of unyielding concrete. She had put out her hands in an instinctive gesture to protect her head and the bones of her arms, though shattering on impact, had saved her life.

Lying helpless then, she had remained conscious for mere seconds, only long enough to feel wonderment that she lived. Tonight, so many decades later, she still did.

"But soft, methinks I scent the morning air," she whispered as the dawn insinuated its way into the bedroom through the mullioned windows. Elsinora was pleased to right herself and stand without Hesper's help. With this success she began the 30,822nd day of her life.

II. Jangled out of time and harsh.

ON HEARING HIS prognosis, Fletcher Mulcaster felt a set of timpani drums roll over his chest. He sat upright in the comfortable chair facing the doctor's neatly arranged and well-polished desk, behind which, it seemed to him, the elderly physician was trying his best to disappear.

"I am so very sorry. There is nothing that medicine can do for you at this juncture," were his words.

"Don't look so stricken, Dr. Schadad. Life imitates art. Think of *Hamlet*. In the end, everyone dies."

"The world will be a lesser place without you and your music, Mr. Mulcaster," said the doctor, with heartfelt sadness. His eyes glistened. He took a moment to adjust his glasses, pushing them back along his nose and then forward into their original position, giving himself the time he needed to resume his composure. He had never fully mastered the skill of professional detachment.

Fletcher, who noticed the gesture, was touched. "I think after all these many years, and certainly after such a profound communication, you should call me Fletcher."

He steadied his breathing, allowing his eyes to travel around the physician's familiar consultation room. Cheerful framed Audubon prints of brightly colored birds decorated the paneled walls. A ficus tree thrived, against all odds, in a sunless corner.

The desk displayed a framed photo of the doctor's family: wife, now deceased, three healthy-looking children, now grown. There was a rainbow-colored paperweight brought home from a summer's trip to Venice, a brass paperknife, and a large plastic ashtray shaped in the form of a human skull, positioned on the desk to remind the doctor's patients not to smoke. And there, lying dead center, was the file folder with his name on the tab, his ominous fate enclosed within. He wondered if Dr. Schadad was the last doctor alive whose medical records were still committed to paper, not as mere blips on a computer screen.

Fletcher reached out and lifted the forbidding ashtray. It was smooth to the touch, ivory-colored and life-like, if that could be said of a skull. He turned it over in his hands. It seemed to say: "You will soon look like me." He set it back onto the desk, none too gently. "How long?"

"Three months would be most optimistic. Less is likely. Enough time for you to get your affairs in order."

"My affairs are seldom in order, doctor, and there have been so very many of them." He shook his head with a bemused smile. "But you are talking about documents, not people, aren't you? Those I shall attend to. Much pain?"

"Morphine will ease you out." He slid a prescription across the desk to Fletcher, who took it gratefully, folded it neatly, and tucked it into his suit pocket like a starched handkerchief.

"Anyone ever beat this?"

"Not to my knowledge, Maestro...Mr. Mulcaster...Fletcher."

"Thank you for being so forthright, doctor. Now buck up. Maybe your next patient will only have the flu."

The doctor stood up slowly, a little awkwardly, his age an encumbrance. He was inwardly somewhat embarrassed that in this delicate moment it was the patient offering words of solace, not the other way around.

Fletcher watched the doctor thoughtfully. Dr. Schadad was still an attractive man, distinguished, with a full head of icy white hair and gray, perceptive eyes. Awkwardness aside, there was a grace to his person, and a kindness in him that seemed as natural as his breathing. He had gotten shorter, Fletcher noticed, as have I, as do all men who touch eighty. Our arches fall, and gravity has its way with the rest of the architecture.

Fletcher was aware of every inch of his own body, now humbled and aching from mortal illness. In his youth he had been favored with handsome features, a strong jaw, deep-set eyes, and thick, black hair giving him the brooding look of a well-cast Mr. Darcy, though underneath his stoic features he harbored a lightness of heart which always surprised people; but when he mounted a podium to conduct an orchestra, or lead his beloved choir, he maintained a commanding presence.

An ancient wall clock struck a tentative, slightly flat, g-major chime to mark the half-hour and instantly Bach's Brandenburg Concerto Number 3 began to play in Fletcher's mind. The tempo was too fast, as though the music was hurrying to be heard before…before what? Death. He took a deep sustaining breath and slowed the music down, bowing his head slightly as if in meditation.

He "had the music," as the Irish would say. Since boyhood he remembered every note he had ever heard, and could play any instrument he touched, achieving considerable proficiency on the pipe organ where eyes, ears, hands, arms, feet, heart and soul were all demanded in order to bring forth its sonorous music, but his claim to fame was as a conductor, where the entire orchestra became an even more powerful instrument.

At the conclusion of the first movement of his inner concerto, Fletcher looked up. The doctor was leaning against the edge of the desk watching him patiently.

He spoke hesitantly. "Fletcher, do you mind if I ask you yet again?"

"About Elsinora? Of course I don't mind. I saw her only last week and she seemed fine. Unlike myself, she appears to be in excellent health. Her current housekeeper watches her with narrowed eyes, though I believe the woman genuinely cares for her. Elsinora is, as always, her feisty self."

"Feisty? I never experienced her as such."

"Over her long life she has appeared in many guises to many people."

Fletcher noticed an expression of disquiet settle into the lines of the old man's face; the eyes brightened while the jaw grew tense. It was a look he had seen before, whenever Elsinora was discussed. Fletcher knew the good doctor still loved her, even after so many years. What a painfully long time love can linger, he mused.

"It saddens me to think of her so much alone."

Fletcher, as was his nature, sought to be reassuring. "Elsinora is no Miss Havisham covered in cobwebs, although she once played that part off-Broadway to much acclaim."

"I read those reviews."

"Of course you did. The acting stopped about five years ago, and she no longer endeavors to tutor or teach, but she often comes into the city to enjoy a play or to attend one of my concerts. And, for better or worse, she has had me as a friend, propping up her saggy moods whenever it's been necessary, for all these many years."

Fletcher sighed heavily, his situation darkening his thoughts. The inner music had ceased. "I plan to visit her the day after tomorrow. As strong as she is, I fear she will take my news very badly."

"But you are being very brave."

Fletcher brought himself to his feet. He shook the physician's hand firmly and smiled ruefully. "Not brave, Dr. Schadad. British. But I must admit, this is a terrible way to start the day."

III. All pressures past.

"BRIEF LET US be," said Elsinora, impatient to be outside in the delicate morning air and away from what she experienced as the tiresome concerns of running a life.

"This one is exciting," offered Hesper, as she read quickly through an invitation, handwritten on heavy blue vellum embossed with gold lettering. "The Academy wants to give you a lifetime achievement award."

"They must be desperate," replied Elsinora.

"No. Seriously. They are inviting you to accept the award onstage at next year's Oscar presentation. They will arrange for your travel and hotel and, oh my, Lance Brilliante will present the award!"

"I saw his work in that ghastly film where he was sucked down a whirlpool, or up a tornado, or maybe it was into a drainpipe. I can't remember which. Just as well. I was not impressed with his acting ability."

"But he is the biggest name going these days."

"More's the pity."

"This invitation is awfully nice though. Will you accept?"

Hesper anticipated the answer before it was given. She had worked for Elsinora for twelve years now, in the beginning hired solely as a housekeeper-cook. Soon the responsibilities of secretary came her way and, because they were compatible, she became a companion as well. She combined the work of three people without difficulty. Elsinora compensated her with three salaries.

"I escaped Hollywood's clutches decades ago, as you know perfectly well, Hesper. I have made every effort to forget I was ever there, and have hoped to be forgotten in return. Why in my dotage would I wish to be shoved under spotlights to be gaped at by a crowd of strangers a quarter of my age?"

"You still keep your Oscars on the mantelpiece in your library, so your work there must have been important to you once upon a time," countered Hesper.

"And once upon a time was quite enough. My Oscars sit next to the laughing Buddha for a reason. To remind me that it is folly to worship invented gods."

"It says here that the award is not only for your work in the movies, but also on Broadway. I know your stage career mattered to you. They mention you were a renowned acting teacher as well, so it really is for a lifetime's achievement." She handed the letter to Elsinora who placed it on the surface of the desk without a glance.

"No."

Hesper was acquainted with the many nuances of tone in which her employer said the word no. This one had the ring of finality, but it had been tempered with a touch of gentleness in consideration of Hesper's disappointment.

She retrieved the letter and read it through again. Though it would be a disruption to their well-ordered life she decided that this was far too important an honor for Elsinora to dismiss so readily. Uncharacteristically, she decided to press the matter further, just a bit.

"Why not talk the proposal over with Fletcher Mulcaster, before I send a reply?"

"Hesper, really. You can be most annoying." Elsinora sighed. "When is he coming by?"

"The day after tomorrow."

"Good. Be sure to contrive the potent sangria that he likes so much. I will mention the matter to him, but I can tell you right now, he will agree with me. He knows better than to mount an opposition that will fail. You could learn from him."

"Mr. Mulcaster accepts awards all the time."

"Fletcher is still working, and he loves standing in the spotlight. You don't take up conducting unless you enjoy being at the epicenter of attention. Bake up some of your almond cookies to go with the sangria. Those are so delicious. Now I'm going to go outside for awhile. Reading, thinking. Rewards come from within."

Smiling a relieved smile to be free of the office, Elsinora arose and walked carefully out, without her cane, a book in each hand. Today she carried Shakespeare's *Hamlet* in her left, and a journal in the right.

She left Hesper with the tasks of tidying up the desk, paying the bills, and doing whatever else was necessary to keep Arden Manor, her overlarge home, in proper running order.

The house, built a century past, was of granite with a slate roof and stood in a secluded spot on the shore of a small, private Connecticut lake. With the exception of the trim lawn and an enclosed terrace garden Elsinora had allowed acres of the spacious property to return to an expanse of wild meadow fringed with new growth forest, offering sanctuary to native creatures. She had purchased her home with the money invested from her film career, as well as the settlement she had received from the stage accident. She maintained it with the funds that arrived periodically as her movies underwent a series of reincarnations on television, videotape, DVDs, and streaming channels.

Arden Manor was located close enough to New York City for her to commute when a challenging acting role, one she had actually been interested in playing, was offered to her, and for the classes she taught at prestigious Thespian Atelier. She was past all those pursuits now, but she loved being rooted here in this gracious house.

Having a beautiful home in which to retire is compensation enough, she thought. A lifetime achievement award indeed! The arrogance of these puffed up people, preening and prancing about and bestowing honors on one other! She laughed softly. She wasn't having any part of it. She supposed the offer was well-intentioned, but her forty years of reclusiveness should mean something to even the most thick-headed promoter, should it not?

She wasn't the first celebrity to run for cover. Greta Garbo was famous for repeating: "I want to be alone." Hedy Lamarr refused even to see her own family. Katherine Hepburn was happiest alone; not that Elsinora particularly wished to be solitary, and she had no family left to avoid; but her life, as she had carefully arranged it, was a private one, seemingly a concept that was unknown to current generations.

As she made her way slowly through the house she passed the library and peered in to view the line of Oscar statuettes on the mantelpiece. She hadn't paid any attention to those gilded and gelded apparitions for a very long time. It was Hesper who kept them from gathering dust. The late morning light danced in from the French windows and caught their golden curves. They glistened seductively. False fire, she thought.

Achieving the garden room Elsinora threw open the doors to the terrace and stepped outside. She stood quietly for a few moments enjoying the view of the expansive lawn, the shimmering lake, and then with a satisfied smile she proclaimed with her well-trained voice: "And this our life, exempt from public haunt, finds tongues in trees, books in the running brooks, sermons in stones, and good in everything."

Having delivered the line from *As You Like It* to her personal satisfaction she smiled, thankful to be once again standing in a spotlight of dazzling spring sun.

IV. In duty bound.

HESPER, LEFT to her responsibilities in the confines of her well-appointed office, took Elsinora's concession to confer about the achievement award with Fletcher as a small victory.

She turned her attention to a bill from the plumbing company, which was marked overdue, and was not. She considered marking it overcharged and sending it back, but decided instead to have a sharp word with their bookkeeper. Other mundane tasks would make up her morning, though her mind kept coaxing her away from the paperwork on her desk to visions of Hollywood.

Hesper Ford had a husband, though she seldom mentioned him to Elsinora, or discussed the part of her life that ran alongside his. She assumed her employer was disapproving of Barton, as was Hesper herself, but he needed attention from time to time and she was his wife, so periodically, dutifully, she made an appearance at the apartment they had once shared. Living apart was a choice they now agreed was best for them both.

At the age of fifty-two Hesper was content in the work of maintaining Arden Manor and in caring for Elsinora, whose unbending nature made day-to-day choices easy and the running of her home conflict-free. Hesper simply arranged everything to Elsinora's satisfaction and although from time to time it was necessary to mention the occasional doctor's appointment (always resisted) or the prescribed egg (always declined),

Hesper had determined, long ago, that there was nothing to be gained by entering into arguments with her employer. She had nothing to learn from Fletcher in that regard.

Hesper did not mind the fact that her own choices and desires often needed to be subjugated to those of Elsinora. It was Elsinora's home, after all, and it was Elsinora's life she was employed to assist. The result was a harmonious working arrangement and, of course, the very substantial paycheck. The truth was that although eccentric, and often remote, Elsinora Dean Harding was unfailingly kind to her, unlike Barton.

It was a fine morning. After clearing the desk and setting the table for lunch, Hesper assured herself that Elsinora was settled comfortably in the Adirondack chair by the lake. Then she returned to her bedroom and packed a small bag with her overnight needs.

Hesper, who was blessed with an unusually even temperament, gave little thought to herself, but because she was going out she paused before her bedroom mirror. There was her fifty-ish face looking back at her, composed, colorless, and pleasantly plain. Bland, she thought, but she was clean. She was neat. She was healthy. Those attributes were good enough. She wondered for a moment how she would look if she managed to exist into her eighties as Elsinora had done. Not much different, she supposed. She tucked a strand of graying hair back into her bun and, satisfied with her appearance, thought no more about it.

This morning Hesper felt glad to be out of her housekeeper's role. A change now and then was good for the soul, she believed, though her needs were modest. She had chosen a comfortable, if somewhat dated, blue suit for her time in the city. She also wore sensible shoes as she planned to window-shop and have a stroll in Central Park after paying her respects to the remains of her marriage.

She made her way to the front entry hall, a spacious room in which the rare visitors to Arden Manor were received. The hall had been built to impress, and Elsinora had left it as she found it when she purchased the house. There was an intricately tiled flooring which Hesper kept waxed to perfection, a cavernous ceiling, arched windows, life-sized family portraits of God-knew-who, and even a suit of shining armor standing guard just inside the door below a set of crossed spears. What had the previous owner been thinking?

"Now you behave yourself while I'm gone," she whispered to the suit of armor as she passed by.

Having checked for dust or disarray as she crossed the room, and finding none, she settled herself in an antique Savonarola chair, one of a pair that kept each other company near the outer door, and there she waited patiently clutching her small valise, her fingers opening and closing the clasp with a satisfying snap as she anticipated two days of personal freedom, albeit some of the time sacrificed to her husband.

Robbie and Geraldo Fitz-Marco would arrive momentarily. These two men were long-time friends and admirers of Elsinora. They were always enthusiastic when called upon to help out. Robbie was tall and reserved, Geraldo short and rotund with a smile that almost never left his rosy face. As unalike as the two were in appearance they were always thought of, and referred to, in the plural like salt and pepper or ham and eggs.

The queer old men were a pair of retired drama critics, and both had been entranced by the glamorous Elsinora since her earliest acting days on the New York stage. They had remained devoted to her for fifty years, not just because for a short time she had become Hollywood's darling in the golden era of big screen movies, but because of her indisputable talent as a serious actress, and her incredible knowledge of Shakespeare, the performance of which she had taught at the Thespian Atelier for so many years. And they, unlike some people, respected the choice she had made in mid-life to avoid the garish spotlight, to only appear in roles that interested her, in plays she respected, often on obscure off-off Broadway stages.

Hesper knew that Robbie and Geraldo would look after her elderly charge adequately. Of course, Elsinora had ritually declared she did not need looking after, but Hesper insisted that if she didn't, the house certainly did. It was enormous and though beautiful, it was old and something was always going amiss. On that basis Elsinora agreed to the men's presence from time to time when Hesper requested a weekend away.

Hesper liked Robbie and Geraldo well enough and judged the pair to be almost competent. She suspected that they were both in their late sixties, although they took great care in maintaining youthful appearances. Their hairpieces were first-rate and she suspected "work" had been done on their respective lean and chubby faces. They would attend to Elsinora's needs and manage any unforeseen problems, calling Hesper swiftly back if needed.

She knew that once she was gone the three old people would sit around gossiping about Iago or Hamlet or Macbeth quite ardently, as if they were problematic next-door neighbors. They would eat potato chips and order in pizza and drink too much and have a very good time together.

Whenever she stepped outside the domain of Elsinora, as she was about to do today, the concerns of her personal life reasserted themselves. She was particularly troubled by Barton's most recent project, and the demands he was making on her in its regard.

Hesper heard the sound of a car as it pulled up to the front entrance, and she stood up, smoothing her skirt, ready to go. She felt, only at that last moment, a peculiar reluctance to depart. Too late, she thought, as the doorbell chimed. She opened the door to the eager faces of Robbie and Geraldo.

"We told the taxi to wait for you, dearest Hesper."

"Do you need a hand with your bag?"

"How is our darling Elsinora today?"

"Oh, you do look nice."

Their words came tumbling out, and before she could understand her sudden resistance to departure she had been bundled into the cab. An hour later the taxi pulled up outside the familiar address in midtown Manhattan and she understood it perfectly.

Crossing the empty lobby and standing at the apartment door she hesitated again. There was something oppressive about this place, the building's entrance, and the door itself with its too-many coats of glossy black paint and broken peep-hole. The apartment was on the ground floor of a solid pre-war building, jammed between two modern high-rises that blocked all the light. There was absolutely nothing to recommend it but the convenience of being in the heart of the city. It wasn't run-down, and the outdated public spaces were kept clean enough, but it stood without character or charm housing tenants like Hesper and Barton who had moved in decades before and refused to move out because the draconian rent laws rendered it unaffordable to live anywhere else in the city; people who, like most New Yorkers, had imagined wild success was in their future when they were young, and knew better by middle-age.

She leaned forward, pressing her ear to the thick wood. She could hear Barton, who was expecting her, rooting around inside. She imagined him, unkempt, unhappy, prowling about like a caged bear. She had nothing for him, yet felt there was nothing for it but to enter. She was, after all, Mrs. Barton Ford.

She stood there a minute longer before taking out her key. It was like staring at a doorway to nothing.

For better or worse, Hesper took a deep breath, put the key in the lock, turned it, opened the door, and stepped inside.

V. The matter that you read.

ELSINORA DEAN HARDING was possessed of a spectacular memory. On days like today when the weather was fine, her habit was to sit near the edge of the lake in the bright red Adirondack chair that was missing a slat. There she mused, turning the years of her life over in her mind like the pages of a novel, letting her associations ebb and flow, though they tended to keep circling around the puzzles that still troubled her. Of late she had felt an impulse to write her memories down. She had begun to make entries in a handsome, satin-covered journal meant for her eyes only. Her love of literature demanded that she impose some order to her thoughts, to arrange her memories reasonably, to make some sense of them. She was enjoying the challenge.

It was difficult for her to hold a pen for very long. Although the splintered bones in her hands and arms had knitted back together decades ago, her joints began to protest if they felt mistreated. So she wrote only a little at a time. There was no rush.

The Journal of Elsinora Dean Harding
May 1st, 2024
I have often wondered what Hamlet's life would have been like if he had survived that bloody last act. He was, all told,

responsible for the deaths of eight characters: Polonius, Ophelia, Rosencranz, Guildenstern, Claudius, Gertrude, Laertes, and himself. But what if he had survived that poison-tipped sword, if he had been left alive with his loyal friend Horatio at his side?

Left to pick up the pieces of his life and go on, what would he have felt in old age looking back on the deeds of his youth. Guilt, shame, regret, anger? Would he have led a life broken in spirit? Or might he have found love again and in its healing embrace found the strength for a life of accomplishment and pride?

I have not been responsible for the deaths of so many people as Hamlet. One. Arguably, two. They sit, unable to rest, in my conscience even now, so many decades later.

I know that reminiscence is a gift, granted to some, denied to many. It is a luxury to be able to think over my whole life, yes, but also the meaning of that life and, to put a finer point on it, the meaning of life itself.

To have been or not to have been? That is my question.

Elsinora leaned back and looked upwards. Today the sky presented her with a panorama of puffy white clouds. Her eyes travelled down to their reflections moving across the water like a pod of gentle white whales swimming along the surface of the lake.

It is a day when I feel grateful to still be alive, not one of my dark days when I don't see much point in carrying on. I have endured such hopeless days bereft of light and enjoyment throughout my life, bleak days that arrive and depart of their own accord, so I am not surprised when they periodically come to visit me now in old age. I have learned

over the years to quietly wait them out, knowing that they,
like the clouds, will pass; but I have no need of such forbear-
ance today.

The humidity is low so my joints, which have grown
truly impractical, are not yet demanding apology. The sun
is warming the winter from my being. Inside and out there
is lightness.

She laid her journal aside and picked up her worn copy of
Hamlet, bound in soft brown leather, a material no longer used
in book-binding, gentle on her fingertips. She decided to open
it at random and read a line or two, eager see where the words
would send her mind. Her finger fell upon a line by the mad
Ophelia: "There's rosemary, that's for remembrance. Pray you,
love, remember."

The year was 1944 and her remembered self was standing before a librarian's desk. She was four years old, and her
nose did not quite clear its edge. She held the selected volume
clasped to her chest, her fingers aware of its weight and size.
The book seemed to pulse with life as her heart beat against the
shiny cover enclosing its precious pages. It was her first time in
a library, and this was her first selection.

"Hand me the book, dear," said Mrs. Kellogg, a woman of
imposing size wearing thick spectacles and displaying a brooch
of many colors on her high, ruffled collar. She was holding a
metal date stamp at the ready. Elsinora slid the book onto the
desk, past the sign reading SILENCE PLEASE, and watched fascinated as a card was slipped out of the pocket inside the back
cover. The stamp came down on a black ink pad with a satisfying thunk, then onto the card, which was about to be slipped
back into sleeve when the librarian hesitated.

"This is the date by which you must return the book," she

said, pointing with the stub of a yellow pencil to the newly inked line. "Otherwise you will be charged five cents for each day that it is late. Do you understand?"

She nodded.

"This is a book for third graders. Will your mommy read it to you?"

"I can read it all by myself."

The library in this dying Ohio town was a quiet place, empty at present but for the two of them, and the librarian had seemed amused by her; a tiny, precocious child with soft Shirley Temple curls wearing a blue checkered pinafore. Mrs. Kellogg handed over the book.

"Will you show me?"

Obligingly, Elsinora began with the title: *"Uncle Bennie's Bedtime Stories. Volume One.* By Benjamin Herbert Johnson."

Mrs. Kellogg smiled approvingly.

Although the remembered face of Mrs. Kellogg had faded over the years, her smile, like that of the Cheshire Cat in *Alice in Wonderland,* lingered in Elsinora's mind, shining up through time, merging with the shimmer of haze hovering above the lake's surface. Mrs. Kellogg's smile was unexpectedly tender, softening the lines of her well-worn face, and it was an encouraging smile. Elsinora had need of encouragement. As she opened the book and prepared to read what was inside, the heavy doors of the library were flung open and her mother, her angry mother, grabbed her by the shoulder.

"There you are! Do you want to scare me to death?" She was shaken so violently that the book dropped from her small hands onto the floor. "If you ever run away from me again you will get what's for."

As Elsinora twisted free to retrieve the volume, her mother spoke to the librarian, whose smile had vanished into a frown of woman-to-woman disapproval. "I'm sorry to be so loud, Mrs. Kellogg," said her mother, "but she was right next to me in the grocery store, and in the next minute she was gone. Like to give me a heart attack. A woman out on the sidewalk said she saw her come running in here."

She turned back to her daughter. "Why did you do that?"

"There are books in here."

"Well, they are not your books. Put that back and come along."

Mrs. Kellogg spoke then in a voice that was low and calculated, holding the unmistakable weight of authority, "She is checking the book out."

"How could she do that with no library card?"

"I was just about to issue her one. What is the child's name?"

Her mother's mouth pursed in exasperation. "Her name is Nora Ellen Dean, but she refuses to answer to any name but Elsinora, which she made up herself and—oh, we don't have time for all this!" She took the volume roughly into her own hand and slapped it back onto the desk. With a defiant look at the librarian she began to pull Elsinora towards the doors.

"Wait a moment, Greta Dean," said Mrs. Kellogg, again using a commanding, but somewhat gentler tone. The librarian had watched the children of Warrensville grow up and turn out over the years, and from behind her desk she kept abreast of all the goings on in the town. "A book can keep a child out of a peck of trouble. You've got your hands full all alone there with Kingsley away at the war, God save him. Let her take it. She can keep it. You won't be sorry."

Her mother, hearing truth in the librarian's words, reluctantly returned and awkwardly accepted the gift.

"Thank you, kindly" she managed to say, not accustomed to generosity from other women. She handed the treasure to her daughter.

Elsinora, recording the scene in her journal, added:

I have only loved one other person in this life so purely as, in that moment, I loved Mrs. Kellogg. I have kept the book all these many years because when my eyes fall upon it, I think of her with endless appreciation.

A voice from the house interrupted her reverie.

"Elsinora, dear one. It is almost time for our luncheon."

"I hear you, Geraldo. I'm coming back," Elsinora replied, her thoughts divided between 1944 and 2024.

Startled by the sound of their voices, a large white heron stalked out from its hiding place among the reeds and stared in Elsinora's direction.

She had once, at a Manhattan dinner party, been told by a peculiar man who was wearing a spotty tie and a gold ring on every finger, that the heron was her spirit animal. How such a man could know such a thing, if there was such a thing, had amused her. The elegant bird was by nature patient, the man had informed her, dabbing at his greasy chin with a napkin as he finished up his roast chicken.

This heron was a beautiful creature, graceful, observant, and reserved. The bird turned away and stood quietly again, eyes upon the water waiting for a fish to emerge from the clouds.

"Good morning, Mrs. Harding. I'll help you inside," offered a visiting nurse who had come silently up behind her. "I will do a quick check before you and your friends have your lunch," she said officiously. "Here, let me help you out of that chair. You haven't been trying to read in this glaring light, have you?"

"Only my own mind," she replied.

The nurse extended a hand which Elsinora ignored. She lifted herself up into a standing position, pushing against the chair's broad, flat arms, one hand clutching the journal. The volume of *Hamlet* slid from her lap onto the grass.

"It's like you are sitting in a big red bucket," said the nurse, bending to retrieve the book for her.

"So much depends upon a red Adirondack chair."

The nurse, finding no meaning in the remark, ignored it and attempted to take Elsinora's arm to help her towards the house. Elsinora shook her off.

"I can do it myself!" So much for my heron-like patience, she thought.

Elsinora walked with careful steps across the smooth, green lawn that stretched from the muddy edges of the lake up to the flagstone terrace, appreciating the pink flowering trees and fuchsia azaleas as she went. She paused to ponder a bed of pansies bordering the herb garden by the patio, and stared down at their new little faces which seemed to look right back up at her.

"There's rosemary, that's for remembrance. Pray you, love, remember. And there is pansies, that's for thoughts," she quoted. Then added, "I never did care much for Ophelia, but at least she died romantically."

"I am sorry for your loss," said the nurse.

"Oh you are not!" replied Elsinora. "You haven't a clue who Ophelia even is." And she preceded the confused woman into the house.

Once inside Elsinora submitted stoically to the further annoyances of the nurse.

"Your blood pressure is a little elevated."

"A recent brush with hypocrisy," Elsinora replied.

The nurse inserted a tongue depressor into her mouth and peered down her throat. Her heart rate and oxygen levels were noted. Her eyes were looked into, and her glasses cleaned. She stood on the scale to be weighed and measured, but when the nurse started asking questions about her digestion, which to her was a private matter, she felt she had endured quite enough.

She dismissed the young woman as gently as impatience would allow, and proceeded eagerly to the dining room.

Before taking her leave for the weekend, Hesper had prepared a meal that would also be enjoyed by Robbie and Geraldo. She knew the men would prefer a steak or pork chops, but Elsinora ate only plants and did not allow what she referred to as dead animals into the house. It was Hesper's unspoken belief that the vegetarian diet was Elsinora's way of dealing with the physical insults of great age; some people ran to doctors for every ache or bump, others popped pills, some turned to prayer. Elsinora ate spinach.

"Oh look at this feast that Hesper has left us," enthused Robbie, who for all his wiry build was a great lover of food.

There were wedges of honeydew melon with lemon served on austere white bone china, followed by butternut soup with nutmeg and cardamon, perfectly grilled tomato slices with a Balsamic reduction, and baked peppers stuffed with saffron rice. For dessert there was a compote of baked pears with brandy sauce.

They ate together quietly and companionably for awhile. Then Geraldo broke the silence with a suggestion.

"Maybe we could plan a little party for your birthday next Sunday, Elsinora. What do you think?"

"Eighty-five is a grand number," chimed in Robbie with a smile.

"We can invite all my dead friends," replied Elsinora, "though I fear that even this grand dining room will not be large enough to accommodate them all."

She waved her arm at the enormous expanse of polished mahogany table with its twenty-four matching chairs that had once been intimate with the rumps of many a famous person. But that was years ago, before the death of her husband, the stage and screen director, Oliver-Paul. Fellow actors had enjoyed the meals presented here, but also politicians and noted business men who were the money-bags of her husband's endeavors. He never invited another director though, wanting no one to steal his limelight. All ghosts now.

"So, that would be a no?"

"Yes, a no. I have grown faint of parties. Now take the rest of this afternoon for yourselves. I'm going to nap and read. Please excuse me, but I won't be having dinner tonight. I haven't much appetite in the evenings anymore. Order in whatever you like," she said, folding her linen napkin, which signaled the end of the meal.

Replete with compote, the men nodded, then began to tidy up and put the dishes in the washer. Following Hesper's written instructions they began to lay the kitchen table for Elsinora's breakfast in the morning, for they all knew she preferred to wake up to an orderly house.

Looking up from their chores they watched the elderly woman arise from the table and, taking her books, for there were always books, she left the dining room on measured steps.

"She remains such a beautiful woman," whispered Robbie.

"For all her many years," agreed Geraldo.

"I am loving the way she piles up her silvery hair onto her head these days."

"Yes, it reveals that still graceful neck."

Her features were elegant and her skin, though not without lines, glowed with health. And those sky-blue eyes, they thought. She had been famous for those eyes and they remained clear and wide, seeming never to miss a thing, and the alertness giving her features an unexpected youthfulness.

"It helps when you are old to have been beautiful when young," said Robbie.

Meanwhile, Elsinora made her way to the library, her favorite room, where she settled herself in a maroon velvet Queen Anne chair, well-worn on the arms, deep in offered comfort. After listening to some Bach harpsichord music and then a Mozart piano concerto she drifted off into a pleasant sleep and awoke from her nap feeling refreshed and content.

Using the intercom she requested a cup of Earl Grey tea, which the men were pleased to bring her along with some English biscuits. Respecting her desire for solitude they withdrew to the recesses of the manor.

The morning's cloud-whales in the lake had put her in mind of *Moby Dick* and she perused the floor-to-ceiling bookshelves, arranged precisely according to the Dewey Decimal System. The novel was where it should be and although she knew her eyes would tire, she took down the heavy book, resumed the luxury of the chair, and placed the volume on her lap, before deciding to write another entry in her journal.

I relish the feel of a book in my hands, any book. I am always soothed by the sight of ink on paper, and I enjoy the scent of the humanity trapped within the pages. Rereading a well-worn favorite is a particular pleasure as it offers the discovery of something new within the old.

I believe that every book a person chooses to read changes their life forever in ways subtle or obvious, so one must be careful when opening a book.

As the reader's brain absorbs the march of words across the pages, their neurons enliven, connect, and re-connect, forming new patterns of thought; the sentences they read transform the person into a slightly different creature with each turn of a page, influencing how they will live, where they will go, what they should fear; even determining the kind of person they might choose to marry, or whether to marry at all. Like beckoning spirits, the lines of a book, the words of a script, the verses of a poem lead the reader ever onwards...one phrase after another, prodding souls gently, relentlessly, along the passage of time towards their demise.

What have all the books I have read made of me? I wonder. What kind of person has emerged at this time of life from the thousands of volumes I have absorbed as the decades passed; from the scripts I have read, and the parts I have played? A precocious child became a withdrawn adolescent, then an eager college student, an energetic lover, a successful actress, a wife, a movie star, a woman cunning enough to murder, a skilled teacher, and now at the last, simply an ancient woman clutching a book?

The fragile child I once was, standing before the librarian's desk, did not know it was transformation that would occur, did not know that is what she desired.

She only knew she must read.

The elderly woman who Elsinora was now felt the weight of fatigue descending like a heavy curtain down through her being so suddenly that even the prospect of arising and undressing for bed seemed impossible. The pen slipped from cramped fingers onto the floor where she let it lay.

This is an unwelcome feature of my age, she thought, awakening from a nap bursting with energy, and then as if someone has pulled a plug, feeling it all drain away. Rather than attempt to write any more, or to read as she had intended, she closed her eyes and slumped back into the enclosing wing of the armchair where Robbie would find her still sleeping the next morning and, for a moment, fear she was dead.

VI. Not to be.

FLETCHER MULCASTER WAS puzzling over what to do with his belongings. No one younger than fifty would want his brown furniture, finely hand-wrought as it was. Nor would they care for his library, extensive as it was. People nowadays sat on re-cycled plastic chairs and read on screens. He could think of no friend who needed furnishings, or had the room for a thousand books. Elsinora had taught him to love books when they were young, bless her, but her own library was more extensive even than his own.

And the clothes. What was he to do with the clothes? His Saville Row suits and Grenson black dress Oxfords, all polished to a mirror finish? They marked him as a privileged white male; the kind whom slender young persons of any and all genders would doubtless assume had abused his privilege, although he had not. He had worked his way up the bars of the musical ladder from absolutely nothing. He should be forgiven for dressing well when he became successful, and frankly his profession required it. He could hardly stand in front of a philharmonic orchestra dressed in jeans and flip-flops. He would choose the most elegant of his extravagant wardrobe to be buried in and then— well, he must think of something. He wondered if there was a charity eager to collect used tuxedos.

He did not want to die. Did anyone in their right mind?

There was too much music yet to be heard, to be played, to be conducted, to be composed. What if the realm of death was silent? He shuddered at such a possibility.

Surrounding him was a recording of the triumphal music of Beethoven's 9th symphony, a recording by the Vienna Philharmonic under his baton when he was guest conductor. The joyful sounds filled his sitting room, a radiant emanation from his state-of-the-art Bose sound system. That particular item had cost a pretty penny and was entirely worth it. Joshua, his protégé, would appreciate it. He would leave it to Joshua.

The final golden chords of the chorus began to overpower his thoughts, to enter his soul as they unfailingly did. He knew the translation of its swelling message from the German libretto as well as he knew his own name: "Seek him in the heavens: Above the stars must he dwell."

Why then was he fussing about *things?* There was no necessity to give another moment's thought to what he owned. Ownership was the concern of the living.

When the music reached its conclusion Fletcher stood for a moment in the silence that was not silent, but a continuation of the throbbing music in the stillness of his mind. Then, feeling suddenly wobbly, he sat down and poured a forbidden drink from one of his several remaining bottles of Macallan Scotch 18. No need to waste *that* on survivors, he thought, although Elsinora would have an appreciation for it.

Elsinora. Telling her would be tough, and he couldn't bear the idea of her attending his funeral. Theirs was a relationship that belonged to life. He would assign her some curious task to keep her mind busy and her person well away from the cathedral during those solemn services. She would do as he asked because she loved him, and it would be better for her to be preoccupied elsewhere rather than holding herself together while falling apart at a public funeral. People always stared and murmured whenever she appeared. She certainly wouldn't want scrutiny at such a vulnerable time.

He feared she would have little amusement left in her life without him. He had enjoyed his role as her personal court jester, as well as being a serious helpmate through all the decades of friendship; and she had been unfailing in her support of him when he had doubted or failed in his own efforts. She could not help him with death. Death was personal. Everyone goes it alone.

He would leave Elsinora the rest of his Scotch, along with a substantial legacy which she surely did not need. What else could he do for her? He hadn't chosen to go first.

He must tell her soon before his physical powers diminished further. The illness had come on fast, and he was fading faster. Dr. Schadad said there would be no remission. Chemotherapy might retard the inevitable, but would incapacitate him in the process, so he had decided against any delaying tactics. He must inform her while he was still upright and cheerful and able to walk with a steady tempo. He must not mince words or show fear. He mustn't weep. Her last memory of Fletcher Mulcaster would be of a man still strong, confident, and serene. Perhaps that would be a comfort to her. His assurance would be a comfort for him to think it was a comfort for her.

He smiled at himself, noting that he was still fretting about future results. How could he not? Though the future was not his business anymore. It was a relief, in a curious way.

"Oh dear," he gasped. The sudden pain in his abdomen was vociferously explaining why Scotch was now forbidden to him. "Oh, my. Bye bye Macallan 18. More the better for Elsinora."

He made his way to the enclosing softness of his sofa, stopping to restart his Beethoven again, and to take another pill against his distress. To calm himself while the pain subsided he began to make a mental list of all the things that were no longer his concern: the choice of anthem for this year's Christmas service, the disintegration of democracy, that stack of magazines that should be read through and thrown away, the dentistry he had been avoiding, the rogues running the government, the melting of the Arctic icecap, the search for where in all of England his mother might be buried, the over-population of the planet, an overdue American Express bill, raising the money to get the cathedral's organ refurbished, guiding Joshua's career, watering the orchid; one concern tumbling after another. He should have his unfinished to-do list chiseled into his tombstone. Perhaps everyone should, it would make cemeteries more interesting.

He was growing sleepy. The medication was working.

"I shall live only in the present moment as if I were an enlightened being," he murmured to himself, and took a long, slow breath which he rather enjoyed as the pain receded. Perhaps, he thought, the Buddhists are onto something. Or the drug addicts. Then, as he drifted downwards towards a deep sleep, he passed swiftly through a dream of his long ago lost mother. She held him in her arms. She whispered a promise. Was it her voice? Or Elsinora's? "I shall never let you go," she murmured, as he seemed to disintegrate into the dancing notes of a new concerto.

VII. They come not as single spies.

"Is she still asleep?" asked Geraldo of Robbie who had just returned from checking on Elsinora.

"Quite, quite down, but in her library chair. She must have slept there all night."

"What shall we do then?"

"I think we just let her sleep."

"Breakfast?"

"I'd rather wait for her to join us. Let's have a look around to satisfy Hesper."

"I'm not at all comfortable with prying about."

"It's for a good cause, Geraldo. Maybe we'll find something that will make a wonderful contribution to the wonderful book Hesper's husband is writing about a wonderful woman."

"I suppose it's all right then."

"You would think there would be old diaries around here somewhere. She always has a journal at hand nowadays."

"If there were diaries, Hesper would have found them by now, but let's have a peek in the closets again."

"No! I can't do it. It didn't feel right before, and we didn't find anything anyway. We both know Elsinora cherishes her privacy."

"I suppose you're right. Then let's look through her old scrapbooks again. She wouldn't object to that, so it won't bother your conscience. After all, we were the ones who compiled them for her as Christmas gifts. I'm not sure she has ever looked at them though."

"We certainly won't find anything new in those scrapbooks."

"No, but it will be enjoyable just the same. I'll read your reviews of her performances to you, and you read mine to me."

In her library, Elsinora, who was no longer in the least asleep, listened to their conversation on the manor's intercom. She was angered about this poking about in her past in the interests of a new biography that Hesper's untalented husband was determined to write, and which Elsinora had no intention of letting see the light of day. Like Hesper, the two men had been recruited as spies, and like naughty children they would need to be taught a lesson, one they would well remember.

Elsinora knew how much Robbie and Geraldo loved her. She listened to them as they read aloud their rave reviews of her first days on the Broadway stage before Oliver-Paul had gotten hold of her, taken control of her life, and pushed her in front of those wretched Hollywood cameras. They were not bad, the reviews, not bad. Geraldo and Robbie had always been sweet on her, but the other New York critics had concurred. She had been damn fine on a stage.

She did not relax her vigilance until the men had tired themselves out looking at old photos and Playbills, news clippings and autographs, and had put the scrapbooks away.

She arose and began to ready herself for the day.

Her dream during the night had been a kind one. She and Maurice had been walking together peacefully, hand in hand, down an endless hospital corridor following a pure white heron.

VIII. Past is prologue.

THE FOLLOWING DAY, after Hesper's return, and the men's departure, Elsinora sat comfortably at the kitchen table, glad for the resumption of their normal routine.

Feeling nostalgic she had asked for a large bowl of Cheerios, now christened with soy-milk, and sat staring into its soggy depths. She would let Shakespeare guide her writing again today. She reached for the volume resting by her bowl. *The Complete Plays*, and inserted a finger into its pages randomly. It rested on a line from Othello: "How poor are they that have not patience! What wound did ever heal but by degrees?"

How apt. She opened the journal to her past. It was 1944 again.

There I am. Nora Ellen Dean, sitting at the square kitchen table which is covered in worn, red-checkered oilcloth, wishing for my father's promised return. I missed him terribly, and to a lesser degree my Uncle Conroy, my father's younger brother, who had signed up to fight alongside him in the war against Japan and the Nazis. I was barely two years old when they left, but my father, stationed in Austin, Texas, and having been assigned to a safe stateside job involving army requisitions, had visited home at every opportunity, hitching rides on cargo planes between Camp Mabry and the nearby Erie Proving Ground.

The last time he came home, before he was reassigned to Europe, he had picked me up and held me close. His brown wooly army uniform had a soft, scratchy feel. He had looked at my face for a long, long time. He had blue eyes, like me. He had said he loved me many times during the brief visit, but as I was held aloft in this last embrace he said only, "remember me," and then he put me down gently, turned, and was gone.

I remember his essence, his spirit; warm, loving, playful. A handsome man who filled our home with sweet smelling pipe smoke and deep, rich laughter.

He was sent across an ocean to England. I knew about the army. I knew about war. I knew about death. At the age of four I had taught myself to read, and so I knew more about the world than anyone around me could possibly have guessed.

There were no books in our home, so I began by working out words on the cereal boxes at the breakfast table, gripping them in my tiny hands, holding them close to my face: Wheaties, Cheerios, Rice Krispies. Soon I discovered newspapers which were delivered each morning along with the milk bottles. I struggled with the adult words and ideas, searching for news of my father inside the paper's inky folds.

It was in a newspaper that I found the advertisement for Uncle Bennie's Bedtime Stories, Wholesome Reading for Young People.

Grandma Dean, who often visited, explained the meaning of wholesome to me, hugging me all the while. Armed with wholesomeness, I slid off her lap and ran to my mother, certain that she would approve of such books and would grant me a set for my fifth birthday. I received a plush monkey instead.

"Practice patience, dear," counseled my grandmother. "Christmas will come soon."

On some days my mother used the newspaper to wrap up the garbage before I could get hold of it, so I would sit in our small pantry and read the labels on the cans and boxes that lined the shelves: Green Giant Peas, Aunt Jemima Syrup, Lemon Jell-O, Dried Beef. I hungered for words. Spaghetti. Macaroni. Tomato. Potato. Sometimes I fell into a kind of stupor in the dark recess of the cupboard and then watched through half-closed eyes as the letters came to life. Chopped. Scalloped. Minced. Fortified. Reconstituted.

My mother, Greta, bereft of my Father, shouldered the task of raising me, her peculiar daughter, all alone. She thought I was abnormal, and my ability to read at such a young age frightened her.

"There will be time enough for all that when you get to school, Nora Ellen," she declared from within her perpetual cloud of cigarette smoke. "That's what I say."

My desire to read seemed not to matter to her. In the time and place where I grew up it was still believed that children were to be seen, not heard, and to always do what they were told. I was supposed to be in my room playing with dolls or outside with the neighbor kids, none of whom I particularly liked.

Instead, dutifully practicing patience, I would sit on my swing dragging my feet slowly back and forth in the deepening grooves of dirt. I thought a great deal, about a great many things.

Elsinora pushed the cereal bowl aside. She stood, and taking her journal called out to Hesper, just as she had done as a child.

"I am going outside."

It was another fine day and she wanted the warmth of the sun on her head while she harkened back to her childhood. She slowly slid herself down into the red chair and rested the journal on its wide flat arm. On an impulse she bent and removed her shoes, enjoying the feel of the soft dewy grass between her toes. She wished the chair was a swing.

She again took up her pen.

I was a lonesome little girl, but I had a next-door neighbor who took an interest in me. Her name was Mrs. Richie and she was a tall, thin woman with fiery red hair, black at the roots. When at home she always wore an apron with the words "The Kitchen Witch" printed on the front, though she was not witchy at all. There was a window positioned over Mrs. Richie's sink with a clear view of my back yard. When I knew she was standing there, washing her dishes and watching me, I felt a little less alone.

Sometimes Mrs. Richie would walk over and bring me freshly baked cookies on a round tin tray decorated with pink roses. Chocolate chip cookies were my favorite although peanut butter with real peanuts ran a close second. "What do you have on your mind today, Nora Ellen?" she would ask, and then she would actually listen to my answer. That was the best part. Better even than the treats.

I would tell her about what I had read in the newspapers. She wasn't frightened by my intelligence, though neither she nor I knew the word for my unusual talent...hyperlexia...the ability to read at an early age.

One chilly morning when a December frost covered the ground, Mrs. Richie came over with Christmas cookies. I still remember the red and green sprinkles on the creamy white icing.

"Perhaps you would like to have a book," she said. I was confused. The cookies were cut into the shapes of bells, Christmas trees, and snowflakes, but no books.

"Here," said Mrs. Richie producing an actual book from her apron pocket. "This was my son's first grade reader, but he has grown up and gone away to the war like your Daddy. I've kept it all these years as a memento. Do you know what a memento is?"

Cookies, a book, mementos? My head was whirling.

"A memento is something that reminds you of a time that has passed." She handed me the book, Fun with Dick and Jane.

I received the gift in amazement, barely able to get out the words of thanks before running inside to explore the contents of the precious book in the privacy of my room. There I encountered Dick and Jane and Sally and their dog Spot for the first time. They were almost my contemporaries in age, and Jane looked a lot like me, her blond hair in a page-boy instead of curls, her neatly ironed dresses a match for my own. I soon realized these children, who came to life as I read about them, were leading well-scrubbed small-town lives similar to my own; but they were trapped in the pages of the book, doomed to never grow up or to leave. They were, I was quick to decide, a pretty lame lot. They didn't imagine things or have interesting thoughts like I did. The only line I really liked was: "Run, Sally, run."

Unaware that I was being impolite by criticizing a gift I shared my opinion of the stories with Mrs. Richie, who laughed and gave me a second book: Tales from Shakespeare *by Charles and Mary Lamb. These stories were the carefully condensed and manicured plots of the Bard's major plays. There is only a shred of Shakespeare's genius left in these condensations, and as an adult I know they are much reviled by Shakespearian scholars. They are actually quite pathetic but they will always hold a place in my affection. The book was given to me with love and there was enough left of Shakespeare's plots and characters to nourish my small child's imagination.*

After reading about Hamlet, the Prince of Denmark, who lived in the castle of Elsinore, I decided I would change my name to Elsinora. I imagined I would live with my father someday in just such a castle.

Short letters from my father arrived occasionally from Europe on thin yellow paper, which mother would read silently with a mournful expression.

I made every effort to get hold of those letters and read them, though I found them very odd. There were big black blobs where some of the words should have been.

Dear Greta. We are shipping out on the [blob] next [blob]. Both brother Conroy and I are in good health and spirits and long to be in the fight. Do not worry. We will first go to [blob] for more specialized training in [blob] before going into combat. Please know we are both thinking of you and Mom and sending love. Give my little Nora Ellen a hug from me. I bet she is growing up fast now. xoxo
Kingsley (and Conroy)

Footsteps were approaching in the present.

Elsinora returned from her past.

Hesper appeared, wearing an apron, coming to outside to check on her.

"You remind me of Mrs. Richie," said Elsinora.

"Who?"

"A childhood presence."

"The morning's paper has just arrived, along with a new book."

Hesper placed them on the arm of the chair, and stood facing Elsinora, with hands on hips.

"No shoes?" She shook her head from side to side, suppressing a look of disapproval.

Elsinora shook her head up and down, suppressing a smile.

"Well, I'm going to fry you an egg. Your visiting nurse said you are to have one egg a week, and today is the day.

"No."

"It's not meat, Mrs. Harding, and you do need the iron."

"If a chicken could, like a crab, go backwards, it would become an egg."

"If I could go backwards, like a crab, I would be a less patient companion than I am today."

"But I would not be less pliable. I've had my cereal. Now I would like some fruit."

"What kind?"

"Do I dare to eat a peach?"

As Hesper retreated to the house on a quest for fruit, Elsinora pulled the newspaper towards herself, but realized as she did so that she was not inclined to read it. The news would cast a dark shadow over the morning. The wars of the present day were unconscionable vicious wars, the politicians were revolting malevolent clowns. The criminals were madmen without guile or conscience who went about shooting children in their classrooms, women in their supermarkets, worshippers in their church pews. In the face of such daily outrage, people went about warily, with the ever-present knowledge that they could be the next soft and random target.

Elsinora knew that the Dick-and-Jane-world of her childhood

had been as much a fantasy as her imagined castle by the sea, but now she lived in the richest country in the world, disgraced by the highest homeless population, where the avarice of corporations laid waste to the planet, where the heedless rich lived without conscience, leaving the poor to cling hopelessly to disintegrating safety nets, their children left without proper education or decent medical care.

Her generation, born in the death throes of World War II, had failed to turn civilization towards life, and so the devastation had come full circle, only now it was America, not Europe, that was the killing ground, though no one called it a war.

"It is not, nor can it come to good," she murmured.

But what could she do about any of it at her great age? As a college student she had marched in protest against the Vietnam war, and for civil rights, later for women's rights. She had sent money to just causes, tutored literature to children living in under-served neighborhoods, and voted for poor Hillary who had not understood that a few ill bethought words could change the history of nations. She wished she could believe that the troubles of the world would be solved by younger people, but she had little faith in the young and less in solutions. Perhaps she had, indeed, lived too long.

With a sigh she set to work on the crossword puzzle, but there were too many clues referencing rock bands and television shows she had never heard of, so she decided to sample the book that had just arrived, a first novel by an unknown author. She picked it up and read the title: *Practice to Deceive* by Bess Arden. Nice name, she thought, and it might be amusing. If it was she would regain her good spirits.

IX. That duty done.

D R. MAURICE SCHADAD was melancholy. He rummaged around in his office putting his personal belongings into a cardboard box. There wasn't much for him to take. He was leaving his medical practice, his consultation rooms, and all its contents to the young doctor whose internship he had supervised a few years back. He had judged that the woman had the makings of a proper doctor. She was smart, energetic, and had stayed basically sane through the tribulations of medical training. Those were his minimum requirements; but most of all she listened; to him, and to patients, and to patients' families. She cared. And so it was into her hands that he would deliver what had been his world.

He would continue to consult out of his home, only on Saturdays, and only in order to loyally follow a few of his oldest patients. He would see them out or they would see him out, whoever went first.

The family portrait went into the box. From a drawer he took out a photograph of his late wife, taken just before her final illness. She had been a beautiful woman and had died a contented one. He sat on the edge of his desk, as he had once sat on her bedside, and stared into her smiling likeness. He had loved her in a particular way, a comfortable, understandable way which had become the obstacle to the consummation of what was, he still believed, the great love of his life. Love preventing love. It must happen often, but no one ever thinks of love that way. He never looked at his wife's photograph without thinking of Elsinora.

He dropped her image into the box where she would be close to those of their children and grandchildren, all grown and flown.

He noticed the scent of the empty room; antiseptic soap, rubbing alcohol, iodine, and he supposed, something of himself as well. He opened a window and in so doing saw a lovely day outside. He would have sufficient time now to indulge such a day.

He picked up the plastic skull with its mouth gapping open to receive cigarette butts. Some people were still mindless enough to smoke, so perhaps he should leave it, but it really was macabre, and could hardly be thought of as a welcoming gift to the new physician. He dropped it into the wastepaper basket where it lay grinning up at him. "Goodbye, old friend," he muttered.

He sealed up the box using a roll of adhesive tape, wondering when he would next open it. Most likely, never, he thought. He placed Fletcher Mulcaster's file and several others in the black leather medical bag he had been given on graduating from medical school. How many years ago? Better not to calculate.

All of life felt like a leave-taking now.

His future appeared to him as blank as a sheet of fresh white paper; not a very large one; but when he imagined inscribing something on it, something new, something satisfying, he found himself writing with invisible ink.

X. Whose common theme.

L ATE IN THE afternoon, after reading most of the newly
arrived novel and finding it to her liking, Elsinora made
a note instructing Hesper to send money to its author. She
frequently sent contributions to new authors from a numbered
account. She liked to be an anonymous support of young writers
who showed promise; those attempting literary novels on serious themes, without the inclusion of graphic sex or gratuitous
violence, and without the coarse language that was so common
in what passed for literature at present. Those were her conditions. It was an enjoyable pastime and she hoped the money
she sent, in substantial amounts, arriving with only an unsigned
thank you note, would encourage the writers to continue. Over
the forty years of her reclusiveness she had discovered and
bank-rolled a good many first time novelists, some of whom
were now well-known and respected authors. It was a private
pleasure.

Elsinora was now settled in her library chair. There were
few enjoyable activities that her elderly body still allowed: the
sitting-down pastimes of reading, listening to music, eating,
remembering, thinking, conversing, and writing were the quiet
pleasures she was left with and they suited her.

"Me, me, me," she said, chiding herself a little, and tapping
a finger on the journal. "Well, why not?" she added. "My

memories are interesting to me, and no one else will ever read it."

Elsinora had played all the acting roles that she had wished to play, written all the scholarly papers she cared to write, travelled to all the places she had once longed to see: the Paris of Hemingway and Proust, Fitzgerald's Riviera, Tolstoy's study preserved in his Moscow home, and Woolf's lighthouse off the Cornish coast. She had wandered Dartmoor with Sherlock Holmes in search of the Baskerville hound, and she had traveled to Denmark's Kronborg Castle in Helsingør, which Shakespeare had renamed Elsinore, to visit her namesake. Italy had offered up Romeo and Juliet's Verona, and an old *palazzo* in Venice was the legendary home of murderous Othello, its cramped ghetto held Shylock, and its streets had been graced by Portia, whom she had very much enjoyed playing in two different stage productions.

She had spent a long time in the Stratford-upon-Avon church where Shakespeare was buried, and wandered the streets of Oxford, Cambridge, and London encountering the haunts of her heroes and heroines around every corner. She had always suspected there would come a time in life when travel would become impossible, so at every opportunity she had boarded a plane and flown into the pages of her beloved stories.

Well, she thought, that time has come. She wouldn't be climbing Mt. Everest or taking up marathoning any time soon, so she opened a copy of *Hamlet* at random, and without looking ran her finger down the page. Where would the lines take her this afternoon? "When sorrows come, they come not single spies, but in battalions."

Oh, dear, she thought. 1945. A year that would shape her life through all the decades to follow. She was only five years old. The war was four years old. The Allies were certain now of victory, though fighting in Europe was known still to be fierce.

I waited anxiously to hear word of my father, of his hoped-for discharge and homecoming. Each day I was disappointed. His letters continued to arrive, but far less often now. They came from somewhere in France. My mother, discouraged, often burned them with a lighted cigarette, letting the ashes fall into the sink to mingle with the remains of dirty dishes, but sometimes a note for my Grandma Bessie Dean was enclosed. These would be handed to me intact. I would take them over to Grandma in the nearby Homestead, a sturdy old stone farmhouse that had been in our family since it was built a century before.

Grandma Bessie, having lost her husband long before I was born, lived a solitary life, cleaning and canning and embroidering. She was always welcoming when I entered without knocking, arriving through the wood-shed and into the warm sugar-infused scent of her kitchen. She would smile, hold out her arms and announce to all the Homestead ghosts with pretended dismay, "Now just look what the cat has dragged in!"

It was here that Kingsley and Conroy had been raised. Much of the farmland surrounding the Homestead had been sold off during The Great Depression. On those lost acres developers had built rows of small identical houses standing in neat lines where once there had been rows of onions and potatoes. One of those houses was where I lived with my mother. The Homestead land that remained surrounded the farmhouse for a couple of acres on each side. It was slowly being taken over by nature, which I loved, though I knew the neglect of the property troubled my grandmother.

Sometimes I would gather up apples from the old orchard, or pick blackberries in the brambly lanes, but mostly I explored the untended land, dense with wild vegetation and the beginnings of new forest. I tried to imagine the abundance of vegetables, and the fields of rye and wheat it had once offered up out of its rich, black soil.

Whenever a letter arrived Grandma Bessie would share it with me and give me the hugs that my father wished me to receive. Just the sound of the loving words, sent from so far away, made me happy. I longed to be able to write back to him and tell him about my new name, so much prettier than plain Nora Ellen, but there was no way for me to reach him.

After the letters were read I would hide them in a cigar box under a loose floorboard in the tool shed. The box was embossed with the words "King Edward Mild Tobaccos" on the lid, and "Imperial" on the side, and carried a scent of my father who had enjoyed a cigar now and then as a change from his usual pipe. They were my mementos.

Elsinora now lifted the lid of the cherished box with the few precious letters inside. She inhaled deeply, but the ancient cigar smell had vanished long ago.

"What's in the box?" asked Hesper, who had come silently into the library to check on Elsinora.

Elsinora held up the heavy military medal that was shaped like a silver heart with George Washington's profile in the middle hanging from a purple and gold ribbon. Then she dropped it onto the terrible final telegram.

"A king of infinite space," she said and shut the box with a snap, placing it inside a small metal safe which she locked with a twist of a key.

"Memorabilia, I would guess by the look of it," ventured Hesper.

"Of my father."

"You have never told me about your father."

"He died when I was a young child. Killed in World War II. He was one of the 7,200 men designated missing in action and his body was never found. So there is no story to be told."

"Your mother raised you all alone?"

"My mother was occupied with her own troubles and later with my wounded Uncle Conroy when he returned from France. I brought myself up with the help of a great many authors."

"What was she like, your mother?"

"A small paragraph."

"Whatever do you mean?"

"Her obituary was in the local paper. A small paragraph."

Hesper saw Elsinora's lip tighten, a sure sign she would say nothing further.

"I came to ask if you would enjoy a brandy before bed," she offered.

"Yes, I would like a brandy." Elsinora knew she was being terse with Hesper, but the questions had made her feel cross. Was Hesper asking out of genuine curiosity, or was she gathering tidbits for her husband's odious book?

"Would you like to watch a movie tonight?" inquired Hesper. "Robbie sent over a video of the Andrew Scott *Hamlet* and said you will love it. Geraldo said you will despise it."

"Very thoughtful of them to send over their disagreements, but not tonight. I find I am quite tired."

"You must go to bed early."

Elsinora thought that Hesper had spoken very much as her mother had once done, pressing a cold hand against her five-year old's forehead. "You feel very hot, Nora Ellen. Yes, you should go right to your bed and I will bring you an aspirin."

She remembered this fever well, for it was the beginning of the mysterious illness that followed the dreadful news of her father's loss, conveyed in two abrupt telegrams; one sent to her mother, one to Grandma Bessie. They both were the same, except one said "husband" and the other said "son":

THE SECRETARY OF WAR DESIRES ME TO EXPRESS HIS DEEP REGRET THAT YOUR HUSBAND (SON) MASTER SERGEANT KINGSLEY DEAN HAS BEEN REPORTED MISSING IN ACTION SINCE FOURTH AUGUST IN FRANCE IF FURTHER DETAILS OR OTHER INFORMATION IS RECEIVED YOU WILL BE NOTIFIED. ULIO THE ADJUTANT GENERAL

No further information ever came from the army or the government. Her father's body was never found. There was no funeral, no memorial service. The medal arrived in the mail. He was simply gone.

For a long time Elsinora had imagined that her father, her *missing-not-dead* father, would come walking in through the front door when least expected. As time passed, and her hopes began to fade, she determined never to forget him. The scents of pipe smoke and Brylcreem could summon him. She would stare for hours at his photograph which her Grandma Bessie kept inside a silver frame on the bureau of her cramped bedroom. In it Kingsley appeared both kindly and serious. His eyes seemed to follow her around the room, watching her without comment. Sometimes she read to him. Sometimes she danced for him. He appeared so handsome in the grey and white photo, turning slowly to yellow and then beige under the glass. The picture was placed on her own bureau now. She had never stopped loving him.

Hesper returned with the nightcap.

"Would you like me to read to you?" she asked, her voice gentle.

Elsinora sipped the brandy, and whether it was her companion's kind offer or the alcohol's warmth, she felt herself soften. She knew Hesper to be loyal. She had chosen to stay and care for Elsinora during the pandemic rather than to live with her husband Barton. She had told Elsinora about his idea to write the biography and agreed not to tell tales about her. Perhaps Hesper should be given the benefit of the doubt, and the brandy had made her suddenly feel talkative.

"After my father went missing in action, I was alone with my mother and I became very ill."

"What illness did you have?"

"I've never known. It was dramatic and undiagnosed. I could not walk, so at first polio was feared, then a spinal infection. I slept a great deal, ate almost nothing, and spoke less. This was before antibiotics were widely available so there wasn't much to be prescribed but bedrest. I missed a full year of school, but as I had skipped first grade before falling ill I ended up back with my contemporaries who stared at me when I returned. I suspect I was pale and a bit wobbly, like some alien creature.

"In the year when I was bedridden, and on the advice of the school principal, my mother allowed me books, though she never offered to read to me. Mrs. Kellogg, the librarian, brought them. My teacher brought them, and my neighbor Mrs. Richie gave me a well-worn Webster's dictionary. It is a treasure that I still own. My small room began to resemble a library which pleased me as stacks of volumes, read and unread, piled up alongside my cot. My mother, immersed as she was in her own grief, had no strength to object."

"So that is where all this began." Hesper gestured at the thousands of books that surrounded them.

"Yes. I went through the children's classics swiftly. *Heidi, Lassie, The Hardy Boys, Alice's Adventures in Wonderland, The Wind in the Willows,* and the long awaited *Uncle Bennie's Bedtime Stories.* I was not the first, nor will I be the last lonely child to fall headfirst into a pile of books for solace. Sometimes I met them in the very stories I read, *Anne of Green Gables,* Jo in *Little Women,* and later Nancy Drew. I was happy to move into the adult classics, discovering Twain, Dickens, Austen, the Brontës, Hawthorne, Wharton."

"No television?"

"No, thank God. The books possessed me. Their imagined landscapes beckoned my mind to palaces and grand country houses, to attics and artists' studios, dungeons and dens of thieves, cafes and cathedrals, cheap hotels and the occasional oases of luxury. Though I was trapped in my small bed, my legs as useless as limp rags, my mind had hiked moors and deserts and mountains, swam in the seas. For this reason, in some shockingly sad way, it was a good year. Slowly my appetite returned and I began to recover my physical health.

"On my return to grammar school a boy I had once rather liked asked me if I still believed in Santa Claus as he was quite convinced of the flying fat man's existence, sleigh, reindeers and all. I was, and not for the last time, stunned into speechlessness by a schoolmate's inability to distinguish fact from fantasy. Think of it, Hesper. I had just worked my way through *Shakespeare's Complete Works,* amazed at the difference between the children's summaries I had first encountered in the book by the Lambs and the real plays, rich in every human triumph and failure, every horror and delight to be found in life, and the most glorious language. In that moment, standing before the cheerful, credulous boy, I saw no point whatsoever in remaining a child."

"What happened then?"

"I was bumped up from second grade to fourth, which was the only thing the school principal could think of to do with me. The older children, particularly the boys, seemed large and unfriendly to me, but one of the girls, Doris, her name was, had shot up even taller than the boys, and she became my friend. She liked to read too, but mostly books about science.

"There I sat, among those giant children, my feet dangling, a tiny girl more fictional than real.

"Then life abruptly changed again. Uncle Conroy came back from the war."

"Are you all right?" asked Hesper, suddenly concerned. "You just went all pale."

"I'm alright, but the long-ago me and the present me are both suddenly quite done in for today. I'd rather not talk anymore this evening."

The two tired women said their goodnights.

I shall write about Uncle Conroy tomorrow decided Elsinora. It was time for him to be faced. She remembered that Fletcher would be coming for a visit on the morrow. That would lighten the day, she thought.

XI. Smile and be a villain.

UNCLE CONROY. HE had returned with a limp which he was ashamed of, and a scar across his forehead which he was proud of. Elsinora believed that there was no understanding Uncle Conroy. Not then. Not now, but she felt she must, at last, understand why she had done what she had done.

It was a rainy morning and Elsinora opted for the living room. She did not wish to bring Conroy into her library. It was with reluctance that she began to write.

My uncle moved back into the Homestead to console his grieving mother, or so he said. He spoke of my father only once as Mom and Grandma and I sat before the fireplace. His head was bowed, looking down at his shoes so we could not see his face. There was anger in his voice.

"The fighting was fierce," he told us. "It was dark, and I lost him in those damn French hedgerows. I was shot in the leg and another bullet grazed my head. I went down. I woke up in a field hospital and expected him to soon come to visit, but he never did. I never saw him again."

As he said this he looked up and pointed at his scar. Both Mom and Grandma cried, but I was all cried out by then. I sat staring silently at Conroy until he slid his eyes in my direction. There was no sadness in those eyes. Only an emptiness, surrounded by anger, which scared me.

About a week later, on what had seemed an ordinary day, my mother asked, "How was school today?"

"Fine," I replied ritually. Actually it was more than fine. I sucked up knowledge like a sponge and was never happier than when I was learning something new. She began a familiar litany.

"Are you going out to play with Doris?"

"Yes."

"Don't go near the lake. There are snakes. And you could drown."

"We are going to the playground."

"Don't get hit with a swing."

"I'll be careful."

And then the conversation took an unexpected turn as I received the news that would alter my life.

"We are moving in with Uncle Conroy at the Homestead. We will pack up this weekend. You better go down to the grocery store and get some boxes for all those books of yours or they will have to be left behind."

"I don't want to go to the Homestead," I immediately protested. I loved the farm, but didn't want to live there with Uncle Conroy. Nothing felt right about it.

"Oh, don't be silly," replied my mother. "We were always meant to live in the Homestead. After Grandma passed away, of course. This tacky little house was only meant to be temporary. Your father would have inherited the farm, but it goes to Uncle Conroy now. We'll be getting out of this cracker-box and living where we belong."

"Is Grandma dead?" I was horrified.

"No. Grandma Bessie will go to the old folks' home where she can be properly cared for."

"That's not the way it's supposed to be!"

"Nothing is ever the way it is supposed to be, Nora Ellen. Best to learn that while you are young."

"No!" Elsinora exclaimed aloud.

"Is something the matter?" called a concerned Hesper from the hallway, where she had stopped on her way to replace a flickering lightbulb.

"Just leave me be!" snapped Elsinora. But seeing Hesper's hurt expression as she appeared in the doorway, she added more softly, "I'm sorry. Thank you, I'm in the midst of writing and trying to remember something and I really need to be left alone."

"What are you trying to recall?"

"If I knew that I wouldn't be trying to remember it."

"Well, I'm not about to put up with your sulky moods," my mother declared. "Like it or not, you are going with me to the Homestead."

I rushed to my room and slammed the door. Going to live at the farm without my father, without my Grandma Bessie, was all wrong. I felt it. I knew it. I cried myself to sleep.

Elsinora awoke in the present with a start, an empty tea cup in her lap, her journal having slipped to the floor. She was confused and disoriented as she heard herself protesting loudly, "I won't go!"

"You really should," said Hesper firmly who was standing in the doorway again, holding a cell phone, evidently in the midst of making a doctor's appointment for her. "The doctor can't do an MRI here. He wants a look at that heart flutter the nurse reported."

"I am in perfect health," Elsinora protested, though the room seemed to spin as she tried to bring her mind under control.

"How do we know that if you won't see a doctor?"

"We know that *because* I won't see a doctor. The body is meant to be healthy, sometimes to be sick, and finally to die. I fear that today's doctors, with the rarest of exceptions, don't see it that way. They find out your failings and give you medicines which make your failings proliferate. I'm old. Being old is not a medical issue. I will soon die. Dying is not an illness. It is a natural occurrence, a transformation. Hindus believe that the moment of leaving your body is a time to achieve enlightenment. Christians believe it is when you meet God. Buddhists believe it is when your essence transmigrates to another life. I'm not a Hindu, a Christian or a Buddhist, but I do know that death is nothing that requires a doctor. It is the one moment in all of life that is perfectly safe!"

The two women stared at one another. Elsinora to collect herself, Hesper to frame a measured response.

"You say you are in perfect health and in the same breath that you will soon die."

"If not now, then later. If not later, then now. The readiness is all."

Hesper's face showed the same look of exasperation that her mother's had once done. "Mrs. Harding, may I say with all due respect that sometimes you are quite impossible."

Ignoring Hesper, and feeling unusually angry, Elsinora retrieved her journal from the floor and opened it to the disturbing pages.

My mother would, of course, have the last word. Parents did. Our tract house next door to Mrs. Richie was sold. My Dick-and-Jane-life came to an abrupt end.

It wasn't that I disliked Uncle Conroy. He had been a welcome visitor in my earliest years when my father came home with him on leave. Conroy drove a pink Cadillac convertible, and drank whiskey with milk chasers. Once he brought me a sissy-looking kewpie doll won at a carnival, which sat unloved on a shelf in my closet and did not move with me to the Homestead.

On those visits he laughed and smiled as he played cards with my parents and Mrs. Richie. Canasta it was called. The four adults shoved pennies back and forth across the rickety card table as the hands were won and lost. At the end of the evening the pennies were counted, the winners were announced, and all the pennies were gathered up and put into my piggy bank. Those were cheerful times. Even my mother smiled when she was dealt a good hand.

Uncle Conroy didn't look at all like my father. He was shorter and had missed out on being handsome, with a weak chin and curiously mis-matched eyes, both brown, but one much lighter than the other. The oddest thing about him though was his left ear which everyone called a cauliflower ear. It had been deformed by a blow to his head, evidently delivered by his father when he was just a toddler. Everyone had made fun of him in school, Grandma told me, until he started issuing his own blows. I often stared at the cauliflower ear fascinated, but only when he wasn't looking at me.

Conroy lacked seriousness. I didn't feel safe with him as I had when my father was nearby. I felt that he made a perfectly fine uncle, a funny guest, a lively member of the family; but he was not a replacement for a father.

"You can have your Dad's old room," he announced the day before the move. "All his books and trophies from

childhood are still in there. Mom saved everything he had like it's some kind of sacred site."

I had loved going into my father's childhood room when visiting Grandma. To have my father's possessions around me would be a kind of comfort.

Mother seemed pleased about everything concerning the move, and this was confusing, as she had mostly been sad since the war began, in other words, all my life. Of course I wanted my mom to be happy, but why now when it was finally understood that my father was not coming back. Ever.

"I don't want to go."

"Well, you really should."

"Make me!"

"You know perfectly well I can't make you do anything, Mrs. Harding," replied Hesper.

"Exactly!"

Hesper sighed in defeat. She would call the doctor in the morning and cancel the MRI.

Elsinora was aware that Hesper considered her difficult, but she did not consider her demands to be excessive. She simply wanted to be comfortable, have a book to read, and to be left alone to think, to write; but people were always at her with one demand or another, with their ideas about how she should be, and what she should do. She was tired with the lot of them: doctors and nurses, parents and teachers, directors and agents, administrators and lawyers, husbands and friends. The current batch meant well, she supposed. She sighed deeply. It was all over. Could they not see the simple truth for what it was? Her life, her loves and hates, her crimes, her successes, her tragedies, all were history now, as one day they would be for everyone.

"Do you wish anything else, Mrs. Harding?" asked Hesper in her most professional voice.

"A lifetime achievement award, a brandy, and some blessed silence. And I do appreciate your patience, Hesper. I am sorry to be so troublesome. I'm thinking of a time in my life when everything changed. It has tired me out and confused me, but I'm not quite ready for a nap."

Elsinora made her way to the library, took the cigar box out of the small safe, and removed the note from Grandma Bessie, carefully preserved among the other memorabilia. She held it to her nose, but no trace of the old woman's lavender perfume remained. It had vanished with the scent of cigar.

Now, having surpassed her grandmother in age, Elsinora wondered how the old woman had felt with her life behind her, shunted away to the old folks' home. Her mother had said she had asked to move there after hearing of Kingsley's death, which seemed curious to Elsinora, even at the time. Her mother explained that her Grandma Bessie was tired of life and wanted to be taken care of. Her mother assured her that it was best for everyone. "Everyone" for her mother, was her mother.

When had Grandma Bessie become silent? Elsinora recalled visits to the old age home when they had talked together, even laughed, but then abruptly at some point, a short time before her death, she had ceased to speak altogether.

Elsinora remembered those last strange, silent visits clearly; how her grandmother would watch her attentively with a placid expression, but remain completely mute. There was talk of a stroke. Some people thought she had become senile, but Elsinora knew better. Her grandmother's eyes were full of intelligence, deep pools of awareness, circles that seemed to see everything but reveal nothing. Her steadfast silence was a personal choice, a decision to hold everything within.

Then Elsinora had been given the note. It had been folded tightly, handed to her by the silent woman during a holiday visit. There was no Christmas tree at the home, but colored lights had been hung haphazardly around the dismal sitting room. A smell of pine boughs swaddled the usual old people smell. A stuffed Santa Claus leaned, lopsided, in a corner, smiling malevolently. The whole place was the definition of creepy. Why had Grandma Bessie chosen this place to live out her last years? *Had* she chosen?

Elsinora had given her a tin of cookies which she had baked and decorated herself. In response, a bony hand reached out and clasped her own. A note hastily ripped from a notepad was surreptitiously slipped into her palm, and a cautionary finger was raised to the old woman's lips.

Grandma Bessie had shared a secret with her! She remembered her eagerness to return home and be alone so she could unfold the paper. Perhaps it was just a thank you note, but even that would be a privileged communication.

Greta Dean, who had not come inside to see her missing-and-presumed-dead husband's old, mute mother, sat in the car in the driveway, puffing on Camel cigarettes and listening to Christmas carols on the radio. Joy to the World.

"How was she?" she asked, when Elsinora climbed into the back seat.

"Fine. The same." Elsinora knew her mother didn't really care. The interior of the car stank of old smoke and suddenly felt unbearably claustrophobic.

"I think I'll walk home."

"You will not! A truck could skid right off the road in this weather and kill you."

And so, clutching the note as tightly as Grandma Bessie clutched her Bible, Elsinora had endured the ride while Bing

Crosby crooned "I'll be Home for Christmas" into the smelly automobile.

When Elsinora was at last alone in her room she carefully opened the folded paper. It was jaggedly ripped where it had been attached to the notepad, with perhaps its beginning word lost to the tear. Only six words were legible, scrawled in Grandma Bessie's handwriting:

...death is not what it seems

Whatever could it mean? Why had she given this to Elsinora?

She never told me. I never stopped loving my Grandmother, but without any conversation the visits engendered frustration, restlessness, and sadness every time I went, and so as time passed I paid visits less and less often. The place where the old woman withered away in silence did not seem to me like a home at all, but the shabby waiting room of a funeral parlor. I finally stopped going altogether.

Elsinora began to quietly weep.

My abandonment of Grandma Bessie, that poor self-thwarted being, is the most profound regret of my life. I turned away from someone who had loved me, someone in a hard, unknowable place who was, perhaps, asking for my help. I do not seek forgiveness for myself. There is no one to forgive me.

The only person I ever told about this note was Fletcher. The words, like every sentence I have ever read, affect me still, a sentence, delivered from the soul of one person to the soul of another.

...death is not what it seems

When I was finally given the means to understand those words, when I grasped the note's full implications, what I did was necessary. Wasn't it?

She put down the pen.

Elsinora was determined that her own death would be accomplished by her own hand. And in that hand she would be holding the note, for it had become her justification, her exoneration, if that was even possible.

At present she would live on.

XII. Together with remembrance.

"**H**ELLO-HO-HO!" FLETCHER SANG out gaily as he crossed the lawn towards Elsinora. "I have come to tell you that I'm dying."

"Who isn't?" replied Elsinora, as he kissed her on the top of her head and then sank into the blue Adirondack chair next to her red one.

They both laughed, Elsinora unaware of the truth of what he had said, for they always laughed at life's absurdities when they were in each other's company.

"Oh, look! Almond cookies! Yum."

Elsinora poured each of them a glass of sangria from the pitcher on the folding table that Hesper had thoughtfully set up near to hand. Both of their chairs faced the placid lake, so they watched each other sidelong, from the corner of their eyes.

He has always been a classically handsome man, she thought, but with each decade he has grown more so as some fortunate men do. He certainly remained imposing, English slender, with a full head of silver hair. His quick, black eyes could oversee every movement of a full orchestra, or pin the right notes into a soprano's performance. When he took the podium before a concert he was admired by many a matron even at this advanced age.

Remembering her promise to Hesper, Elsinora consulted

with Fletcher. "The Academy wants to give me a lifetime achievement award. Is that not preposterous?"

"I want to give you an award, too; The Fletcher Mulcaster Award for putting up with me for a lifetime."

"Seriously, Fletch, I haven't been in a film in forty years or on a stage in fifteen. Who is even left to remember me, let alone care?"

"Someone must. You were special, Elsinora. Everyone understands that but you."

"I was miserable in Hollywood. You remember. For those six long years I was bullied into it by Oliver-Paul, pushed around by powerful men who put me under contract so I had no say in parts I played, mobbed by the public, falsified in the press—"

"But stunning on the screen."

"Seriously, should I haul this ancient frame back to such a place? What for? To provide strangers with the thrill of seeing what age can do to beauty?"

"You know, dear one, that you will do exactly as you please. My vote would count for naught, even if I had a vote. You won't go and they will end up giving the award to some deserving actress who has kept at it, getting tummy tucks and facelifts until she looks like a Barbie Doll that's been microwaved by mistake."

"You are scandalous, Fletcher. Just what I need on a day when I'm in a grump. But to be fair, Hollywood is a man's world and the women there must take extreme measures to survive in it."

"I'm glad *you* did. All in your past now."

"The past seems to be very present lately. I've made a project of trying to remember my entire life. I've begun a journal."

"A memoir? Private old you?"

"I've run into the old puzzle."

"The missing thirteenth year?"

"Yes."

"Almost the whole year, the one before you arrived. I know I was alone at the Homestead with mother and Conroy. Grandma was in the old folks' home. Mom lost a baby. That's all I've got. I can't remember any details. It's all a blur, then there you were, and everything clears up again like windshield wipers going on. I must have told you things about that time when I was still a child. Can you help me out?"

"I'm afraid not. At fourteen you were almost mute. Like your Grandmother. And I was so out of place, too shy to ask many questions. We seem to have begun new lives starting when we met. Why is it so important to you at this late date?"

"I'm trying to understand why I did what I did. You know of the situation to which I refer. I thought if I pieced all my life together, I might understand myself finally, perhaps attain some peace of mind before I die."

"Ah. Yes. Peace. Death. Which brings me to the reason for my visit today."

"Since when have you needed a reason to visit?"

"I'm afraid I meant it, about dying, Elsinora. I know this will be an awful shock for you, but you must be told. The doctors have declared my condition incurable. So I've come to say my farewell to you."

He had initially made his announcement so light-heartedly that she, though she knew him intimately, had missed his fatal undertone of seriousness or perhaps defended against it, but now his words penetrated, and she shrieked.

"Oh dear. Oh, *no!* You *mean* it. Oh hell!"

Elsinora turned to face him directly and saw it was true. Inside herself, something important crumpled, shriveled, and started to hurt very badly, but she thought only of Fletcher.

"Are you in pain? I hope you are not in pain." She reached out and gripped his forearm.

"Quite the opposite. The potions that issue forth from the medical establishment nowadays vanquish the pain and lift me into what some would call 'a happy place.' I sense the pain is in here somewhere, but I don't often feel it."

She kept a hand on his arm, as if to steady her balance although she was seated. She was trying to take in this dreadful news and expel it at the same time. He was here. She could touch him. He would not always be here. But he *must* always be here.

Fletcher continued now. His manner composed, his voice now at its most serious. "The drugs are a blessing, but among the many blessings of my life, our friendship is foremost. You know this, Elsinora, but I wished for you to hear the words spoken aloud by me. I want to say how much I have depended on our relationship throughout my life, how much I have adored you. How much I have enjoyed being 'us.' You have been my lifelong treasure."

She wanted to speak to him of her own love in words as beautiful as those he had spoken, but he lifted his hand, his conductor's hand, placing a finger to her lips.

"I know," he said tenderly.

His voice lightened again and he relaxed back into the chair and smiled. "So many years," he said. "So many grand adventures. In so many places. Wherever my mind travels, there we are."

"Almost seven decades," she replied, reaching inside herself, past the ache, searching for the lightness she knew he was asking of her. "Remember our climb together up Mount Kilimanjaro?"

"I remember we looked at it in an admiring fashion when we were drinking martinis together on the sundeck of that Tanzanian wildlife lodge, but we never climbed it."

"A Tanzanian vacation. Whose idea was that?"

"Mine, I suppose. I remember that the cocktails were excellent."

"I did not enjoy the roar of the animals in the dark."

"In Venice there was only music."

"We kept returning to Venice."

"It was a city that mirrored our souls, beautifully battered and entirely improbable. Wherever did we come from, Elsinora?"

"And then there was Normandy," she whispered.

"Perhaps we should not think of what lies in Normandy just now."

"Fletcher, you know you saved my sanity and probably my life when you joined our family. You came bearing love and music and humor into a childhood, which I see, so clearly now, was filled with sadness and loneliness."

"And I brought a good deal of trouble, too. Remember the time we stole apples from old man Jeppe's orchard? Your friend Mrs. Richie saved us from a tanning by quickly baking all of the apples into a pie. We ate the evidence."

They laughed again, perhaps too heartily. He was determined not to let the conversation become maudlin.

"And Fletch, I remember an occasion when you thought you heard a ghost in the attic and were so frightened you jumped out of your bedroom window."

"And you, brave little Nora Ellen, heard me shrieking and ran to my room and followed me out. I landed on your mother's prize rose bush and you landed on me. I can still feel the thorns in my butt whenever I conduct Vivaldi's *Summer*."

"Where were the adults?"

"Conroy and Greta?" He laughed. "They were never adults. We were born older than the two of them put together."

She continued to peer at him, seeing no signs of illness or distress, silently praising modern medical science for keeping him from pain, admiring him for the brave front he was wearing for her like a perfectly pressed tuxedo shirt.

He gazed at the lake, keeping his emotions as calm as its surface. She could tell he was hearing music because his fingers were tapping lightly on the arm of the chair, keeping time to some private melody. Where, she wondered did the notes that only he could hear originate? In the quickening breeze, the rustling of the leaves, the ripples on the surface of the lake? He would not allow her to know if he was hurting, and he would expect her to help him in this task by controlling her own feelings, not letting the present tragedy tarnish these last moments together as they exchanged and augmented their treasury of recollections.

Fletcher, oh dearest Fletcher, how can life be life without you? She asked herself silently, wanting very much to throw herself into his arms and sob, but he was conducting this meeting like a concerto and they had moved from *adagio* to *allegro*. She managed a smile. "Remember when we were fifteen and tried to have sex and you found out you were gay?" she asked, struggling to keep her voice light.

"Gay. That word, as you know my dear one, did not exist back in the day, at least as it applied to me. I was a homosexual, the dreaded deviant, fag, queer, poof, pansy. I was thought to be pathetic, but certainly not gay."

"And I was very unkind."

"Just in the moment. Once your clothes were back on you were much more reasonable."

"I've been called many things in my time, Fletcher, but never reasonable."

"You can be forgiven. You were in shock, I suspect."

"I was in love."

"And still you are, my dear. Any woman who gets naked in my presence is in love with me forever."

"I'm likely to have been the only woman to have had that experience."

"Point taken. Of course, you are the only *woman*."

"Oh, such beginnings."

He sighed, changing the tempo again. Largo. Looking at her directly he said with a hint of solemnity, "And now the end is nigh."

"I don't want you to die."

"Death doesn't matter now. Now matters now."

"Perhaps we should die together, Fletcher. It could be arranged. I know just the thing, and we could—"

He held up a restraining hand. "I admire your talent at arrangements, but I think in this instance, if you would not mind, I would like to reach the final chord with a clash of my own cymbals."

"I shall be so very sad, Fletcher." She said it evenly, as a fact, not as a whimper.

"But, Elsinora, you have always been sad, and you shall only have to endure this particular sadness for a very short while. You'll soon follow me. Within this very decade, I suspect."

"Even so, it will be too quiet in the world without you."

"Not at all. I have a young protégé, Joshua, whose talent makes the grand organ vibrate throughout the cathedral so that the very walls absorb his music and can barely remain standing; the stained glass windows quiver their panes with their shock at his talent. He shall perform variations on the melody of God Save the King with a *full* orchestra at my funeral. I did the arrangement myself."

"Why God Save the King? That's the British National Anthem. Isn't that blasphemous or something?"

"It is the same melody to which My Country 'Tis of Thee has been set, so the blasphemy was accomplished long ago by

Samuel Francis Smith. It pays homage to my roots, one foot in England, one in America."

"Straddling the Atlantic."

"It has always been an uncomfortable stretch, if you must know the truth."

"However shall I endure the funeral?"

"Oh no, my dear. We must not think of that! No funeral for you. My job in this long life has been to lift up your spirits. Up, up! And funerals are always melancholy affairs at best. No. While I am being laid to rest, as *they* put it, and shoved into a hole in the ground, as *I* put it, I insist that you go to New York City and buy yourself a many-feathered hat."

She frowned in dismay. "No one wears hats nowadays."

"And when have you cared about what other people do, or don't do? I remember so well how beautiful you appeared under the veiled hat you were wearing in the final scene of *Anna Karenina,* and how the camera pulled back slowly away from the railroad tracks so as not to show your poor severed head, and then that final image: the glorious scarlet hat rolling away down the embankment." His arm circled in the air.

"Just kitsch, that shot. Oliver-Paul always went in for that sort of sentimental rubbish, but the picture did well."

"Do you ever miss him?"

"Oddly, sometimes, yes, not much."

"But you still miss your father a great deal."

"The first loss."

"Perhaps I shall be the last."

They were quiet again, all levity passed, and together they gazed out over the deep, uncaring water. "My father. Methinks I see my father," she quoted.

"I know, my dear." He patted her hand that still rested possessively on his arm.

"And always, only, ever, in my mind's eye. From some things we never recover, do we?"

"Perhaps you live too much in remembrance," he chided gently. "I want you to know something, Elsinora. I am content with what you did on that dreadful day, long ago in Ohio. The day that still bedevils you. I know you worry at it like a cat with a crooked claw, but truly, it is all right. And it is long since past."

"Perhaps I should not have told you, but you had a right to know, and you are the only person I have ever told. After all, he was your—"

"—you knew you could trust me with your life, whether I approved of your actions or not. And now I will take your secret with me to my grave."

"Have you ever wondered how Hamlet might have felt had he survived that final scene where his mother dies, and he forces poison down his uncle's throat, and—"

"I can't say as I have, Elsinora," he interrupted, arching an eyebrow."

"Haven't you wondered what he would think of himself if he lived to be as old as we are?"

"I can honestly admit it has never crossed my mind."

"You haven't imagined what Hamlet would be pondering? Would he be racked with guilt? Would he still be unsure?"

"Nope. Not even once."

"Well, I have and I'm almost certain he—"

"Lay. Your. Past. To. Rest. Elsinora."

She heard him. She took a deep breath, sitting silently then, just being with Fletcher, who seemed more alive than ever before.

He slid his arm from beneath her loving hand, took another sip of the sweet sangria, and then with an admirable grace arose from the chair, unfolding his body into an upright position.

"And now I must go. Don't be sad on my behalf, dear one. I've had a long rich life, full of music, more lovers than I can count, and the world's best companion, my sometimes cousin and my very naughty, very haughty, oldest and most dear friend, Elsinora Dean, to whom I now make a last request."

"Anything, Fletcher."

"You are to leave instructions to be buried in the new feathered hat when you die. Wherever I am, I want to see you coming."

It was her turn to try and struggle up from the chair, wanting to embrace him, hold him, keep him close, just one last time, but he would not allow it.

He placed his hands on her fragile shoulders and gently restrained her. He stood silently behind her now. She could hear his breathing. His precious breathing.

"*Finale,*" he whispered. "Death is not what it seems."

He kissed her on the top of her head, turned and walked away, leaving her to face the landscape alone.

In the shadows beneath the willow tree the white heron stood unmoving and majestic, one straight leg immersed in the murky water, the other bent. The water was dark now, its surface uneasy below a heavy cloud. The warmth of his kiss was carried away in a sudden gust of wind.

XIII. Dirge in marriage.

"So the spy has come in from the cold," said Barton, greeting his errant wife.

You wish! thought Hesper. He thinks he is being clever, while getting the situation so totally wrong.

She had just entered her husband's airless office on another of her dutiful visits.

"What's new with Elsinora?"

"You might first ask after me, you know."

"Sorry."

Hesper sighed. She must tell him something, she supposed.

"She seems troubled," she replied after some careful thought, hoping to get today's conversations over without giving anything substantial to Barton. Elsinora had trusted her with some childhood memories and she was keeping them. "Ever since her cousin Fletcher came to see her she has not been herself. In the past his visits always buoyed her up. Now she mopes. She will not say what passed between them."

Hesper sat down in a straight-backed chair, and put her feet up on a nearby stool to encourage her circulation. She blew on the hot coffee in a paper cup she had carried in, willing it to be cool enough to drink.

Barton, his face blanched to unhealthy gray by the light from the screen, looked up from his sticky keyboard. His eyes narrowed.

He looks like a weasel, thought Hesper.

"Fletcher Mulcaster. Always the dark horse in the story. *The New York Post* photo showed him right beside her leaving the funeral, when her husband died so suspiciously."

"Yes, yes. The questionable death of the late, great Oliver-Paul Harding. I know. I know. You've told me your theory a dozen times, but the woman I care for is not capable of murder."

"Then why did she give up a stellar acting career, and go into hiding right after the bastard croaked?"

Hesper flinched at the cruel words her husband seemed to use more and more of late. "She fell off a stage, Barton, and almost died. That might be reason enough. And she did not go into hiding. She stood in the front of classrooms and taught for thirty years."

"Well why does she refuse to talk about her past with you? Old people gibber on about their lives all the time."

"Not every elderly person does so. She doesn't."

"But she was a *star*. The biggest star of her day."

"As you have said a thousand times. Stop speaking to me as if I am braindead. Do you think I don't know who she was, or who I'm working for?"

"I was just making a conversational point. She was important."

"Being important to the public doesn't mean her personal life is public property. And some people, people like Elsinora, simply prefer to be reclusive. She is still refusing to consider accepting that lifetime Oscar award, by the way."

"Damn her! If she would accept the award she would be the center of attention again. It would revive some interest in her and would help my book sales."

"*If* you can manage to write the book."

"I'm blocked. Don't rub it in. A little fresh information from you would help. So there is nothing new out of her?"

"Nothing," Hesper repeated, trying not to sound exasperated. "I told you. She's as dried up as you are at present. She almost never speaks, she goes nowhere. Has no appetite. She is drinking too much. She ruminates."

"The old cow. Do you suppose she is becoming senile?"

"Barton! Please don't speak of her in such derogatory ways. She has never been talkative, but this current silence is profound. I think something is hurting her. Fletcher's recent visit, whatever occurred between them, has struck her dumb. I'm seriously worried about her."

"The person you should be worried about is me, Hesper."

"I worry about you consistently, Barton. I worry that you are becoming obsessed with this ridiculous idea that Elsinora is an evil woman. You have no grounds to think so. She is a good woman, and your biography should be about all the light she has brought into the world with her acting and teaching and philanthropy. That's what you said it would be at the start. Now all you seem to want to do is frame her for a murder."

"Murder sells."

They were at an impasse, both thoroughly opposed and angry with the other's point of view.

"Do you think she is becoming like the grandmother who never spoke?"

"You wouldn't know anything about that poor woman if I hadn't told you, and I wish now that I hadn't. You twist everything I say. Elsinora has all her wits about her. She has gone quiet for some personal reason."

"Well, you will have to find out what it was that Mulcaster said to her. Cheer her up, for God's sake. Or argue with her. Do whatever it takes to get her talking again. I've only got the barest of an outline here, and it is full of Grand Canyon-sized holes. The old newspapers mostly carry her theater reviews, and the movie magazines are not to be trusted."

"You've told me all this before." Hesper could not keep the weariness out of her voice.

"Maybe she and Fletcher were lovers."

"You know perfectly well he is her first cousin, and he is gay as a goose."

"Illegitimate cousin."

"Fletcher and Elsinora are close friends, Barton, but you'll find no scandal there, much as you would like to discover one."

"Who's side are you on?"

"Yours, of course, Barton," she said automatically.

He heard the edge of falseness in her voice and scowled at her. "At least Fletcher Mulcaster is famous. That will sell some copies, whatever their relationship, but I need details, Hesper, specifics. I need the younger years filled out. All teenage girls write diaries. Still no sign of one?"

"Her adolescence was almost seventy years ago. If she wrote a diary it has doubtless been lost or destroyed. Lately she has begun a journal, but she keeps it close at hand."

Barton's eyes widened.

Now he looks like a frog, she thought, ready to jump right into the muck.

"You must get your hands on that journal!"

"What would you have me do? Knock her out? Maybe Robbie and Geraldo will have coaxed her into telling some more show business tales this weekend, a backstage story or two."

"Those silly old queers have been pretty helpful on the theater years."

"Oh, that's mean, Barton. When did you get so mean? You promised me the book would be a tribute. That is the only reason I agreed to be helpful. It doesn't sit right with me anymore."

Barton shrugged and turned back to the smudged computer

screen, to the scandalous biography he was failing to write of the rich and once-famous Elsinora Dean.

Hesper sipped at the coffee which had gone cold and bitter. It tasted of cardboard and she tossed it into the bin.

Barton's past books had been carefully researched and well written. They sold well, and he had a reputation to maintain; but for her to be retrieving the memories of Elsinora, like a dog bringing a dead duck to a self-satisfied hunter, was demeaning. Housekeeping may not be a profession, she thought, but nevertheless there were standards, unspoken rules to be kept, and she wasn't going to betray them.

His plan was to have the book finished, copy edited, and ready to go to press the moment Elsinora died.

Hesper did not like to think about her employer's demise. When Elsinora stopped breathing Hesper would be instantly out of work and it wouldn't be easy to find another position as comfortable and lucrative. Fifty is not the new thirty, she knew. Her body had begun to tell her so. Her knees and her back were sending signals to slow down.

If Elsinora died and she was unable to find another live-in employment, where would she go? She had no desire to return to this apartment with Barton. When had their relationship begun its long, slow exhalation? Perhaps when they failed to produce a child. Perhaps when he had been so adamantly opposed to the idea of an adoption. Once content, they simply hadn't flourished. Now, as they grew farther and farther apart, the walls of this apartment felt closer and closer together. And they needed repainting, she noted.

Hesper had decamped during the pandemic. It was supposed to be a temporary arrangement. They needed her income so she moved into Arden Manor instead of coming and going each day as she had been doing in prior years. She found that she liked living in. Certainly the commute was easier. The two women had decided, without words, to be kind to each other as the world around them staggered under the impact of the unknown virus and came to a fearful standstill, death hanging vaporous in the very air.

Once they were in complete isolation Hesper had washed every can and bottle that arrived when groceries were deposited outside on the patio, and she did many of the household repairs herself, rather than summon in workmen which would risk possible exposure. Together, in their enforced confinement they watched as the surrounding lawns grew into weedy fields and emboldened wildlife emerged to retake the property.

Elsinora ordered books by the dozen, discovering new authors and sending them money. She seemed to need draughts of literature the way Inspector Morse needed beer. Hesper, though married to a writer, had never been much of a reader, but she began, with Elsinora's encouragement, to enjoy her employer's much beloved pastime. Sitting side by side in the evenings with their chosen books, the boundaries between them had begun to loosen and an uncertain friendship began to grow.

As the months passed, Hesper had phoned Barton often and sent him daily texts, often issuing warnings about hand-washing and social distancing which he probably ignored, but she had refused to visit him in person until after the vaccinations made it possible to do so with only limited risk. She had convinced herself that this abandonment was best for them both.

Looking at him now, she recognized that she still held threads of affection for him that persisted from the past, her early years with a young Barton, ambitious and smart and talented as he had once seemed to her, before his self-importance swallowed him up; before he had stopped seeing her as a desirable woman, and before he began taking her wifely services for granted.

Alone during the pandemic he had grown sullen and coarse, and he had developed a paunch which she very much disliked. She wished she could feel only one way about him, but the movement of time had a way of complicating her emotions.

Hesper glanced around at his messy office now, and knew, without taking a tour, that every room in the apartment would present the same shambles. She could not abide such disorder. When she took an overnight away from Elsinora, and dutifully paid Barton a visit, she stayed in a fastidious AirB&B on the next block.

She could not help the angry thoughts that came rushing in. If he wanted her back, he would clean the place up, wouldn't he? If I was not a Catholic I would divorce him, wouldn't I? She touched the cross that hung from a simple gold chain around her neck.

Keeping Elsinora alive for as long as possible was the best possible course for the foreseeable future. With that thought in mind, she renewed her determination to get her employer active and speaking again, to help Elsinora out of her current malaise; not for Barton, but for herself. For Elsinora.

XIV. A crafty madness.

ELSINORA PACED FROM one end of the house to the other avoiding Robbie and Geraldo, who lurked. Fletcher had told her in no uncertain terms that she should lay to rest the guilts, recriminations, and uncertainties that swarmed about in her past like flies on a corpse, but they would not lie down and die, and until they did she felt she could not go peacefully to her grave. At present she felt buried alive, with all her imperfections in her head.

"I cannot make my mind calm down!" she complained to herself. All afternoon she had been surreptitiously sipping at brandy, though she could not tell if this made things better or worse. Sometimes she opened the cigar box and looked at her Grandmother's note, or the gun Uncle Conroy had given her. Now and then she would plop down in front of her iPad to see what the YouTube algorithm would send in her direction. This morning a cathedral concert conducted by Fletcher popped onto the screen and this had sent her spiraling downwards. She had sprung up too quickly, spilling some of the brandy onto the iPad. She paced in a vain attempt to outwalk the grief that she felt.

Finding herself in a long hallway between the living room and the garden room where the unadorned, off-white walls of the corridor held no interest, she dragged a lightweight aluminum chair from the conservatory into the narrow confines, and sat down where she had never placed herself before. She found the chair, with its generous cushion and sturdy armrests quite comfortable and felt an unexpected calmness in the sterile space. It was like sitting in nowhere.

At last she opened the journal, hoping that writing might bring some steadiness.

> *I see no further point to striving onwards into a future without Fletcher. No one could possibly understand what he has meant to me, my always available unavailable man, the gay, insouciant cousin who snapped wit like a whip, brought forth music like a God, and whose dry humor and sharp sense of irony had made my life tolerable even in its darkest hours.*
>
> *Fletcher has always hidden his true self like an oyster in a shell, for he has a tender soul. He once explained that the music of the universe sang to him, gentled him in the midst of life's hardships. He had turned to me, and only me, with his troubles. We were each other's strength. Life without Fletcher is unthinkable. Unimaginable. Alas, I must think of it, and imagine it, and I find it intolerable. When the knowledge of his impending absence became a reality to me, revealing a world in which I would exist but Fletcher would not, my brain convulsed.*

Using all her will she placed her mind in a time when they were young and happy.

> *It was Fletcher who put me on the stage and has orchestrated much of my life, both before and after my catastrophic marriage. Fletcher ceded his prime position to Oliver-Paul*

when I insisted I must be wedded to the man, but not without warning me first. He told me, without equivocation, that Oliver-Paul's ambitions were far more important to Oliver-Paul than any of my feelings or desires. Of course Fletcher was right, and I soon found myself living in the center of my husband's preoccupations, but in the parentheses of his emotional life.

On my wedding day Fletcher had whispered to me, "Never give up control of your own money." Having seen Uncle Conroy sell off the family land and spend the money on drink, I listened to Fletch and I held onto my income with an eagle's claw, causing endless rows with Oliver-Paul, but I can now live well as a result.

She pushed her mind back further in time to her college days. There he was. Fletcher, mischievous young Fletcher, barging excitedly into her dorm room.

"*Hello*-ho-ho! This is I, Fletcher the Pain."

"Hail to your grace."

"Listen, my dear," he said excitedly. This is important."

"Go away. I'm studying. There is a quiz in American Lit tomorrow." She tried to shoe him away, holding up her notated Hemingway. "The bell tolls for thee."

"Oh, put down the damn book. Whatever the assignment is, you will doubtless have read it, and probably memorized it, by the fifth grade. There is something else you must do."

She stuck a marker in the book and looked at him skeptically.

"Now here me out. They are casting *Hamlet* over in the drama department. You have always adored that play. You re-christened yourself after its castle, for God's sake. Please go over and audition. I've been asked to write incidental music for the production and I want you to inspire me."

"I've never acted, Fletch, you know that. Besides, I'm not fond of naïve Ophelia. She is too much under the thumb of all the men in her life, and that's the only role I would be right for. Now go along. Find a nice, brawny Laertes or a devoted Horatio to inspire your melodies."

"No, no. *Not* Ophelia. I want you to play Hamlet. They haven't found anyone in the whole department that satisfies the mad professor who is directing the production."

"A female Hamlet?"

"Yes, all very daring for this old pile of rocks and ivy in which we find ourselves entombed. And you would look cute as hell in doublet and tights, sword at your side. I might fall in love with you."

"You already *are* in love with me. You just can't let yourself believe it."

Their mutual laughter seemed to echo up from the past and along the corridor in which she now sat. She returned to her journal.

To be Hamlet or not to be Hamlet. Now there was a question.

I went to the audition, partly to satisfy Fletcher and partly in the grip of a strange compulsion, as if some force born of a lifelong fascination with the play was drawing me towards the theater. Until that moment the emotional prince had been a dependable friend, living out a black and white existence quietly inside my volume of Shakespeare's Complete Works; and whose moods mirrored my own nature. He had been a companion on many a dark day, his words never failing to astonish me.

When my turn came to audition, I walked from the wings onto the center of the stage where I stood encompassed in the glaring circle of a single standing stage-light. I was suddenly tremendously nervous, feeling sure I would make a colossal fool of myself. I didn't need to hold a script because I knew every one of Hamlet's soliloquies by heart.

The director spoke from the darkened auditorium.

"Elsinora, you have a very apt name, and a very in-apt gender, but you are here so do go ahead."

As I spoke the first line of the monologue I had chosen— "Oh that this too too solid flesh should melt"—something unexpected happened. I felt myself vanish. It was Hamlet who stood in the glowing circle of light. I was inside his very skin. I looked out at the world through his mournful eyes. Hamlet's mind had replaced my own. His feelings were mine. And oh, what feelings!

The relief I felt at the loss of myself was enormous. The joy I felt in being another person, especially this brilliant and murderous Dane, was extraordinary. This was the most surprising moment of my life, and it was then that my quite unanticipated career as a stage actress began, there on those bare college boards. I had dumbfounded the director and he gave me the part. I triumphed. I transferred from the English to the Drama department all within a few months.

"Oh, Fletcher, thank you," I whispered.

By graduation I knew I was deeply talented and I was eager to go to New York City. It was an era when Shakespeare, Ibsen, Tennessee Williams, and Eugene O'Neill could find stages alongside Rodgers and Hammerstein, Cole Porter, and Neil Simon. Ticket prices were reasonable and there were audiences enough for every taste. It was Broadway before Disney. I had, of course, heard the discouraging stories of so many out-of-work young actresses, but that was not to be what awaited me.

I returned to Warrensville for a week after graduation, and it thoroughly displeased Greta and Conroy when they learned I would not be staying. They had expected me to come home, teach school, or take over the local library in order to make a steady income and look after them as they aged, not that they deserved it, but I was determined to pursue a stage career.

"You'll be mugged! You'll be raped!" My mother had wailed. And now, for the first time, with fresh, college-educated eyes, I saw that my poor mother was insane.

Uncle Conroy gave me his service revolver, tucking it into my small suitcase, saying it was for my protection.

The Cleveland bus station was cold and smelly, with homeless men asleep in dark corners. I remember that I was shivering as I sat waiting for the bus, but I think it was only from excitement. I carried the one suitcase with my best clothes, my father's photograph, the gun, and The Complete Works of William Shakespeare. The rest of my library was packed away, stored at my friend Doris's house so Uncle Conroy wouldn't sell it, or just toss it away for the fun of it. All I could think was: Run, Elsinora, run.

My mother had instructed me to sit directly behind the bus driver for reasons of safety. She actually said: "You never know what terrible men might be riding on a bus. You must be very careful of men, even if you like them, and keep yourself pure for the man who will someday be your husband."

Who was she, I thought, to be telling me how to conduct myself, after she had married her husband's brother within a month of his death. And what advice! It was like her head had gotten stuck in the nineteen-thirties. It was, however, the threshold of the nineteen-sixties.

*I took the front seat as my mother had directed next to
a handsome Marine private, no doubt headed for Vietnam.
When the bus got to Pittsburgh, he took me willingly to a
hotel, and then to bed. I discovered I liked sex. I never knew
the soldier's name.*

*The following morning, the Marine was gone, and I took
the next bus, from Pittsburgh to the city, carefully select-
ing the front seat again. This time the space next to me
remained empty. I leaned back as the bus rolled me towards
the future, and I enjoyed the pleasure of having both obeyed
and disobeyed my mother on the same journey.*

Elsinora's hand had grown tired, as had her eyes. She leaned
back in her chair as she once had leaned back in the seat of
that long-ago bus, but something felt very wrong now, and it
was only a moment before the memory of Fletcher's impending
death came crashing back into her mind.

She shook out her hand, and rubbed her eyes and took up
the pen again. It was necessary to continue. To keep away from
the unbearable present she would write of the past, all night if
need be.

*Once in Manhattan I started out as many would-be
actors do, working as a waitress in a diner. I stayed in a
spartan room in the YWCA on Eighth Avenue for six dollars
a night. I remember standing by the window mesmerized
by the number of people on the sidewalk below, and the
unknown, backlit lives playing out in the opposite buildings.*

*I began going to open-call auditions as I knew all
unknown and out-of-work actors must do, and my fate was
waiting in the short, stocky form of a famous off-Broadway
producer. His name was Ned Schulz. Long dead now.*

"Well, well, what have we here?" I heard him mutter to his assistant when he first saw me.

Ned Schultz was casting a line of pretty young women for the chorus of the Greek tragedy, Iphigenia in Aulis, and one of the women would also understudy the lead.

I gave a deft reading of the Euripides text, and Ned was pleased. He gave me the coveted understudy role, because I knew the play, understood it, and read well. He was, in spite of his eye for fresh young actresses, a serious producer. I looked the part, was the right height, and I fit in well with the other women. Better still, I would fit his casting couch, which was quite real and not very comfortable.

"Come by my office this evening, say at ten o'clock," he had said with undisguised meaning, "and we will go over your contract together."

I look back through the years now, and I smile a forgiving smile at my young self. It was decades before the MeToo movement, and back in the day I knew these unsavory arrangements were often part of the deal. Show biz, they called it. It was a fleeting, and not entirely unenjoyable, alliance of which I am neither proud nor regretful but, nevertheless, I decided not to let it happen again. I wanted to succeed by my talent alone.

The Grandfather clock in the distant living room struck ten, jolting her forward into the here and now. Elsinora stretched out her arms and legs slowly. Her body had stayed too long in one position. Her back was aching. She struggled to her feet and made her way to the cabinet for another brandy.

"Should I?" she asked herself, eyeing the bottle the way her mother had eyed the cookie jar. "'Tis medicinal brandy, methinks," and she poured herself another.

Elsinora was teetering a bit, but she was determined that as the alcohol was slipping her mind to happier times she would, tonight, keep drinking. She returned to her seat in the hallway and reopened the journal.

I enrolled as a student in The Thespian Atelier, and felt a home there immediately. I made friends easily. I soon discovered, that besides being talented, I was quite savvy about what to audition for, what roles to accept or turn down, and my career as a serious actress began to be real. I loved every moment in a rehearsal hall or on a stage or in an acting class. I was only anxious when I was waiting in the wings before going on in a play. Once on, I was on. I shed my unwanted self, became another.

I remember how an empty stage seemed like a gigantic book, its pages sprawling open and onto which I would step, and out of which emerged the living people enclosed within. It was said that I gave life to the characters I played, but it was they who gave life to me.

The second most surprising moment of my youth occurred when I realized that if I was playing the part of a beautiful woman I became beautiful. I ceased to be the somewhat pretty, underdeveloped Nora Ellen Dean of Warrensville, Ohio and became glamorous. It was magic. In reviews I was called stunning, magnetic, alluring, ravishing; and at first I was unbelieving, but soon had to admit it was so. I took pleasure in the illusion.

Alas, when I was alone between roles I was, as I had been throughout my life, a restless and unhappy soul. It was my fallback setting. I had secured a small apartment at the top of a brownstone in the West Eighties. There were friends in the building, other actors, and a kind landlady. I read books, as I had always done, and now I listened to Leonard Cohen's mournful ballads which somehow soothed me.

I knew what I should feel: happy at my fine health and for my good fortune in a notoriously difficult career; enjoying, maybe even loving, the occasional admirer I chose to take into my bed. I knew by my twenties that my inner life had a name, melancholy.

I chose to concentrate on my work. I studied, and learned, and honed a natural talent into an exceptional skill. In time I was becoming famous and that led to more work so I accepted it's inconveniences—agents, managers, publicists, stylists, accountants—as necessary. Soon these supposedly well-meaning people were managing my life in the way adults had once controlled me as a child.

But Fletcher, as in my youth, was nearby rising in his own career while mine took off, speaking sense and nonsense in exactly the right balance to be a helpmate to me. Oh, I must not think of him just now. I'll write about Oliver-Paul. No! My old heart beats too rapidly when I—

The pen dropped from her hand. The hall seemed to be tilting. She thought perhaps that she should lie down, but felt oddly secure in this isolated spot. She did not wish to summon Robbie and Geraldo, her erstwhile caretakers, her own personal Rosencranz and Guildenstern, the faithful pair, who were most likely already asleep in the nearby guest room while Hesper was away again dealing with her unholy marital situation. She swallowed down more brandy. Oh, she thought, the choices we women make, poor things! With few exceptions the lives of the women of her generation had been organized by men. Though exceptional in so many respects, in this regard she was not: Kingsley, Conrad, Oliver-Paul, Fletcher—

Elsinora knew that by writing she was hoping for a way through her sadness, but when she looked up the vision of a life emptied of Fletcher's presence disorganized her thoughts much as the loss of her father had done when she was a child holding the fateful telegram. Missing in action. It meant dead. Her father was dead. Action was missing. All her little girl's hopes had come to nothing. And now in her eighties she couldn't even harbor illusions of hope. She knew too well the finality of death.

An illness will overcome me again, she thought. Perhaps I will cease to walk, and be unable to tolerate any food but candy. This time I will not survive.

She didn't care.

The last shot of brandy hit her suddenly and she dropped the glass onto the carpet next to her pen and watched it lie there, still and empty, not a drop of goodness left inside.

Slumping in the chair she tried to command her mind, to order it to work properly, but it now lurched and cascaded through time. She had drunk too much and could no longer make her thoughts behave. Instead, memories appeared and disappeared at random, like a Marquez novel or a Rushdie or Murakami, with reality and fantasy all in a tumble, the images flaring in a wildly unpredictable manner, like the flames in a roaring fire.

Exhausted from her attempts at mental control, Elsinora, like an army general retreating to a bunker uncaring of the whereabouts of his disordered troops, at last surrendered and let her thoughts run where they would. She had just been on a Broadway stage, but now she was sixteen, arranging books in the Warrensville public library where she had worked throughout her teenage years, and where she had once fully expected to become a librarian like the late, much-loved Mrs. Kellogg.

In the next moment she was thirty-five having been devoured

by her charismatic husband, Oliver-Paul Harding. There they were attending the Oscars in Santa Monica where their latest movie had been overlooked, but her performance had received a nomination.

She had told Oliver-Paul when she met him that she was satisfied with her theatrical life in New York, that she was not the right kind of actress for film, that she did not have the ruthless strength of the women who prevailed in Hollywood. He said none of that mattered and, just as Fletcher had predicted, he steamrolled right over her objections. She had the looks, and talent, and brains, and working with that material he, Oliver-Paul, with his own talent, business savvy, and ambition, would make her into a star, and for awhile, in spite of herself, he had done just that. She was the oil poured onto the flame of his directing career, which was his actual concern in life.

How insistent he had been that they show up at those Oscars, arm and arm, dressed like royalty, and wearing big movie star smiles.

"I don't want to go!" she protested.

"Your gown has just arrived, my dear one," he replied with a self-satisfied smile, "and you look magnificent in gold. We must go forward like the spectacular couple we are, onwards onto the red carpet. Big smiles, Babe!"

There they were, sunk into their seats in the monstrous auditorium, cameras swinging aloft scrutinizing their intimate expressions and gestures; her smile was a feat of acting, while he naturally relished every moment of the attention. There they sat, a stunning pair, magnanimously applauding other nominees.

She had won again. She had cared a great deal about her performance at the time, but not a bit about the award she was handed. She acted as if she did. She did that well, too. The Oscar mattered to Oliver-Paul.

None of the showing-off, the glitz, or the glamor had anything to do with the fine art of acting, the beauty of creation, the perfect loss of self that she so loved and needed and found only upon a stage.

Her reckless mind rocketed far from the Academy Awards stage and fast-forwarded into Oliver-Paul's well-attended funeral. Her dress was black. Fletcher was seated at the organ console playing mournful hymns in that austere Presbyterian Church on Fifth Avenue. All of it was the opposite of Hollywood unreality. At least she didn't have to smile.

In the next moment she was hurled back to her Uncle Conroy's hospital room watching him struggle for breath, and then she saw his coffin as it was swallowed up on the slowly retracting tongue of the crematorium's horrific, fire-breathing maw.

Now she was falling from the raised platform of the Broadway stage, down into the unlighted orchestra pit, her back arching and her bones cracking as she hit the floor. Pain. Blackness.

She kicked at the empty brandy tumbler, as her disordered brain charged forward offering seductive promises: death would come as a release; death was rest; death was the peace she had always sought; it might be wondrous: she might undergo a miraculous reincarnation as half the world believed; or she might reunite with all those friends she had lost. Perhaps her spirit would sail forth from her body and soar, thrown like a sword through the ether, into some alternate universe of experience. Might not Oliver-Paul's spirit await her, or even her father's? Would she recognize him? Would she bump into her mother? Hi, Mom, no need to worry about me anymore, I'm dead. Or would Grandma Bessie be there to take hold of her ephemeral hand? Would Grandma speak again? That would be wonderful. Would Uncle Conroy be there? The thought was chilling. There was a remote possibility of heaven she supposed, with God and judgment, insipid music and annoying angels, but she didn't believe in God.

She believed in Shakespeare: "The undiscovered country from whose bourn no traveler returns..."

Yet it seemed an impossibility that she, this matrix of living flesh, of memory, of thought, of pulsing emotion and desire, this Elsinora, would simply vanish as if she had never been. There was no way to imagine nothingness.

"Death is not what it seems."

"What did you say?" asked Hesper who suddenly appeared in the hallway having returned from her most recent wanderings. There she stood, her face arranged in a combination of concern and disapproval. Somehow it was morning again.

"I was speaking to myself."

"Here, in the empty hallway."

"Yes, and sleeping in the hallway, too. I must have become medicinally drunk."

"So it appears."

"And where are Robbie and Geraldo?"

"Haven't a clue."

Hesper flushed. "You've been here all night in that wretched chair alone?"

"And I still breathe. Imagine that."

"Are you hungry?"

"No."

"There must be something you would like to eat."

"Funeral baked meats."

"You don't eat meat."

"It's from *Hamlet*."

"Is that what he ate?"

"Hamlet, as you know perfectly well, is a character. An act

of imagination. He doesn't exist and therefore he eats nothing."

"Sometimes, I cannot make sense of you, Mrs. Harding."

It was always upsetting when Hesper sounded like her mother.

"Nora Ellen, really! You would think after all the books you've read there would be some sense in your head," declared Greta.

"Ribbon candy."

"What?"

"I will eat ribbon candy. Like we had at Christmas."

"You will do no such thing, young lady. Candy will rot your teeth."

"You better let her have the candy, Greta," interposed Mrs. Richie who was standing next to her mother at the bedside. "She is starving herself, poor child. At least it might keep her alive until a doctor figures out what to do for her."

"She doesn't need a doctor. She needs a good hiding. She is just being stubborn."

"Well, neither you nor I are going to give her a hiding. That's for fathers to do and she hasn't got one anymore."

"Kingsley would never lay a hand on her. That's half what's wrong with her. Spoilt her, he did."

"He hardly had time to do much spoiling. She was just a mite when he went to the war."

"You're right. I don't suppose she even remembers him." Greta started to cry, whether from frustration or sadness or concern was unclear.

"I've got some of that curly candy she's asking for leftover from Christmas," said Mrs. Richie. "I'll go get it."

"Thank you. Oh, what will I ever do without Kingsley?"

"I lost my Bill to a bad heart six years ago this November. We women carry on. We do our best. You will find a way, Greta."

Elsinora felt warmed to know that Mrs. Richie was once

again looking out for her mother as well as herself. While the women talked over her she was re-reading, *Hamlet.* If Greta had been Hamlet's mother she would warn him to stay away from the battlements and never play with swords. She smiled.

Elsinora knew her mother loved her as well she was able, fearfully, without curiosity, and therefore without any understanding. It was the small love of a small woman; one capable of moderate affections and annoyance, of envy and disappointment, of niggling worry about what the neighbors might think. Anyone who was not like herself was thought to be suspect, and her daughter could not have been more unlike.

Her mother hadn't bargained for widowhood or single parenting when she married Kingsley Dean, doubtless in the hope of some security after her orphaned childhood and a loveless upbringing among distant relatives who called her Regrettable Greta, and thought of her more as a servant than as a family member.

Elsinora felt a softness towards her mom for loving her, and for doing her best in an ill-suited role, but this sentiment was stained with pity, much as she felt for Oliver Twist or for the poor, much-abused Jane Eyre.

When Elsinora was older, after reading her way through *The Forsythe Saga,* she had reason to wonder about her parents' marriage. She thought she understood her mother's part in it, but why had her father married Greta? What she remembered of her handsome father was that he was an unusual man who preferred reading to hunting, dancing to sports, listening to showing-off; she imagined that he could have had his pick of women. Although she would never really know, Elsinora had come to believe that her father had chosen her mother because she was the woman most in need of his love.

Had the war not interfered, had he lived, he might have

soothed Greta's anxieties, honed her brittle edges, brought forth tenderness instead of strictness from her bruised and frightened soul.

Well, there they had been, stuck with each other: two orphans in the storm of life…a depressed, worried mother who did not know how to be a mother and a willful, bookish child who did not know how to be a child.

"How about Cheerios?" interrupted Hesper. "You always like a bowl of that old standby."

Hesper was seriously worried about Elsinora who had completely lost her appetite and turned her nose up at every offering but brandy.

"Ribbon candy."

"What?"

"When I was a child I became very ill. I would eat only ribbon candy. It was the only thing I could keep down."

"No one can live on candy."

"That's what my mother said, but I did, and for a very long time. I have a taste for some now. And no, I am not demented."

Hesper bent to retrieve the brandy tumbler, and with some prodding of the recalcitrant Elsinora, achieved her agreement to take a restorative nap. She went out like the proverbial light.

Robbie and Geraldo had reported that while Hesper had been away Elsinora agreed only to tea during the entire weekend, and had seldom talked, never smiled. Hesper was vexed that they had not called her home.

Ribbon candy. Perhaps it would be a start. It contained a little nourishment which might whet Elsinora's appetite after three days of virtual starvation.

How Barton would enjoy this bit of arcane history. A childhood illness was of some interest in a biography. Was it benign enough to tell him? She wasn't sure. And that mother! Letting a child live on candy. She shook her head in dismay. Everyone had to be some way, she knew, but no one was the way they should be.

If Elsinora continued to refuse food Hesper knew she would soon be forced to summon the doctors, but as this might signal the beginning of the end, she hesitated. If Elsinora went into a hospital or a nursing home, the manor would be closed up and she would be immediately unemployed.

Hesper went to her computer and brought up the grocery site. Ribbon candy!

XV. Give thy thoughts no tongue.

RETIREMENT WAS NOT suiting Dr. Maurice Schadad. Not a bit. The only day of the week that he now fully enjoyed was Saturday when he consulted with a few steadfastly loyal patients with minor complaints, whom he thought of as the-worried-well. He saw them mostly because they were lonely, as was he. He knew this was a common condition in old age.

And now there was one less patient. One who had truly been ill. He refolded *The New York Times* and threw it onto the breakfast table. It skidded into his half-empty cup of tea and almost knocked it over.

Fletcher Mulcaster was dead. The news coverage alongside the obituary reported on how the shocked city was mourning its great musical icon. As his personal physician he, more than any other, was prepared for this unwelcome news, but no one is ever truly prepared for the black figure of death when it arrives, only to swiftly disappear with a loved one forever hidden beneath an inky cloak.

He had, of course, done all he could for the famous musician, consulting with the top specialists, personally reviewing the cutting edge research, but nothing could have saved Fletcher from the fast moving illness that had lurked inside him, demanding his life and silencing his music.

As sad as he was himself, his mind had flown to Elsinora.

She would be heart broken. He desperately wanted to call her, perhaps console her, as he had once done so long ago, but that time was ancient history, buried under decades of absence. Was it possible he could now reach out to her?

He took his cell phone from his pocket and stared at the screenshot on its glowing face. Some time ago he had replaced the informal snapshot of himself and his late wife. Now he gazed at a preciously young Elsinora as she had appeared on stage in the role of Juliet. He had captured her image from a celebrity site on the internet. He touched her cheek with his forefinger.

He knew she had never married again after the death of Oliver-Paul…after…himself…but so beautiful a woman must have taken lovers. Fletcher, of course, would have been too discreet to mention them in their brief conversations about her over the years. The thought of Elsinora in the arms of another was hideously painful.

He laid the phone facedown on the counter.

He finished his tea and dropped the newspaper into the bin, placed the breakfast dishes in the dishwasher, wiped down the table carefully and dried it with a dish towel. He walked the few steps to the laundry room and deposited the dishtowel in the washer. He kept his kitchen as clean as an operating theater.

He looked down again at the resting phone.

He had no right to disrupt her life, to interrupt her grieving for Fletcher; not after the choice he had made to remain with his wife in his long, long marriage; no right to speak to her after forty years of silence.

XVI. Mourning duties.

ELSINORA, TREMBLING, HAD enclosed herself in her bedroom and locked the door against intrusion when Fletcher's protégé had phoned with the news that he was now gone. Her grief had begun to howl inside her, and desperate to once again escape the lacerating present she had stabbed her finger into the Shakespeare volume. Her eyes followed her hand down to the place onto which it had fallen; a line of Prospero's, in *The Tempest*.

"What seest thou else
In the dark backward and abysm of time?"

She would not think about her treacherous childhood. She would not try to recover the lost year. Thirteen was gone. But at age fourteen when, like a gift from the Gods, Fletcher Mulcaster had appeared, her memory once more sprang to life. He had arrived at her home, rather like Heathcliff had been brought to *Wuthering Heights,* by Uncle Conroy without any warning. The memory was as clear and sharp as a diamond.

She opened her journal, and with a shaking hand began to write.

On the day before Fletcher appeared Uncle Conroy received a telegram. Stuffing it into his pocket he swore in words I had never even heard before, and announced he had to drive in to Cleveland. He tore out of the driveway like Satan himself was on his tail, leaving both Mom and me without the slightest explanation. Mother, of course, expected the worst.

"It must be another woman," she wailed, and went off to her bedroom to cry.

I allowed myself a brief moment of hopeless hope that he was going to find my father.

Early the next morning when I heard another sling of gravel on the driveway I ran to the front hall, full of curiosity. Conroy swung the door open and pushed a reluctant boy over the threshold. Fletcher stood, just inside the foyer, with a small suitcase in his hand and a dazed expression on his face.

"This is your cousin. His name is Fletcher," Conroy announced. "He'll be living here now. Nora Ellen, as you are camped in Kingsley's old room he can be put in the smaller one next to yours, the one I had as a boy. Why don't you show him where it is and tell him what's what. I need a stiff drink, and I expect your mother will need one too when she hears this news."

"I didn't know I had a cousin."

"Well dearie, I didn't know I had a son! Until yesterday. He has grown up with his mother, a woman named Rosie Mulcaster, whom I don't recall in the slightest, in England, near a place where your father and I were stationed awhile during the war. Now he is here, shipped over by boat and train without an extra dime or a by-your-leave, and only that telegram arriving last night to inform me of his existence, and ordering me to get to the train station in Cleveland in the middle of the goddamned night to fetch him. The mother is too ill and too poor to keep him. Supposedly."

He turned to stare at the silent boy. "He hasn't said a single word. Not even hello. Maybe he's daft. God knows how he got so far as he did with only these instructions pinned to his jacket, a passport, and tickets in the side pocket."

I recall Conroy's fierce expression as he lit a Lucky Strike and blew the smoke in our direction. He turned on his heels, and went down the hall in search of my mother, who was still secluded and distraught in their room. There in the hallway the two of us stood; one amazed, one bereft, both bewildered.

What I saw standing before me was a frightened boy of about my own age. I liked the look of him. He was a bit on the thin side, dressed in strange-looking clothing, and staring straight ahead. He seemed afraid to look around at his new surroundings. I was drawn to him. I took a step forward and laid my hands gently on his shoulders. Our eyes locked. My heart went out to him and it never returned.

Where is my heart to go now?

IN THIS MORNING of unpredicted rain Hesper tarried at her desk, reluctant to engage with the gray, pattering day, one she knew would be difficult.

She stared at the slightly dampened newspaper with its black lines announcing Fletcher Mulcaster's death and immediate memorial service. At last she knew what had been the cause of Elsinora's previous two weeks of despondency. He must have forewarned her. The paper reported he had died "peacefully after a short illness."

The notice caused her deep sadness and also aroused her guilt. She had failed to elicit what had been distressing Elsinora.

And she had been too distracted by her husband's demands.

Although she knew every inch of the house that she kept in such good order, where every object was arranged and every paper filed, she had thought perhaps that Robbie and Geraldo would notice something interesting she could take to Barton, some harmless tidbit of interest that she might have overlooked, so the previous week she had asked them to poke around the manor while they stayed to look after Elsinora. Although they had come up empty, she wished she had exercised better judgment and not involved them at all. It had simply been wrong of her. In fact, with Elsinora so fragile, she shouldn't have left her for a moment.

Angry with herself, she decided to clean. Cleaning always steadied her nerves, lightened her moods.

As she worked her way around the manor, dustcloth in hand, she tried unsuccessfully to ease her conscience. She had been pushed by Barton who was frantic about getting his version of Elsinora Dean down on paper before anyone else seized upon the idea. Although the former star had of late been largely forgotten, exactly as she wished to be, her demise would wake everyone up again. Barton was certain the biography crowd would start writing dizzily the moment Elsinora's obituary appeared.

"We have to be ready when she goes!" Barton kept repeating, but that event could be tomorrow or ten years from now, thought Hesper. People lived to be a hundred nowadays and if anyone could do so, it would be Elsinora.

There had been one unauthorized biography published already, almost twenty years previously, but it was poorly written and long out of print. When a used copy showed up on Amazon or eBay (and Hesper had been told to check for this often) Elsinora would buy it and destroy it. She was fierce about her privacy. Hesper had only agreed to cooperate with Barton's book because he had assured her it would be complimentary, and come out only after her death. Elsinora would never know. But now it no longer felt right because of the turn his mind had taken. What had caused her husband to descend from respectable biography to tabloid journalism?

Hesper was again due to visit Barton on the weekend and he would want to know all the details of Elsinora's reaction to the death of Fletcher. It was unseemly. Perhaps a biographer had to be relentless, but she didn't have to like it.

She pictured his office, overheated, messy, manila files overflowing with newspaper articles and old movie magazines. Stories, true and false about Elsinora's love life, the tragic death of her husband, and about the official police inquiry.

It was true that Elsinora's husband, Oliver-Paul Harding, had died a grisly death; an electric fan sliding from its perch on a granite bathroom counter into his tub. The circumstances had been investigated at the time as there had been salacious rumors printed about their marriage, terrible public fights reported, speculation about an impending divorce. In the end, Oliver-Paul's death was ruled accidental.

And now Barton would not leave the story alone. He declared that the suspicious death of a warring spouse made for damn good copy.

Hesper shook her head in sad disapproval and resumed her work. She had never had the bravery to war with Barton. A few spats were all she had ever been able to muster. She had largely ignored their problems, letting things drift. Deciding to move in with Elsinora during the pandemic had been the undeclared end to their union.

So why was she acting as if she was still his loyal spouse? Why was she continuing to do his bidding, accumulating guilt in the process? Why did she not act on her own behalf and become a free woman? You can take the Catholic out of the church, she thought, but you can never take the church out of a Catholic.

Would Elsinora, who espoused no religion, abide in a loveless marriage? she asked herself. No. She was sure of that. But murder? It was a ridiculous idea! The actress Elsinora Dean had a reputation in her day: willful, difficult to work with at times, a perfectionist, prone to angry demands on the set or the stage, but why would she murder Oliver-Paul when she could more easily divorce him?

And why couldn't *she* divorce Barton when half the time she wanted to kill him? Of the two sins surely the former was of less consequence.

As she dusted the small safe in which Elsinora kept her cigar box and important papers she wondered if there was a will. Hesper would like to see a will if there was one. She was sure to be left some sort of a remembrance. Wasn't she? Some suitable amount of money to see her through until she found her next job? She had hopes. The safe was always kept locked.

She stopped dusting and stood still. She folded her arms across her chest, her posture a part of the decision she was making. Elsinora had received terrible news. It was right for Hesper to stay with her this weekend. Let Barton be damned! She reached up and felt for her crucifix, ran it gently back and forth along its delicate gold chain. No, not damned, but he could stew.

At the sound of a bell, she put the dustcloth down and her feelings aside. She must go in search of Elsinora. She was needed.

Elsinora's bedroom was located at the far end of Arden Manor so that she would not have to hear the clack of computer keys or the myriad phone calls Hesper was required to make in the course of her duties. Unless she wanted to, of course. Hesper knew about the intercoms and cameras connected to Elsinora's devices and, as much as she tried to ignore them she seldom forgot them. She was generally cautious, but setting Robbie and Geraldo snooping about the place had been careless. The two well-meaning men had been caught on camera and come in for a serious scolding from Elsinora. They had been told not to return. What a mess. Everyone spying on everyone else! She was lucky she had been allowed to hold onto her job.

She found Elsinora, as expected, in her bedroom. She looked up with a blankness that revealed nothing.

"We need to go into the city, Hesper," she announced.

"I am deeply sorry for your loss, Mrs. Harding. Mr. Mulcaster was a wonderful man. I shall miss him, too."

There was no reply. Hesper could intuit the tumult inside Elsinora, though her stillness sealed it from view.

"It says his memorial service is at four. They haven't given us much notice. I'll order the car."

Elsinora sighed deeply and seemed to bring herself together. "Doubtless they held off printing the announcement of his funeral until the very last minute in order to limit the number of spectators. We, however, will not be going there. Don't look so startled, Hesper. It is at Fletcher's own command."

"Then where will we be going?"

"Where you go will be your choice. Too bad it is raining. Not a good day for you to shop. But I will be purchasing a hat."

Hesper's eyebrows raised. "We have a great many hats, Mrs. Harding, rain hats, sun hats, knit caps, earmuffs. Why ever do you need another just now, if I may inquire?"

"I'm talking about hats of the kind women *used* to wear, beautiful concoctions that enhance a woman's appearance. One only sees them nowadays in photographs of British royalty. American women walk around wearing baseball caps. Baseball caps are for children. And those pink pussyhats that are meant to make a political statement about women's strength do exactly the opposite. They are cute. Cute is for fat babies."

"I am not quite following this, Mrs. Harding."

"It's not so difficult. I need a hat for a grown-up woman. There is fortunately a proper millinery shop still in business on the Upper East Side. I have made a call myself to secure a private appointment."

"I'm wondering why you need such a hat, if we are not attending the funeral."

Elsinora was silent, thinking of Fletcher. Might he really greet her in the clouds someday? She would wave the red hat. She smiled.

Hesper was at a loss. "Perhaps a dramatic hat is needed because you have changed your mind about attending the Oscars?" she offered tentatively.

"Close, but no cigar."

"What did you say?"

"A quote from Annie Oakley."

"Who?"

"Oh, never mind! I live in a world without reference these days," Elsinora replied in frustration.

Maybe, Hester thought, there was indeed some senility beginning to make inroads into her employer's brain, but she saw an opportunity and took it.

"You had best eat a proper breakfast this morning then. You have sustained a terrible shock. You will need to get your strength up for the city."

"There is nothing wrong with my strength. Have you tried any of this ribbon candy?" she asked holding up a box of the delicately curved red and green sweets.

"I did. Nothing but sugar."

"That is all I can abide today. Oh, and Hesper, a brandy, no a large Scotch, just before we go."

Minutes later as rain beat down upon the car while it hummed steadily along towards the city, Elsinora willed her thoughts away from the cathedral they would be passing with the funeral soon to be occurring inside its walls, the coffin, the crowds in suits of solemn black. God Save the King.

Fletcher had been right. It was the last place she needed to be, though Hesper had shown incomprehension mixed with her usual compliance when Elsinora told her that she was going hat shopping instead. How could Hesper understand her unconventional relationship with Fletcher, their lifetime of unlikely love, or his ability to take care of her even after his death?

As the car proceeded slowly through the congested traffic of the Upper West Side, she returned her mind to the past where she could find a living Fletcher.

Ohio. 1955. She was fifteen. A new war had just been fought, the Korean War, killing people far away that made no sense to her young, defiant mind. She had read all about her father's war, the Holocaust, and Hiroshima in *Life* magazine. Eighty million dead in his war. She thought the world in which she found herself a very wicked place.

An uneasy peace prevailed inside the Homestead at that time, and she was thankful for it. She remembered sitting with Fletcher in the living room, side by side on the old velvet sofa that her Grandma Bessie had cherished. It felt to Elsinora like they were sitting on Grandma Bessie's lap together.

"Fletcher, do you miss your Mom in England a lot?" she asked almost in a whisper, though there was no real need, for the adults were outside, snuggled into the hammock together, drinking their Bloody Marys before dinnertime.

Fletcher got up and crossed the room and turned the television off, then tuned the radio to a classical station, listened for a moment, and said, "Brahms."

"I'm sorry. I guess you don't want to talk about her."

He plopped back down next to her. "I don't think about her very much, to be honest. I don't believe my mother ever loved me and I don't really miss her, but I wish I did. Growing up I imagined it would be nice to have a father who might love me, but look how that turned out. Neither of us have been lucky in the parent department, so it's probably best not to think too much about it," he said, his fingers tapping gently on the worn velvet in time to the music.

Not thinking too much was a new concept for Elsinora. She would have to think about it.

"I know you miss your Dad," he continued.

"I think about him every day. It is almost as if he is right here with me now, sitting over in that armchair, so I'm not sure I am missing him exactly."

"Like he's a ghost?"

"Yes, but not really."

"Has he always been there?"

"Yeah."

"It's your imagination, Els. You have a killer imagination."

"I know."

"Nothing to be afraid of then. He's not an actual ghost."

"But I *am* afraid," she said.

"Of what?"

"I was a baby when he enlisted and five when he went missing. I only saw him a few times when he came home on leave, before he went overseas, so you could say I never really knew him. I'm fifteen now. Shouldn't I be over it? Over him? Yet he is so real to me. Right now he is sitting there smoking his pipe and listening to our conversation. I think I might be crazy. Do you think I am crazy?"

Fletcher looked long and hard at the empty chair, then at her. "No. There is plenty of craziness in this bloody house, but you aren't it. I think you just want your father to be alive so much that you make him up. It's funny. I've got a father now and I don't even want him. Conroy is a jerk. And maybe not even my real father. I had a lot of so-called fathers in Liverpool. Mom sort of collected them."

"Could you ever go back to your mom?"

"No. She made it clear she couldn't take care of me. I'd have to go into an orphanage. She didn't have any money and was going to lose the flat. She thought the best thing was to send me here."

"I'm glad. What is she like, your mother?"

"A solitary note. An e-flat, I would say. Helpless to really connect with another person, to make anything lovely out of life. She was pretty. There were always the men about. Some had money, so we got by, but the drinking was bad."

"Was she musical?"

He laughed. "No. Not in the least. I never heard her sing or even hum. She didn't listen to the radio, except dance music if there was a man there. She didn't know what to make of me for sure. I had a habit of getting caught sneaking into different churches to practice on the pipe organs, then being brought home by the police. I'm not religious but give me the inside of a good church any day than a bedsitter in Liverpool. You can find music in any church, even the Quakers have it. Sort of like you preferring life in the library because there are books there. We have to leave our homes to be us. I wonder where we came from sometimes."

"The Daring Dean brothers of Warrensville, Ohio."

"And where did they come from?"

"Grandma Bessie. That's all I know, and we can't ask her, because she won't say a word."

"There is something wrong with Conroy, isn't there?"

"Yes. But I don't know what."

"It's like he has a part missing. I saw him kill a chicken the other day. With his bare hands. He was smiling."

"Oh. Let's not talk about our parents anymore. Talk about your music."

"Reverend Brown, here at the Methodist Church, says I can play the organ during the day when no one else is using it. There is that old upright piano in the back room here, though I can't get Conroy to cough up the money to have it tuned, but there is a good one at school, and we have our music lessons there."

"It is you who should be teaching them."

"Mr. Gerton is pretty lame, isn't he? All those dumb Sousa marches! A-one-and-a-two-and-a…"

"Gross."

"Adults don't seem to be of much use to us, do they?"

They heard Conroy and Greta laughing as they came into the kitchen where she would heat up the frozen TV dinners. Conroy said something to her mother that Elsinora and Fletcher could not hear, but they guessed it must have to do with sex by the tone. There was more laughter.

"Maybe they aren't monsters, just daft," commented Fletcher.

"Certainly pointless."

"We'll get to New York City someday. I bet grownups are different there. Operas and orchestras and Broadway musicals and all that."

"And the New York Public Library and museums," she added. "We'll go together. Someday." She took his hand.

Fletcher smiled and nodded in the direction of the chair across the room. "Does your Dad like Brahms? Let's just listen to the music for a while." As the next sonata issued from the radio he had sighed pleasurably.

In the New York City of the present, Elsinora's car pulled up to the curb and eased into a lucky parking spot almost in front of the building that housed the exclusive hat shop. The rain continued to fall. Cold tears, thought Elsinora.

As she entered the millinery establishment and was welcomed by a staid, middle-aged woman of uncertain beauty, Elsinora smiled in delight. The shop resembled an overgrown candy store. The stands of many-colored hats displayed upon the skillfully arranged tables reminded her of rainbow lollipops festooned with jellybeans and sprinkles, and cones of feathery cotton candy.

Oh, Fletch!

Soon she was standing before the brightly illuminated mirror admiring her beautiful new hat, of glistening candy-apple red, adorned with scarlet feathers and a veil that both concealed and flattered. She gazed at her image in the mirror, and just for a moment, just for the tiniest slice of an instant, she sensed he was smiling approvingly.

XVII. Thus runs the world away.

ROBBIE AND GERALDO were also absent from the funeral service, though they had known Fletcher well and admired him. As a matter of principle they did not attend anyone's funeral, thinking them barbaric rituals which offered no comfort, and rose no one from the dead.

They had friends who made a point of attending celebrity rites, hoping to see famous people in attendance, but they thought that was ghoulish. They preferred to remember their friends as they had been in life. They dealt with their losses by distraction.

They were standing elbow to elbow at the crowded bar in the lobby of the Imperial Theater. It was the matinee's intermission and the play, a postmodern staging of *The Tempest*, was not to their taste. They were considering whether to leave or, after a strong drink, go back in and tough out the second act.

"Are we just too old to appreciate these revitalizing dramatic experiments?" Robbie asked Geraldo, not for the first time.

"No. It's not us. This version of *The Tempest* is way too odd to be appreciated."

"Caliban is certainly amusing."

"Played by that big black dog."

"And apparently speaking with the piped-in voice of Richard Burton from the 1960's television version!"

"Even Shakespeare, with his mighty imagination, wouldn't believe it."

"Animals have their rights, you know! They have been disen-franchised far too long." Both men started to laugh.

"Well, I should have preferred a different breed in the part. The Great Dane was miscast. Far too imposing. Caliban is but a slave to Prospero after all, so perhaps a hangdog Spaniel or a Basset hound."

"Tell me this isn't a serious conversation."

"Indeed, we are two too old. Let's finish these drinks and make our escape. We can go over to Sardi's before the rush and order that nice fusilli with chicken."

"Unless the chickens are all at an audition for *Oklahoma*."

Chuckling and shaking their heads at the absurdities appear-ing on the current Broadway stages and accepting the reality that the innovations of the modern world were swiftly outpacing their ability to appreciate them, they walked from the Imperial to Sardi's where, in this haven to all people theatrical, they were warmly welcomed.

Now retired, Robbie and Geraldo had been rival drama critics in two leading New York City newspapers back in the day when the city had seven daily papers. But as Broadway weakened, and newspapers died, and fewer shows of merit were produced they had teamed up as movie critics on a chatty television show. This had proved far more lucrative, giving them a comfortable old age. In the process they had fallen in love, and were now settled into their golden years as a contented married couple.

The walls of Sardi's interior were famously decorated, head to toe, with row upon row of caricatures. Actors and theatrical personalities of every generation, both famous and faded, found a place there. It was a moment before the two men realized they had been seated in a red leather banquette directly under the restaurant's picture of Elsinora Dean, and their mood deflated.

"She will be devastated," said Geraldo. "Fletcher was like a brother to her."

"I wish we could be there to console her."

"We could send flowers."

"What good would that do?"

"Just so she knows we care."

"She is very angry with us, and she doesn't need us or she would send for us."

"Do you think she will ever need us again?"

"If we are, we'll be sent for."

"We should never have agreed to snoop, even a little."

"Hesper was very persuasive."

"We've been over all this a dozen times, dear. We wanted to help perpetuate her name, her fame. We thought a biography would do exactly that, and we believed Elsinora would be pleased. It was a colossal mistake. End of story."

"What a dressing down she gave us! I felt seven years old, not seventy."

Her image was fresh in both their minds, standing on the front steps of Arden Manor, hands on hips, refusing them entry, and delivering Hamlet's angry protest: "S'blood, do you think I am easier to be played on than a pipe?!"

They automatically reviewed her performance.

"She was very effective."

"I would say memorable."

"Her voice was strong."

"Her stance was perfect."

"Do you think she will ever forgive us? She has kept Hesper on as her companion, you know."

"Royalty requires courtiers."

"I thought we were courtiers."

"We have never been more than hangers-on. We were never sent for. Except by Hesper."

"Oh, but I have always so admired Elsinora! What a talent. What an intellect. One seldom sees *that* in combination."

"She always enjoyed our admiration, but she never loved us."

"You judge her very harshly, Robbie."

"Well, she *was* harsh."

"Only because we deserved it."

"Speaking of harsh, did you see the reviews for the new *Macbeth* at the Almeida Theater in London?" asked Robbie, eager to turn the conversation away from the unhappy recollection of Elsinora's anger.

"No. Do tell. Is Macbeth played by a lesbian or perhaps by a schoolboy in short pants and a beanie?"

"They actually cast a grown man, can you believe it? And a woman for Lady Macbeth. Alas, it takes place in a Caribbean resort. Evidently Lady Macbeth is holding up a cocktail with an umbrella in it when she says, 'Is this a dagger that I see before me?'"

"They were aiming for *Macbeth, The Comedy?*"

"Tragically, yes."

"Oh, here comes the fusilli with the poor chicken who didn't make it into a show."

"Eat up quickly before some animal rights group barges in and protests."

Their good humor was somewhat restored by the food, the wine, and the discussion of the bad reviews out of London. Their concern about the falling out with Elsinora Dean receded until they rose to depart. Once more her likeness looked out at them from within its enclosing frame. She appeared as she did in her years of youth and beauty, and as she would always appear in their minds.

"She looks in that picture, even in caricature, as she did when she played Ophelia. The best Ophelia of our lifetime by far."

"Every young actress always overacts Ophelia's mad scene. They put on an antic disposition, but the ravings inevitably sound fake."

"Elsinora played it as if she was actually insane. From the inside."

"Her off-Broadway Hamlet was wonderful, too. Few women can play the part, but she pulled it off."

"I preferred her later performance, in the Broadway *Hamlet*."

"I think we have agreed to disagree about which was better, but we both wrote sterling reviews."

"Yes, but you nailed it. 'She played Hamlet not as a man, nor a woman neither, but as a human.'"

"Am I right to remember that she had first played it in college?"

"Yes. It was her maiden performance, if one can believe it. We shall not see her like again."

"That is the tragedy of every great stage performance, nothing of it lasts. At the final curtain all is lost."

"Memory, dear one. We retain the memory."

"We are such things as dreams are made on—"

"Yes. Yes. And there will always be her films."

"And our reviews of her performances. Those will last in the library archives."

With these consoling thoughts Robbie and Geraldo went out onto the darkening West Forty-fourth Street, hastening home through Times Square with its blaze of garish advertisements and actors who could only find work wearing the costumes of frolicking Disney characters.

XVIII. A soldier to the stage.

ON WAKING, COLONEL Arthur Osborne stretched and yawned and stretched again. Nurse Benoit would be coming in soon to perform his morning checkup, and, because she liked him, she would bring his breakfast porridge herself instead of relegating the task to an aide. He would much rather have a big bowl of strawberry ice cream, but you took what you could get in a place like this.

He was the last man alive on this ward who had fought in World War ll. All the other much younger patients were from Korea, or Vietnam, or Afghanistan, or Desert Storm. There was even one fellow each from the invasions of Grenada and The Panama Canal, neither of whom were *compos mentis*. The United States government kept its veterans' hospitals full to brimming with every kind of disabled soldier, and provided them with free cemetery plots, too, when the time came.

Nurse Benoit arrived with a cheery hello, and her thermometer gun which she placed against his forehead, giving him a satisfied smile as she noted the numbers. This procedure always gave him the creeps.

She took his pulse in the old fashioned way, his wrist in her soft hand, and then placed a plastic tray on the rolling table by his bedside, slid the table over the edge of the bed so the tray was positioned within reach and, giving him a pat on the arm, prepared to leave him to his breakfast.

"Special day today, Colonel Osborne," she remarked as she left the room.

There on the tray was the card, just as on every Fourth of July. He smiled. Elsinora never missed. It was always a satisfying pleasure to know she was still alive. If he was one hundred and three today, she would be? He could never quite calculate it. He could only think of her as the young star she had been when he had met her during their one brief, significant encounter. He remembered this in detail.

Right after a Wednesday matinee he had walked through the backstage door into the Broadhurst Theater on West Forty-fourth Street as bold as brass. It was something he had learned to do in the army; just comport yourself like you look like you belong somewhere and no one will think otherwise. He supposed that nowadays Broadway backstages had become security-ridden prisons like everything else, but back then…how long ago…fifty years ago…he had strolled right in without so much as a by-your-leave.

There was Elsinora Dean, sitting in front of a big light-encircled mirror looking so exquisite it had caused him to stop breathing for a moment. She was removing her stage makeup after a performance, as Laura, in *The Glass Menagerie,* a play he hadn't much cared for, but the truth was that he could watch her in anything and be mesmerized. (Often, being a red-blooded sort of man, he imagined her in nothing at all.)

She had looked up, startled at this stranger's sudden appearance in her private dressing room, but at the time he was just a slight, well-groomed man, in an army officer's uniform, smiling his friendliest smile. There was nothing frightening about him. She had no doubt supposed that he was a pushy fan in search of an autograph.

He had never been in a backstage dressing room before, but it looked like the ones he had seen depicted in movies. There was a three-way standing mirror in one corner, a tall folding screen with costumes thrown over it, end tables adorned with flowers, and the dressing table was overflowing with stacks of cards and telegrams and unopened envelopes which he took to be fan mail, next to pots of stage paints, brushes, and combs.

She wore a bright red kimono, and her hair, darkened for the part she was playing, had been pulled back to facilitate the removal of her stage makeup. Elsinora, the central figure in the whole scene, appeared incredibly glamorous to him.

He had quickly and carefully introduced himself, shown her his identification, explained his background, and then come as swiftly as he could to the point of his visit. He was not there for an autograph.

Elsinora paled when she heard the real reason he had come. The color had drained from her face like liquid rushing down a pipe, and she had clutched at her heart, not in a theatrical gesture, but because she was made faint by what he had told her.

"My father," was all she had managed to whisper in response. Tears had appeared in her eyes, quivering there.

"I thought you would want to know these facts about him," he had said. "Nevertheless, I am sorry to bring a report that so distresses you."

She stood up suddenly and closed the dressing room door, then sinking back onto the chair she clutched the edge of the dressing table in an attempt to steady herself, her knuckles white. Her eyes moved wildly, darting about the room.

He had poured her a glass of water from the pitcher on the table, and wanted to pat her on the back or take her hand, but was afraid to touch her. One did not touch a goddess.

"Thank you," she managed to say after greedily swallowing

the water, attempting to regain her composure, remaining as white as if she had seen a ghost. "Does anyone else know of this?"

"I reported it, of course, to the army authorities at the time, but nothing was done in the chaos following the end of the war. Having no proof I could not pursue matters further. Since that time I have spoken the truth to only one other soul. You were but a child, and your mother, with whom I tried to speak, would not let me come into the house, so I sought out your grand-mother at a retirement home. She was the only one, besides myself, who knew."

"Why have you come to me now?"

I have been stationed abroad for most of my career, and so this is the first opportunity I have had to converse with you as an adult. As you are Master Sergeant Kingsley Dean's daughter it seems right that you should know the truth."

"It is right."

He had ventured to ask: "His brother Conroy...he is still—"

"Yes!" she snapped, her voice sharp with anger. "Sadly, yes," she repeated. "He lives at the Homestead. And now we both know what I must do. Promise me you will not speak of this to anyone else."

She picked up a paper knife from the table and turned it over in her hands.

"I promise," he had assured her, warily watching the glint from the knife blade as it revolved in the light.

"On your honor as a soldier, it will remain between the two of us?"

"I swear it."

Distracted, she had asked yet again, as if for the first time. "I can trust you? You swear to silence?"

"I have sworn."

They stayed together for awhile in silence, he standing almost at attention, she sitting still, mired in her own dark thoughts. He had watched as the color slowly returned to her perfect face, as her breathing became regular, as her hands ceased to tremble, as her eyes settled on the knife.

Only then had he noticed that his own hands were clammy and clenched in tension where he had jammed them into his trouser pockets. He realized, as the soldier he was, that he had unconsciously been waiting to be dismissed.

So, as no further words were necessary between them, he nodded politely and left the dressing room, out through the stage door, never to speak to her again, but bound by his vow of silence to Elsinora Dean for all these many years.

Colonel Osbourne's eyes had misted over at the memory. He began to pay attention to his porridge, which had gone cold and thick, but was still filling. Here, in this small, some would say claustrophobic, hospital room, which he would probably never again leave, he could taste the rich earth from which the grains of his cereal had sprung. He could imagine the sunlight and cool rains that had nourished the stalks, and enjoy the sweet taste of its young, golden wild oats. His mind roamed free as a child.

He opened the envelope. Inside was an expensive card with an embossed American flag waving proudly. In her own hand, she had written a simple thank you, so much nicer than the ecards and email notes he would get from scattered great-grandchildren he barely knew, and who doubtless hoped to be remembered in his will.

There, above her signature, was the message, the one that only the two of them would fully understand:

Death is not what it seems.

Nurse Benoit would be quite surprised if she returned to his room just now, and happened to check his pulse.

XIX. The heyday the blood.

A T THE AGE of eight-four Elsinora had long been finished with sex, but sex was not finished with her, or so she had discovered. In the early hours of the morning, well before dawn, she emerged from a dream in which she was a full participant with Oliver-Paul on a dressing room couch, backstage in an unknown theater. They were as they had been when their romance was young, their blood roaring, and their appetite for one another ravenous.

She had awakened abruptly in her narrow bed, with body parts aglow, and knowing there would be no more sleep for the night, she decided to walk down to the edge of the lake. She took her cane, and made her way with slow and careful steps through the darkness, arriving safely at the Adirondack chairs without incident, settling herself in the blue one that Fletcher had always preferred. She would watch for the sunrise. Her multiple layers of nightgown, bathrobe, shawl, and quilt were wrapped around her as tightly as Oliver-Paul's phantom arms had been in the dream, keeping her warm.

In the cataloging of her life she had shied away from the years with Oliver-Paul, and in particular his death, her mind always sliding away when it caught sight of that terrible scene; but her memories of the perilous time were pushing upwards into her consciousness emerging from sleep into waking.

She could picture Oliver's perfect body and how drawn to it she had been after the spindly, bookish boys with whom she had first been involved and the actors who came and went with the shows in which she performed.

Mysterious at the time, lust in recollection keeps its secrets. Fresh from her dream however, an echo of those early feelings returned to be remembered.

She had thought she felt love for Oliver-Paul. How shocking it had been to suddenly feel something so powerful, so real. Desire that was her own and not those of a character she was playing; the kind of love she had read about in novels for years, and had, until that time, believed was only fictional.

Sex with Oliver-Paul had been a mighty thing indeed. He had taken her down like a lion takes down an antelope. Everything about him was momentous;, working with him, eating with him, drinking with him and, most memorably, sex with him. He was a brilliant, ambitious, charismatic director, a genius with actors, a tyrant with Elsinora, demanding always her best performances, and they had done some of their best work together. He cared only for stardom. He wanted fame, and in their marriage as the golden couple he had found it.

The strength of her passion had staggered her: the relentless desire, the pain her wanting inflicted; the transformation of her need of him into rage and despair when it was withheld, and her emptiness after his horrible death, his gutting absence.

"Th' expense of spirit in a waste of shame," she whispered aloud. Oh how Shakespeare had known everything. Everything.

One woman had never been sufficient to satisfy the appetite of Oliver-Paul, alas, not even *this* woman.

After making their seventh movie together, an *avant garde* rendering of the Joan of Arc story that had failed both critically and financially, Oliver-Paul had begun to drink more than even he could sustain, and his actions, always extreme, had begun to seem out of control. Yes. He had hit her, and on more than one occasion. Always contrite afterwards. So sorry. So classic.

Now, in this chill before dawn, she wondered why so many memories which at their first appearance seem only to offer a cornucopia of pleasure often spill out sorrow instead. A kind of entropy of recollection.

Her mind burrowed deep now, into the remembered agonies of Oliver-Paul's demise. The evening had begun at Sardi's. She was that night, like so many nights, furious with him. He had been flirting with Broadway's brightest new ingenue, much like the golden girl she had been not so long ago. The young woman was seated at their table along with a gaggle of other actors having a post-performance supper, and it was obvious to her that Oliver-Paul and this young woman would soon be in each other's clutches, if they weren't already. The more he drank the more openly he made his intentions known, until he became an embarrassment to the entire assembly, including the girl.

Robbie and Geraldo, still active as Broadway critics, and with whom she had only a nodding acquaintance at the time, were seated nearby. They always wrote such wonderful reviews of her performances. It was, she thought, mortifying for them to observe the seamy underside of her life.

When she could bear it no longer she had stood up, and collecting around her what dignity she could manage, had stalked out of the restaurant, feeling the eyes of strangers and friends alike sliding over her like slime. Oliver-Paul had followed and they made it home, her in an angry depression, him in full stagger, and raving.

Once in the apartment she had fled to her bathroom, locked the door and readied herself for bed, knowing he was unlikely to approach her in the state he was in. The morning would bring black coffee and a fight over the breakfast table as had occurred so many times before. She would deal with him then, after her feeling of murderous rage had subsided. How had she ended up exactly as her mother before her, full of despair over an adulterous man?

She was out of dental floss. Her mouth felt furry from the rich food and whiskey. Damn. Well, she would simply march from her bathroom to his and take the floss from the medicine cabinet without a word. Then she would retreat to her end of the apartment, maybe to the guest room which had a lock. The thought that he might try to touch her in his drunkenness, either in anger or lust, made her skin ache. Did she hate him then? Yes. On that fateful evening she had been furious enough to kill him.

She had stomped into his bathroom and there—

Her mind's eye clamped shut, leaving her with only a shudder of misery.

Her stage accident had followed hard upon his gruesome death. Was it an accident? A misstep? Had she, like the Gertrude she was playing on that fateful night, actually harbored a wish to die?

Elsinora watched the rim of sun follow its own glow up out of the water's edge, spilling its silver and gold riches across the placid surface like a wealthy man pretending money meant nothing to him.

In the year after her fall, as she slowly convalesced, she looked at the life she had been living without mercy or pity. She had been blessed with a talent, and had chosen a career which suited her well. Others wrote the plays in which she acted, gave her the words to speak, the emotions to feel, the clothes to wear. In a play, all the decisions about how she should behave and move were made for her by others. She took direction brilliantly.

There was no room for Elsinora on a stage. Only the characters she portrayed. There had been no place for Elsinora on the screen, only the false and flickering images that the movies made of her. And there had been no place in Oliver-Paul's heart for her either.

If she had seemed at times indifferent to other cast members, to lovers, and to her fans, she now realized this was merely an extension of the indifference she felt towards herself. She had, indeed, been playing a part through most of her life.

Only Fletcher had truly known her. Oliver-Paul had caught glimpses, but he had no taste for the inward, small-town girl hidden deep inside the alluring stage presence that first he had witnessed. In his determination to make her into a star he rode roughshod over all consideration as to who she actually was; and because this powerful new feeling, this physical desire for him, had risen within her, she had let him ride.

Elsinora knew herself to be as soft as goose down on the inside, but when she had fallen from the stage she had not floated. She had crashed. She had shattered like a sculpture made of glass. Only the shards remained.

When she had awakened doctors and nurses had hovered around her. They were to be her companions for many months as she lay encased in plaster casts almost from head to toe. And it was they who witnessed the emergence of a new Elsinora Dean from the brittle, protective shell her stardom had provided, like a moth unfolding from a chrysalis.

Now she grasped at authenticity the way a landed fish gasps for water. In her broken state she had no choice but to be vulnerable. The nurses and aides showed her every kindness, and she was warmed by their genuine concern for her. They reminded her of Mrs. Richie and Mrs. Kellogg, and Grandma Bessie. Those would be her three muses, her true guides, no longer Oliver-Paul and the horde of agents, directors, publicists, and managers into whose hands she had so willingly put her life and career, and from which they all had all been happy to benefit.

She was convinced that if she could *perform* characters who were good and kind, then she could *become* genuinely good and kind. She willed it so. She remembered her father's words of long ago: "Give my little Norrie El a hug for me. I bet she is growing up fast now."

Fletcher was amused with her attempts at transformation from diva to human. He watched with wonder as she sweetly talked to the nurses' aides, gave autographs with an appreciative smile, and laughed with the janitor when he told her of his children's antics.

"Are you any happier?" he asked her, on one of his many visits, as he placed a tiny Austrian music box on her bedside table.

"Not noticeably."

"But are the people around you happier?"

"They seem to be."

"Maybe it will rub off on you."

"I'm told by the psychiatrist who evaluated me that I have suffered all my life from depression."

"'There needs no ghost come from the grave to tell us this,' my dear one. Are they giving you pills?"

"I won't take them. If depressed is what I am, then depressed is what I want to feel."

"Are you talking with this psychiatrist regularly?"

"No."

"Just going to tough it out then?"

"Just going to be Elsinora, living life without a script."

"That *is* tough."

He wound up the music box and out churned a version of the Queen of the Night's shrieking aria from Mozart's *The Magic Flute*.

"This is to remind us that there are worse mothers than ours." He bowed with a flourish. "And on those impossibly high notes, I take my leave. See you tomorrow, Elsinora. Have courage."

As her bones knitted and she had grown stronger, there had been ample time to question whether her desire for a more genuine life was, in itself, genuine, and she found that it was, though what it would look like exactly, she had difficulty imagining.

Dr. Maurice Schadad, her attending doctor, gave no thought to her celebrity, only to the mending of her bones and the recovery of her spirit. He seemed unbothered by her self-absorption, and he listened not only to the her litany of physical pain, but to her thoughts and feelings, much as Fletcher, and only Fletcher, had ever done. He never touched her as other than a proper physician would, yet his eyes told her of something more than care. She couldn't imagine what she had done to deserve his tenderness. It was as if he saw a promise within her of the healed Elsinora, of a happy Elsinora, which she so needed to believe was possible at just that moment. Life had provided her with a man who was the opposite of Oliver-Paul.

Handsome, yes, though his fine features and perceptive steel-gray eyes were not what had brought forth her love, her genuine love. It was the growing, life-changing awareness that he loved *her*.

Maurice had wanted many things from Elsinora, first and foremost for her to live and to heal, as he would wish for any of his patients; but then, so like in a novel by Wharton or Woolf, they had connected in the extraordinary way that only people in midlife sometimes connect—when, alas, they are mature enough to know what such impossible emotions will cost.

"I have fallen in love with you," he said simply, his hands at his side, his head bowed, like a schoolboy confessing to having cheated on a test. He raised his left hand to his forehead. The hand with the golden wedding ring.

"And I with you," she had replied.

They were sitting alone in the empty cafeteria at the far end of the rehabilitation unit. Potted plants dwindled in the corners, watercolor prints expired on the walls. Pool of spilled milk congealed under a nearby table. Elsinora, with his verbal encouragement and the support of a metal cane, had walked the entire corridor to this unpleasant spot for the first time since her casts were removed.

"What will we do?" he asked.

"Will you leave your wife for me?" she asked in return, going directly to the heart of the matter.

"No. I fear I cannot."

She could tell from the measured way he said this that he had already considered it carefully. "Because you love her, too," she supplied in a gentle tone.

"Yes. But, and I feel foolish saying this at my age, I love you in a way I've never felt before."

She smiled. "It's a line in a great many plays and novels."

"There is no other way to say it." He reached out and placed his hand on hers. It was the first time he had ever touched her that had not been medically required of him.

"I feel this, too."

"Would you be my lover?"

"No. As you say, I fear I cannot."

"You say no so kindly, Elsinora, but with such finality."

"If I became your lover, and your wife were to find out, would she be hurt?"

"Devastated, I expect."

"And you want me to act in such a way as to devastate someone you love?"

"No. But. Oh dear." He paused. "I'm about to say another line
from a great many plays and novels."

"You don't think you can live without me?"

"That's the one."

"But you can. You will. We are not children, Maurice. I know
all too well what deceit does to a relationship, any relationship; and you and I are not free to be together without deceit.
Everyone will be hurt if we act. And afterwards, for there is
always an afterwards, and because you are the kind of man you
are, you will end up hating yourself. We cannot go there, my
dear one. The most honorable thing we can do, both of us, is
just to go on loving each other as we do now."

"And that's all there is to be?"

"It's more than I have ever had before."

He looked so sad, knowing she was right, there in those
wretched surroundings of smudged tile floors and chrome
tables where, nevertheless, the warmth of love glowed between
them. Again he appeared to her like a crestfallen boy, now
denied a longed-for sweet.

"Love is like a child, That longs for everything it can come
by..." The quotation floated into her mind from far off in
Shakespeare's Verona, and she smiled inwardly.

Elsinora had been where he had not. She had seen Conroy's
infidelities devastate her mother. She had felt the crushing pain
of Oliver-Paul's betrayals. She had played Anna Karenina. She
would not, could not, become the destroyer of another woman's
life, nor of the integrity of this fine man who had dared to love
her; her...the shattered, naked, real Elsinora.

He remained her doctor for as long as she stayed in the
hospital. He continued to do all in his power to restore her to

health. They did not speak of their feelings again. They enfolded them. The love was there, in his eyes, in his caring touch, in her smile at the mere sight of him. Others could see it in the tender glances, the quiet words they exchanged, imagining them entwined with each other behind closed doors, just as she imagined them, as he imagined them, but it was never so.

She left the hospital a month later walking on her own, brimming with this unsullied love. How many years ago now? Forty and a few. She could find that love for him still within her heart. Perhaps he loved her, too. More so for her decision not to destroy his life.

Did his wife, who had, unknowingly, stood between them, still live? Elsinora did not know. She would never inquire. The memory of his sober, compassionate, encompassing care as she left her former life behind and walked, healed, into her new one was fulfillment enough.

"There you are!" proclaimed Hesper with both concern and amazement in her voice. She had herself awakened from a troubled sleep and in checking on Elsinora had found her missing.

"Whatever are you doing out here by the lake at the crack of dawn wrapped up like a mummy?"

"But soft, methinks I scent the morning air."

"Shakespeare again? Were you sleepwalking? You do cause me to worry. Why, you are shivering!"

"The glowworm shows the matin to be near."

"Whatever you say. Let's go inside and get you back to bed. I'll make you some hot chocolate to warm you up."

Hesper took in a sharp breath. Brushing the remaining sleep from her eyes, she helped Elsinora back to her bedroom and then made her way to the kitchen for two cups of cocoa. She returned to Elsinora's room rather hoping to find her asleep again given the ungodly hour.

Elsinora, surprisingly, was sitting up in her bed, resting against the pillows, sipping a brandy and clearly eager to talk.

Hesper sat down in a straight-backed chair near the bedside and waited with growing annoyance for her employer to speak.

"Living such a long a life is a calamity," began Elsinora at last. "One suffers more and more as age accumulates, as the body refuses to run up and down the stairs, as the icons of one's culture disappear into retirements and graves, as the world continues to spawn phenomena with which one cannot possibly cope, as your close friends continue to die."

Here, she paused.

Hesper knew she was thinking of Fletcher, so recently interred.

"Hamlet says we 'can know ought of what we leave behind,' and doubtless he was correct, but nevertheless we try to influence events that will come after our death by writing wills and making deathbed requests. We want funerals arranged and monuments built as if we will be there ourselves to see them. We paint and draw and write and carve our initials into the rocks, into the living trees hoping the world will notice that we were once here. And who will it be that notices? No one we knew in life or can know in death. Why do we do this?" She sighed deeply, not expecting an answer.

Then she continued. "You may perhaps assume I have left you some compensation for your years of service in my will," she continued. "How many years has it been?"

"Twelve."

"That is a lot of service. I believe I have paid you well over the years, but have I ever truly thanked you? I have, most likely, been remiss in that regard. Words of that kind do not come easily to me, but I've never taken you for granted. You have had my silent gratitude all along, and I say it aloud now. Thank you, dear Hesper, for being of so much assistance to me for so many years."

"Mrs. Harding, I—"

"No, you mustn't speak just yet. I do not wish to lose my train of thought. Fletcher Mulcaster has left me a considerable legacy for which I have little use. Perhaps it was his way of being remembered, as if I could forget him! I have instructed my attorney to make the legacy over to you. The acceptance papers for you to sign will be ready shortly."

She raised a hand to keep Hesper from interrupting.

"There are conditions."

Hesper, wide awake now, straightened her back.

Elsinora pulled the bed covers closer and turned at last to the enjoyment of her hot chocolate. She was quiet for a long time, savoring the warm, rich drink, and Hesper became more and more uneasy as the minutes passed, her mind racing back and forth between the words "legacy" and "conditions."

Quiet, as was her habit, she did not speak, but she did fidget. Having finished her own cocoa she turned the empty cup around and around in her hands, and a foot jiggled under her nightdress, ever so slightly.

At last Elsinora returned to her subject. "The conditions. Listen carefully. One. As I have said before, you will stop poking around in my belongings looking for clues to my past like some demented Nancy Drew under the pretense of cleaning."

Hesper felt the sting of the accusation acutely and flinched. And who the hell was Nancy Drew? There was no time to wonder.

"Two! You must find another babysitter for me should you wish time away. Robbie and Geraldo are not to be allowed at the manor again until I give my permission. I have given them a proper dressing down for their snooping as you know. I will need considerable time to forgive them, though of course, I will. They are dear boys but they were led astray by you."

A blush of shame was crawling up Hesper's neck.

"Three. You will stop telling tales about me to that unpleasant husband of yours. He is a pedestrian writer of the third rank, and I will not abide him making me into a monster in some ill-bethought biography after I'm dead. Actually, all those conditions are the same. No more spying!"

Hesper's heart was beating rapidly with confusion. Whereas Robbie and Geraldo were banished, she was being offered a legacy, not a termination notice? She was completely baffled.

"And four, regarding said husband of whom neither of us harbor charitable feelings, you will divorce him."

"What?!" gasped Hesper in genuine surprise. "You are saying I must divorce Barton to—"

"—to receive this legacy."

Hesper's face stiffened. She clutched at her crucifix and stood up abruptly. She could remain the docile servant no longer. "How can you order me to do such a thing? It is not your business who I am married to, Mrs. Harding. This is quite outrageous! My personal life is my own."

"*My* sentiments exactly!" Elsinora shot back. "And without that man poking about in my past, my personal life will be so."

Then in a gentler tone, she continued, "However, in regards to *your* personal life, I'm afraid you have made your marriage my business as well as your own, and I am excusing your misbehavior, dear Hesper, because I know you were caught between your loyalty to your husband and your loyalty to me. I sense your kind heart was not in the spying, yet you participated. It can't have been comfortable. Nevertheless the struggle with your conscience truly is your business, not mine. And may I point out to you that the divorce I require is most certainly not an order. It is a condition, which I have every right to impose."

"Well, I will do no such thing!"

"One million dollars, taxes paid."

Hesper sat down as abruptly as she had stood up, stunned into silence. She had always lived a modest life, some might say a poor one. She knew a million dollars was not an incredible sum of money in the world of the present day, but it was much more than she had ever dreamed of possessing.

"In addition, *and only* if you accept my conditions, thereby the legacy, and continue in your service to me, you may live in Arden Manor after my death until such time as you decide to sell it, as I will put it into your name. I expect it is worth about two million more."

"But, why— "

"My reasons are my own. Don't worry. I am not mad. My attorney protests, but also attests to the soundness of my mind. I have no children to contest my will, I've already provided handsomely for the charities that I support and the authors I encourage. Now toddle off to bed, Hesper, and sleep on the matter. Sometimes we have to decide to be different than we have ever been before. Sometimes it requires a bit of a bump to do so. And now, I need to sleep."

Elsinora held out her empty cup and brandy tumbler.

Automatically Hesper sprang to take them, then in a daze she carried the tray full of empty vessels out of the room.

She was extremely confused by the mix of surprise and gratitude and anger and excitement that swirled inside her. Perhaps this is all just a crazy dream, she thought as she returned to her bedroom.

She had been content in her cozy room with its adjoining sitting room and office for many years and had known that when Elsinora died these rooms would go, as would she. Now the thought of owning the whole house, of living out her life, her retirement years in Arden Manor, perhaps with a house-keeper of her own was overwhelming.

It was the most dizzying moment in her entire life. Her mind was actually spinning, not knowing what she should do and, at the same time, knowing exactly what she would do. There was no hope of further sleep this morning.

Elsinora, certain that Hesper would see sense and agree, now felt that the events she wished to keep hidden in her past were more likely to remain there. With this soothing thought she settled into her comfortable bed, and swiftly dropped off into a sumptuous morning sleep.

XX. Entrance to a quarrel.

RETIRED DETECTIVE SERGEANT Milo Griffith stepped outside McSorley's Tavern for the dubious pleasure of a smoke. A hot summer humidity filled the air of the Lower East Side, but it was still fresher than the musty interior of the ancient bar.

He lit the cigarette and stared at the detritus along the curb. It was an unfortunate time of year in the city, too hot for people to walk to the nearest trash can. There were pigeons poking along the gutter hoping for the emergence of junk food crumbs and adding their droppings to the mess. A mouse, or maybe a baby rat, scurried along in the dribble from a spilled beer bottle towards a half-clogged drain.

The smoke soothed his insides but did nothing to quiet his disturbed thoughts. An unwanted and inappropriate request was troubling him. It was regarding an ancient case, closed long ago. His detective work was being called into question from an unexpected source. Barton Ford was a writer, evidently with some measure of success to his credit, and he was digging around in an old investigation hoping to find a morsel of truth to build up a story, much like the dirty pigeons poking about in the gutter.

This intrusive little man had dared to seek him out, here in the bar where he burrowed each evening to drink a little bit more of his life away, and it had made him very angry. Barton Ford would not return to this bar anytime soon. Milo Griffith was a big man and could still be alarming when annoyed.

As the hours passed, he had stayed at the bar, hardly tasting his beer, and growing more and more disturbed as the man's questions began to gnaw at him. How dare this guy come around challenging his long-ago findings with no evidence whatsoever?

Had the actress Elsinora Dean murdered her director husband, Oliver-Paul Harding? Could it have been a crime of passion? Had he, as a young detective assigned to the high profile case been out of his depths, overlooked some small detail during his investigation? He dropped his cigarette butt into the dirt and lit another.

It was true that he had been young and relatively inexperienced when he had been handed the case. How long ago was it? Forty years? Even longer. Although the incident involved celebrities, not so unusual in New York City, it had appeared to be a straightforward accident from the get-go, and so had not commanded a more senior investigator.

True, he had been predictably mesmerized by Elsinora's glamour, but he had dutifully carried out his inquiry with all due diligence to his supervisor's satisfaction. Now, at this remote date, he had been set to wondering. Had stars gotten into his eyes? Distorted his vision? He could recall it all well enough. One didn't forget such a scene. The electric fan had been improperly placed on the bathroom counter, the cord was too short, and Oliver-Paul had been about as drunk as a man can be without being unconscious. Accidents happen.

Elsinora Dean, perfectly dressed and coiffed at each of several formal questionings, had stated unequivocally that she had heard nothing in the way of distress as she was at the other end of their spacious apartment in her own powder room. She had discovered her husband dead in the tub shortly after the accident had occurred when she entered his bathroom to borrow some dental floss.

Milo hadn't known apartments came as large as the Harding's elegantly furnished home in the mighty Dakota, which stood like a fortress on Central Park West, and had over the decades, behind its iron gates, been home to Lillian Gish, Judy Holliday, Jason Robards, Boris Karloff, Rudolf Nureyev, among others; and in front of which poor John Lennon would one day die.

Detective Griffith had made a point of standing in Elsinora's mirrored bathroom, marveling at the walls of glistening white marble streaked in green like the inside of an Italian church. He had instructed one of his colleagues to cry out as loud as he could from Oliver-Paul's bathtub. No sound had reached him.

Careful of all the details in her story he had checked her medicine cabinets for dental floss. None was to be found amid the cosmetics and perfumes, worth, no doubt, a year of his salary.

He had first questioned her in the massive living room overlooking Central Park.

She was thoroughly believable.

He had questioned her at the police station, and her story did not vary.

She was a renowned actress.

He had talked with her, yet again, when they met by chance in Characters Bar, a midtown watering hole.

It was said that she loved her husband deeply.

It was said that Oliver-Paul had both beaten and betrayed her.

She had tearfully confirmed that all that was said was true.

Death by misadventure was the official ruling, a diverting

phrase when you thought about it. He supposed this annoying writer fellow could be forgiven for thinking there might be a juicier story filed away inside the quietly closed file. It was the stuff of a pulp fiction.

Retired Detective Sergeant Milo Griffith didn't want to think about the Harding case, or any case, anymore. He was old. He had left police work behind twenty years ago. He had been a decent fellow and a good cop. He had worked hard and had been, for the most part, honest. He had functioned within the thick of the city's underlife, seen things he wished he had never seen, solved crimes he did not wish to remember. He had left the force with a clean record, and tried to shake off the grimness of it all like a dog shaking off water.

Sometimes a man's life has played itself out, and knowing that was true of himself, he had felt it wise to let a little peace predominate where once there had been ambition, competition, victories and defeats, loves, lusts, and heartbreaks, of course.

He just wanted to smoke his cigarettes, drink his beers, watch tiny football players run about, entrapped as they were, in the black and white television mounted over the bar, laugh at an occasional off-color joke by one of the establishment's regulars, fantasize a bit about the women he had most loved, and die in his sleep one of these lonely nights without ever knowing the moment when he slipped from life into death. Was that too much to ask? Death by the opposite of misadventure.

His meetings with Elsinora Dean Harding were glimmering memories of his years on the force. He wished to leave them distilled in time.

The last thing he needed was this writer guy coming around, poking into his past, looking for trouble. And for what? Money. It always came down to money. Barton Ford had even made the lame mistake of offering him cash for a peek at the confidential records. Had Milo Griffith still been a policeman he would have arrested the creep for attempting to bribe an officer, and he had told him as much. There was some pleasure in recalling how the writer had scuttled away.

The man had informed him that Elsinora Dean was still alive, something of which he was already aware. An antique now, like himself. There had been scant word of her since she had fallen from the stage and given up acting. She fell within a month of her husband's death. There had been another police inquiry, in which he had not been involved, centering around the stage-hands who had not secured the set properly. No suspicion of murder, but the theater was sued by her management team. He suspected a big payout from the insurance company. There were plenty of witnesses to that accident. An entire audience had watched her go careening down into that pit. He winced as he thought of it.

Since that time she only occasionally appeared on a stage, usually on an obscure one, and never with advertising or billing. Nevertheless, he had managed to view several of these rare performances. He knew she had become a teacher. Of Shakespeare. Who cared about *that* guy once you got out of high school? Why had she done that? He shook his head in perplexity, as he imagined Elsinora Dean stuck in some stuffy classroom, after the amazing life she had lived...mixing with other celebrities, traveling the world, performing at The White House. He coughed, took in a breath of the thick air and sighed. Everybody becomes nobody.

He stamped out the butt end of his smoke and went back into the bar. The familiar hum of old men talking and arguing in the semi-darkness was what claimed him now. Sound and fury signifying nothing. He had heard someone say that once, but couldn't recall where, or who it had been.

XXI. Dost thou hear me, old friend?

Alone in her study, Elsinora dropped the recently arrived letter onto her desk. Why was she never left in peace? First the Academy Award invitation which Hesper had failed to decline on her behalf after all these many weeks, and now this.

She was annoyed with missives that began: "You probably don't remember me—" as they were usually from some minor actor with whom she had once shared a stage, or a student from her days at The Atelier who wanted something from her (a recommendation or an autograph) with which she dealt graciously, but without pleasure. However the remark about being unremembered, though it was meant as a show of humility, was experienced by Elsinora as an insult to her mental capacities. Her memory was a miracle of nature. She remembered everyone. She remembered everything. Almost.

The mental chaos that had ensued immediately following Fletcher's death was a singular occurrence, and understandable. That there were slight disruptions in the smooth flow of her recollections must be conceded. She admitted to the occasional conflation of two events, the hesitation in recovering a proper name. Quite normal at any age.

Her mind had once again settled, and her narrative was orderly. She was proceeding through the years in a proper fashion as she considered and questioned all that she had been, and all of her choices in life.

Only the unyielding walls around the age of thirteen stood in her way. Except for insignificant flashes of mundane events, that year remained empty, and she knew it must conceal some experience that was terrible. She needed to discover what was repressed. She was sure with the help of one good clue her locked mind would surrender, it would encourage her brain to make the necessary connections and whatever traumatic event lay hidden within that year would appear like an image emerging on photographic paper in a bath of developing fluid.

The year's stubborn blankness was akin to the occasional moments she endured when a word or a name would not come to her. Then her mind scratched like an animal at the unyielding wall behind which the elusive word was hidden. True, a few minutes later it would pop into her consciousness, but the momentary void was frightening. She knew this was considered normal for a person of her years but to Elsinora it was a grievous wound to her pride.

If only Fletcher were still alive! She *must* have told him all about her girl's life when he first came to live with them, intimacies simply because she liked him so much, and she would have wanted him to know her, though he always protested that he knew of nothing important. When she had pressed him in the past he would say, "Oh Elsie, that was the year that you said you had pimples, or you had a hopeless crush on the math teacher," and then, instead of everything falling into place…nothing!

High school was all there. Her work in the library, too. The college years were visually seamless, every class, every professor, her first flirtations, and the momentous discovery of her acting talent.

Her fingers drummed on the desk impatiently. Her arthritis

made this a mildly painful exercise today so she stopped. She picked up the letter and read it through again.

"You probably don't remember me but we went to school together in Warrensville, Ohio. As girls we were pals, although because you had been skipped ahead into my class you were three years younger than me. I'm eighty-seven now and have just moved from Albany to the assisted living apartments on Halcyon Circle nearby to you.

Gossip informed me upon moving here that the famous actress, Elsinora Dean, lives near to this town. Of course, in years past, I followed your career when you were an actress, and I felt sorrowful when I heard of the death of your husband and your subsequent fall from the stage.

The people in this retirement home are very nice but all new to me. My husband, family and dearest friends have all passed away.

When I saw the obituary in the Times for Fletcher Mulcaster, you were brought to mind. I remember how close you were to him in high school. In truth I was a little jealous of his usurpation of our childhood friendship. I am truly sorry for your loss. How the world empties itself out at our respective ages!

With these thoughts in mind it occurred to me that you might wish to reacquaint; perhaps talk of old times, share some stories about our long, long lives, over a spot of tea now and again. There is a very pleasant dining room in this facility.

I do apologize if this missive is experienced as an intrusion. It is sent in kindness and meant only as a friendly invitation.

Sincerely,
Doris Graves

Elsinora took out her journal, as here was a memory trap she wanted to step into.

> *Doris Graves. She rings in clear as a bell. Fourth grade. The pretty girl who befriended me: orange-red curls (the boys had nick-named her Orphan Annie), big green eyes, popular, and more importantly, smart. Perhaps I hold the world's record for having been the youngest intellectual snob on the planet.*
>
> *If I was six when we met then she was what? Eight or nine. Doris acted like a big sister during that first year back in school after my long illness. Doris stuck up for me against the big boys.*
>
> *We played together at Robin Hood and Maid Marion, Nancy Drew and Georgia, the Lone Ranger and Tonto in the playgrounds and surrounding woods. I remember we secretly went swimming after the Salk vaccine vanquished the polio virus and it was safe to go to the lake again, though my mother was certain I could drown in a mud puddle let alone a lake. We studied together, and began to grow into teenagers. And then, and then? I am nearing the memory blockade.*
>
> *It is possible that a meeting with Doris Graves will offer up the exact information that I am seeking, but do I really want to know?*
>
> *I wonder what kind of a life Doris has led these many years, in Albany of all places. Perhaps as a wife to some forlorn and long-forgotten state functionary.*

Elsinora smacked her hand down on the polished desktop.

"There are times, Elsinora Dean," she reproached herself aloud, "when you are quite reprehensible. Now you've grown up to be the *oldest* snob on the planet!"

Would it not be the kind gesture to return the favors of so long ago? To help out this elderly woman in her new surroundings?

Elsinora sat up straight and reordered her thinking. The letter had been well written with a firm hand on good-quality stationary. The offer to renew this friendship was courteous. It was considerate. There was no hint of dementia or anything lurking in its grammar beyond the stated desire to meet.

And the terrible reality was that since Fletcher's death, she was feeling something akin to the aching loneliness she had experienced so long ago in that Warrensville schoolroom, as she had felt as a young actress on first arriving in New York City, as she did after Oliver-Paul's death; but most profoundly when she had walked out of the rehabilitation center, leaving Maurice behind forever.

She must tell Hesper to stop pestering her about the Oscars. Hollywood was a mirage, and quite capable of celebrating itself. Yes. She would accept the invitation to have tea with Doris Graves at Halcyon Circle. Doris was real and they were both in need of company.

XXII. Women's fear and love.

THE LEGAL PAPERS were signed. Her legacy was now secured. Hesper looked at her benefactor, who was seated across from her at the mahogany desk. Prim. She was perfectly attired, her hair dressed into one of her silver concoctions worthy of a Victorian matriarch, her hands quietly folded as she waited for the legalities to be concluded.

Lately Hesper had felt stirrings of genuine affection for Elsinora, an emotion she kept to herself in the interests of maintaining a proper professional distance. Perhaps it was suddenly having the expectation of a million dollars handed to her that liberated her feelings. Or maybe it was the surprising bursts of exhilaration she had been experiencing since filing for a divorce from Barton.

"Mrs. Harding. Please tell me why you decided to do this for me, especially given my lapse—"

Elsinora raised a finger to quiet Hesper.

Elsinora turned her eyes towards the paunchy attorney who was gathering up the papers and feeding them into his expensive leather briefcase. He was a competent, self-satisfied man, successful, egotistical, and completely comfortable wrapped in his assurance of male superiority and at least fifty pounds of unneeded fat. His bald head was shiny with perspiration. Hesper knew the lawyer had opposed Elsinora's decision to leave so grand a sum to a person he considered only a servant, a lowly housemaid.

Elsinora continued to look directly at the man until he nodded and left the room, seeing himself out.

Then she spoke to Hesper. Her tone was measured and full of meaning.

"I look at the scenery of the world as built by men. I see the killing grounds in Europe, Korea, Vietnam, Cambodia, Afghanistan, Iraq, Rwanda, Sudan, Palestine, Haiti. I see the trenches of World War One, the devastation of the London Blitz; the aftermath of Hiroshima and Nagasaki; the mass graves of the concentration camps, Auschwitz, Bergen-Belsen, Dachau; gulags, prisons, Guantanamo; the smoking ruins of The World Trade Center. I see strip malls and endless highways where forests once stood, rivers polluted, air growing thick, glaciers melting, coral reefs dying, deserts encroaching. These destructions are the constructions of men, for it is men who have always held the power on this planet; and it is on these sets that we women are directed to play out our lives.

"If I have learned anything in this extended life, Hesper, it is that women must take care of one another."

XXIII. Doubt truth to be a liar.

"**D**AMN IT TO hell!"

The peaceful sleep of Detective Sergeant Milo Griffith was abruptly ended by the sound of a loud crash and a louder expletive.

He had been dozing deep in the bowels of the police archives. A bored rookie manning the street door of the Brooklyn warehouse had glanced at his old credentials and let the detective enter without question, although he shouldn't have.

Milo had located his original reports of the Oliver-Paul Harding death, read through them carefully, found no fault with his detective work of the time, leaned back against a filing cabinet and slumbered.

He had been dreaming of the young Elsinora Dean as she had appeared in her youthful films, her hypnotizing eyes beckoning him closer when the crash occurred.

He was on his feet fast, surprising himself at how quickly his police instincts still kicked in. "Who's there? What's going on?" he shouted.

He rounded a stack of shelving to find Barton Ford, the sleazy writer, sprawled on the floor under a stack of fallen files.

"What the hell are you doing down here? How did you even get in?" he demanded, but he knew already. Barton had greased the right palm this time, that of the delinquent rookie.

Milo made no offer to help him up.

Barton struggled to his feet and tried a weak imitation of friendliness. "Fancy meeting you here, Inspector Griffith," he said, accompanied by a rueful smile.

The detective was not amused. "Yes, fancy. I expect you are snooping around down here looking for the Harding case. Am I right?"

Barton nodded, his expression turning a bit sheepish in the face of Griffith's stoney stare.

"Then you can march right back outta here." He held up the file. "Everything is in order. I've just had a look-see myself."

Barton smirked. "I rattled you then. You heard what I said about the possible murder and you got nervous, afraid you missed something." The man seemed to be taking pleasure in the thought. "And, just like me, you wasted no time getting over here to check on things. We should have shared a cab."

"What of it?" was all Milo could think of to say in response to these unpleasantly accurate remarks.

"Can I have a peek myself?" Barton asked boldly.

"No way, and you can start picking up those files you knocked over. No, wait. Leave them for the copper you bribed to explain the mess you've made. It will serve him right."

"Wait. Just one question. Please."

"What?"

"Did you dust for fingerprints on the part of the fan that was sticking out of the bath water?"

This idiot was actually asking him if he had been negligent in his duties. For the first time in decades he restrained himself from punching someone.

"Do you think I'm as dumb as you? Of course, I checked. Only Oliver-Paul's prints were on the fan. He did himself in, whether by accident or intent. There was no question about it.

So much for your lame theory."

The writer's expression changed from sly to crestfallen. What answer could he have expected? That he, Detective Griffith had let Elsinora Dean get away with murder? What a stupid man!

"Now it's my turn to ask the questions," he said. "Why are you digging around in her past? Why are you so intent on making trouble for Elsinora Dean? You tell me that."

"I have my reasons." Barton lifted his chin.

"Well then take your reasons and get the hell outta here before I have you arrested for trying to tamper with evidence, or breaking and entering, or destruction of police property, or bribing a police officer, or all of the above."

He watched as Barton ascended the stairs.

In truth, Elsinora's fingerprints had been on the fan. "Why wouldn't they be?" he muttered under his breath. They were a married couple, after all. They lived together. Everything in the apartment carried both their prints. It was the explanation at the time, and it stood.

"Why wouldn't they be?" he asked himself again. He tucked the file under his arm, and made his own way tiredly up the stairs.

BARTON FORD, HAVING struck out in his attempt to get the police investigation information with either his offer of money to the seedy old detective, or his attempted raid in the archives sat alone in a tacky pizza joint on Eighth Avenue and pondered his fate. The pepperoni pie he had just demolished had been delicious, but the extra garlic was giving him heartburn. As he drank a second beer in the hope of quelling his discomfort, he tapped his fingers on the sticky Formica tabletop in agitation. His life was not going as anticipated.

To stay in the good graces of his wife, he had needed to tread with care around the former life of the old witch she worked for, trying to winkle out the small details that turn a biography into a bestseller. But now that Hesper had left him, was intent on *divorcing* him, he had no need to be circumspect.

He thought they had been getting along all right until the pandemic. He had been perfectly content and she hadn't complained, but after Hesper and Elsinora had locked themselves in together the quality of Hesper's relationship to him had changed. She had become not only physically distant, but after the worst of the plague had subsided and she had begun visiting him again, she was emotionally distant as well. He had imagined that working together on the tell-all biography would bring them back together, at least enough for her to show up and clean the place now and then, but it appeared to have had the opposite effect.

In some maddening way, although he had stopped loving Hesper years ago, he had been wounded when she left him. There had been no tears on either side and nothing either wished to contest. She had said he could keep the apartment for which she had no affection. She hadn't even asked for alimony. Ah, there's the rub! Hesper would simply prefer to live with that old bag of bones rather than return to him. It was galling.

Because he was certain that Elsinora was somehow implicated in Hesper's desertion he was, more than ever, determined to dig up every speck of dirt about her that he could find.

It had been a damnable coincidence that Detective Griffith had been down in the police archives at the same time he had bribed his way in. He should have anticipated the man would go at the first available opportunity, as had he. His presence had thwarted his own attempt to get hold of the Oliver-Paul Harding files, but the unpleasant meeting had told him something important. He had spooked the old detective. There was probably a good reason.

He was wondering if there was another way to get his hands on the information when a new thought occurred to him: insinuation. Maybe he didn't need evidence at all. There had been speculation at the time of the death. *The National Enquirer* had pointed its smutty finger at Elsinora and run a photo of her leaving the police precinct after making her formal statement. He took the ratty newspaper from his bag and examined the picture again as he had done so often before. She was not beautiful in the photo. She was distraught. Was it grief alone that contorted her features? Or guilt? A countertop fan spinning into a tub of bathwater was an unforgiving murder weapon, providing a hideously cruel death. Electrocuted husband.

In the photograph Fletcher Mulcaster was gripping her elbow, looking solemn. He was there at every turn of her life, including this one. A friend, surely, but also a lover? Hesper said no. So what? A co-conspirator? And Fletcher was famous. Fortunately the man was six feet under, so he could write anything he pleased about him.

Barton made his decision.

He would write that there had been a cover-up; that the movie studios had been involved to protect their star's reputation; that the cops were corrupt. Damn the evidence and damn the consequences! The day Elsinora was too dead to sue him, he would publish. Elsinora was childless, with no family so there was no one to come after him. Detective Griffith wouldn't have a legal leg to stand on even if he could afford a lawyer, even if he heard of the book, even if he cared, even if he was still alive by the time it was published.

It was he, Barton Ford, who would have the last word. He would write Elsinora Dean's history with murder and intrigue at its core. If anything sold well in this benighted country it was a conspiracy.

Elsinora dead. That was a consoling thought. Hesper, abruptly out of work, would have to find another job bowing and kowtowing to some other old broad. Probably she counted on Elsinora leaving her a little something. Hah! Fat chance. So much for her!

He belched and felt better for it.

He would find a young woman, or two, or three, and have himself some hot sex.

He glanced around the pizza joint, and decided this was the wrong sort of place in which to go on his hunt. It was full of weirdos. There was too much blue hair and too many creepy tattoos at the nearby tables. He would find a different haunt, some place uptown and classy. He would do so as soon as he finished this beer. He burped and patted his belly. Or perhaps his pursuit of attractive women would meet with more success after he lost some of this weight. Maybe he would join a gym. He imagined a whole new chapter in his life, full of success and money and adventures.

Do it, Barton, he ordered himself. He belched again and reached for his roll of Tums, wiped the pizza grease from his chin, and ordered another slice.

XXIV. Be the players ready?

As Elsinora was arranging herself for the afternoon meeting with Doris Graves, she realized she felt nervous, which was unusual. The feeling was akin to the stage fright from which she had suffered waiting in the theater wings before an entrance such a long time ago. It returned to her now, what standing backstage in terror had been like, wondering if her legs would hold. She was not afraid of forgetting her lines. Her childhood ability to read had matured into the skill of memorization. Awaiting her cue she was too much herself. In those tense moments there stood the self that had to be exactly who she was, where she was; a trapped prey with no escape.

She knew that the paralyzing fear she had encountered before every live performance belonged to the unseen child facing a fresh opportunity to be noticed and approved...or disliked and pitied. Who would be in that night's audience? Uncle Conroy or Mrs. Richie?

There was aways a rustle or a cough that issued from the great beast of the waiting crowd, reminding her of its hungry presence, and every night a different animal. Her breathing was shallow and she could smell the theater dust in the tight breaths she managed to take, mingled with her own nervous perspiration, and then the cue would come.

She would step out upon the stage, Elsinora melting into

nothingness, the dazzling stage lights transforming her into the made-up creature of the night; magical Titania, clever Viola, mad Ophelia, tragic Blanche, the ever-faithful Sonya, the merciless Lady Macbeth. Those women felt no stage fright. They were busy being alive.

Elsinora sat down on the edge of the bed to ponder her strange anxiety. Meeting with Doris would not be a performance. Performances were things of the past. She had found her real self, decades ago after the fall from the stage, and had seldom felt other than confident since. Why would she be nervous about spending some time with an apparently harmless old woman who had once been a dear school friend? True, it was possible that Doris might tell her something about the lost year, but that was exactly what she was hoping for, wasn't it? Perhaps she was confusing excitement with anxiety. It was unlikely that anything Doris could say would have the power to hurt her now, sixty years on. Yet her memory of that year had doubtless remained cloaked for a reason.

So what performance was she asking of herself today? She closed her eyes, letting her mind drift back to those earliest of school days and slowly she realized where her nervousness was rooted. It was the child of six whom she could see, pushed ahead three grades, still shaky from a year in the sickbed, and painfully shy. She had wanted Doris, the older classmate, to see her and know her and like her. Those ancient feelings had returned.

"Well, I'll be damned," she said aloud, just as Hesper entered the room. "And you didn't hear that," she commanded.

"Hear what?" asked Hesper with a smile. "Are you ready to go? Oh, you have chosen the watered silk I like so much."

"Is the driver here?"

"Waiting."

Elsinora, her dressing accomplished, stood up and picked up her purse. "To England."

"What?"

"It is a line from *Hamlet.*"

"Hamlet goes to England?"

"He is set upon by pirates before he gets there."

"I doubt we shall be attacked by pirates between here and Halcyon Circle. Do you know you have been referring to Hamlet a great deal lately?"

"Of all the parts I played, Hamlet was my favorite role."

"I have read how you played a man's part well."

"Sometimes, one must. Let us away."

XXV. Heart's core.

Nurse Benoit was pleasantly surprised when Colonel Osbourne asked for pen and paper. He usually tapped out his infrequent messages slowly with one fragile finger on the iPad which a great-great-grandchild had given him so that he could watch the old movies he loved so much. The Colonel had learned to send emails and play a number of word games on the device as well.

"All I can offer you is plain stationary from the office."

"That will do," he replied, wrapping his tartan blanket around his shoulders. It was pleasant, he thought, being out of the bed for a while, sunk deep in this armchair. Nurse Benoit always encouraged him to move about, but at one hundred and three almost everything hurt when he did so, his left leg with the old war wounds ached unrelentingly.

Before going to retrieve the paper Nurse Benoit hovered about straightening up the room, pulling a table to the front of the armchair. She was curious about what the Colonel was up to. The old soldiers in here often wished to remake their wills as the people they knew and loved disappeared one by one. Colonel Osbourne was lucky to have anyone left to write to, she mused. She rather marveled at him. Amazingly, she would have to live her own life over again three more times just to approach his great age.

These elderly people were relics, repositories of the past, living histories, she believed. Nurse Benoit was especially fond of Colonel Osbourne as he had fought in World War II, advanced as a foot soldier right over the ground and through the village from which her own grandparents had been forced to flee from the Nazis. He was her special hero, and the knowledge that he still had loving people in his life pleased her.

He sensed her interest and looked up.

"I will write to a secret friend of mine," he said. "The one who never fails to send a Fourth of July greeting. Every now and then I send her a note to let her know I am still alive, and where I am, and no, she was not my lover, more's the pity. This time I want to thank her for being a bright star in my otherwise quite ordinary life."

Nurse Benoit was graced with the awareness that a person's soul never ages. As the body weakens and fails there remains inside the same person who has always been living there, now trapped, like an animal in a collapsing cage. She attended to the aged bodies. That was her job. But she always spoke to the young person who dwelled in the cage.

"Well, I am sure she will be delighted to hear from you," replied the nurse. She placed a pen and an envelope on his tray, and stood quietly, watching him as he began to write. Yes, he was able to do so legibly. "I'll just go to the office and get you the stationary."

He put a restraining hand gently on her own. "You, too, have been a bit of brightness in an unexpected time and place, Nurse Benoit. You are unfailingly kind to the ancients in your care. Do you know how exceedingly rare that is? You are a treasure."

His eyes glistened.

"Will you tell me about your special friend someday, Colonel Osbourne?"

"Oh, no, I mustn't," he said, holding up the envelope on which was written the name *E. Harding* with a Connecticut address. "We have a secret between us that can never be revealed. I think it makes her less lonely to know another person still lives who shares this mystery, and admires her for what she has done."

Nurse Benoit knew, of course, that she could do a quick internet search and discover the Colonel's mysterious correspondent. She also knew she wouldn't, and he knew she wouldn't. Respect was a value honored within her family, and she brought it to her place of work.

"You make me even more curious, she laughed, "Will you never tell?"

He smiled, rather an impish smile, she thought. "I will need a stamp, too, dear Nurse Benoit. One of those *forever* stamps, I think."

XXVI. In remembrance of ourselves.

THIS IS A nightmare, thought Elsinora, as she entered the dining room of Halcyon Circle, holding firmly to Hesper's arm. Tea was indeed being served, but instead of the cozy parlor she had envisioned she faced a large starkly modern dining room crammed with dozens of jabbering people. Those well past their prime predominated and most were encompassed by visiting families, even children, who were running about noisily. There were wheelchairs and walkers crowding the spaces between the tables and a clatter of crockery, cutlery, and loud voices all of which her ears were unused to hearing.

As she turned to escape she caught a glimpse of the woman who must be Doris Graves making her way determinedly through the chaos. How strange that she was recognizable again after sixty years of separation. It was her crooked little smile, left after her lip had been repaired from a minor childhood mishap. And her intelligent eyes. The red hair was now white, but curiously it was cut as it had been in childhood, short and sweet. She was wearing a well-tailored suit in flattering lavender with a beautiful long scarf of purples and blues. She was waving her hand excitedly, like a young girl.

"I'm sorry, Elsinora," she said as soon as she was within earshot. "I'm new here. I didn't know about Family Day at Halcyon Circle. Quite overwhelming, isn't it? But cheerful.

Come, there is a patio outside my room. No one else will be there. You still prefer to stay away from crowds, no doubt."

"Unless they are seated in a theater, paying both a high price to see me and absolute attention."

Doris laughed, and the two women took a moment then to stare at one another, seeing the fresh faces of the past hidden behind the well-worn masks of the present.

"This is Hesper, my companion of late," introduced Elsinora, still holding tightly onto Hesper's arm, just as a small boy with more jam on his face than on his bread careened past them using a wheeled walker as a scooter. "Hesper Ford, please meet Doris Graves, my companion of early."

"This way to safety," said Doris indicating the doorway through which they had entered.

In the hall, away from the noise, Elsinora said in a stage whisper. "Wait, Doris, I have an idea."

"Why Elsinora, you say 'I have an idea' in the way you did when we were children, and you had some mischief in mind."

"There is a driver waiting outside with a nice roomy car. Let's go to New York City and have our tea at the Plaza. My idea, my treat. The Palm Court is a pleasant place and you and I can talk properly there. No one recognizes me when I'm out in public anymore. My age is a wonderful disguise. Hesper will have a little unexpected time to shop in the city. What do you say?"

"I say that is just the kind of mischief I would like."

On the way into the city they had driven past Arden Manor, and Doris had exclaimed at its grand size and the verdant lawns.

"It is amazing what a few hit movies have provided for me," said Elsinora. "And fortunately they don't make you pay back anything if you star in a clunker. I chose that great pile of stone for the view over the water and the way the original owner embellished the top edges of the building with crenellations."

"Your castle by the sea. Because it reminds you of the setting for *Hamlet?*"

"You have quite a memory, Doris."

"It would be hard to forget your fondness for that play. Few other children would choose to go near Shakespeare."

An hour later the two women were seated at a quiet table for two. The drive had given them the time they needed for their initial inquiries and reacquaintance. Doris had remarked in person how sorry she was to hear of the loss of Fletcher. "He was incandescent, wasn't he?"

"Literally, the light of my life," agreed Elsinora. "Now his absence leaves me in shadows."

"No one at our age is without their dark places."

As the tea progressed Elsinora found that she was pleased with the reunion, and her nervousness had swiftly dissolved into the warmth of Doris' friendliness.

The room surrounding the two ladies sparkled, the waiters hustled, the well-brewed tea and carefully constructed cucumber sandwiches were delicious. Desserts awaited them on a tiered silver tray. Though the dining room was busy it remained blessedly quiet. They felt they had stepped back into another era, and discovered that in this environment they had fine appetites.

"It seems we have been fortunate regarding our brains," remarked Doris. "I seem to still have all my marbles, as you clearly do. I feared that awful header you took off the stage might have set you up for memory loss. Of course I followed your calamity in the newspapers when the accident happened, but mention of it soon faded away. I take it you made a full recovery?"

"You could say that. I recovered my senses certainly. I'm left with some physical mementos. A wrist here, a shoulder there."

"And you gave up the theater and making movies right afterwards to everyone's astonishment."

"I continued to perform on stage occasionally, if obscurely. It is a challenging art form. I couldn't just walk away from acting. It was the razzamatazz of celebrity that I loathed. That, and a load of other bad habits is what I walked away from."

"I don't recall you having any bad habits. You always had your nose stuck in a book."

"I lost myself in those books. And in our make-believe games. Later, when I was acting, I lived as a heroine in a fictional world, and thought I was a good deal more important in the scheme of things, on stage and off, than I actually was."

"Don't all young people think that way? You were very shy when I knew you."

"It's true that I was withdrawn as a child, but I had a lot of success at college after I started acting, and later here in New York. I became very full of myself and quite prideful. Celebrity goes to one's head, until the celebrity's head goes to the floor."

"Well, the Elsinora Dean I knew was just the spindly, scholarly girl who lived in that monster of a farmhouse. You preferred to go to my home after school, and I understood."

"What did you understand, Doris?"

"Well, about your mom and your uncle. And, of course everyone felt sorry for you because your dad had been killed, and—"

"And…?"

"Oh, Elsinora, do you really want to reminisce about those ancient times today? I thought we just might catch up with each other a bit. You could tell me about being famous, and married to Oliver-Paul Harding, and Hollywood, and how you keep busy these days, and I could share some of my own life, not that it is, or ever was, as exciting as yours."

"The celebrity years may look exciting from the outside, I

suppose, but for me getting out of Ohio was the most exciting part of my life, being on campus, sitting in a great college
library, stepping onto the stage in that first college play. I'm sure
your life had its adventures, too."

"Your head was always full of the stories you were reading,
and I expect later in the parts you were playing; whereas I've
lived my life inside the minds of other people. Being a psychoanalyst entails a more sedate life, but it is rich and interesting in
its own way. I've been able to see the world through the eyes of
so many different people."

"Yes. A psychoanalyst." Elsinora considered, then she took
the plunge. "I expect your work demands a fine set of marbles,
and I would like to call upon some of them."

"Those days so long ago were unhappy ones for you, Elsie."

"Not when I was with you."

"We had our adventures, didn't we, Lone Ranger?"

"Yes, we did, Tonto." Both women laughed, but then Elsinora
grew serious again. "You know, Doris, I have felt like the sole
keeper and watchman of our long ago adventures. It is wonderful to remember them *with* you. But I must admit to having
a memory problem, a lapse. I can't recall much of anything
about my thirteenth year, until Fletcher arrived. I've sifted and
sifted, and except for Mom's miscarriage and a few visits to my
Grandma Bessie before she died, I remember nothing clearly.
Oh! My goodness! You were there! I think I remember that you
came to my Grandma Bessie's funeral with me. How kind you
were."

"You were beside yourself, and it was a grim affair. All the
funny smells, everyone in black clothes, your Mom attempting to read out those passages from the Bible when she wasn't
completely sober."

"Genesis. Grandma Bessie wanted readings from the book

of Genesis. Adam and Eve, their sons, serpents, apples. She had written those instructions down somewhere."

"That is exactly what you would remember. What book she had chosen."

"I've wondered if my amnesia could be as a result of that plunge in the theater, but I am fairly certain that the blankness was there before I fell, that it is psychological in nature, the result of a repressed trauma, which is right up your alley. So any light you can shed on that year would be a gift."

"Oh. My." Doris hesitated. "I should not characterize it as light, or a gift." She sighed. "Why does it matter to you so much? It's all so very long ago."

"Everyone faces death in their own way, Doris, most by denying that it will ever happen to them. Some, like Fletcher, by putting everything in order. My way entails reviewing my life. Assessing its value. Perhaps forgiving myself for things I have done and about which I am not at peace. I've been writing everything into a journal. I need all the pieces in order to render a proper judgement."

"I am unsure, from what you say, if you are hurting yourself or healing yourself. I suppose that is not for me to know. Let us enjoy these cakes, while I think this through."

DORIS IS AS I remember her, mused Elsinora. She is concerned for my well-being. How did I ever let her slip out of my life?

Finding herself in midtown and at loose ends while the ladies were enjoying their tea, Hesper strolled down to Fifth Avenue to peer into the upscale windows of the department stores. Tiffany's had drawn her attention. She looked in knowing that now she could march right in there and buy something she fancied.

She was aware of feeling happier. It wasn't the money

particularly, though that had relieved her worries about the future, nor was it entirely due to being free of the burdensome marriage to Barton. Her lightness of heart seemed to arise from the softening taking place in her relationship with Elsinora, beginning when forgiveness about the snooping had been so generously given.

Hesper had always felt appreciated by Elsinora even though the old woman could not easily express personal feelings, but lately she had begun to issue a steady stream of small compliments, and to ask for less housekeeping and more companionship. This resulted in some awkwardness on Hesper's part as the professional boundaries had always been comforting to her, a safe enclosure wherein she could perform her daily tasks knowing who she was, and that she was doing the right things in the right way. The definition of her duties seemed to be slowly melting away.

She recalled overhearing her mother talking to a neighbor about her when she was an adolescent.

"Hesper is a nice girl, but I fear she will never bloom. She doesn't push herself forward. She is quite plain, but seems complacent about her looks. I expect she will get on in life, but she will never amount to much. Never stand out."

How things heard at that age stick!

Had she led her life to give truth to her mother's assessment?

She looked closely again at the diamonds on display in the discreet square windows of the store she had never dared to enter. Maybe she *could* develop a taste for that delicate diamond necklace or those sparkling sapphire earrings. She took a step towards the door, then retreated.

"I'm a housekeeper, not a debutante," she said aloud, turning away from the jewelry store to windowshop further along the street.

She glanced at her phone. Nothing from her employer.

Hesper had found it cheering to observe how swiftly the two elderly women had fallen comfortably into conversation with one another during the commute, sketching in the outlines of their lives during the sixty-some years they had been apart.

If she had still been spying for Barton she would have many new childhood incidents to convey, gleaned from the ladies' conversation. It was a relief to be free of that uncomfortable obligation. Barton could snuffle around all by himself now! She smiled.

Once the ladies had been settled at the tea table Hesper had loitered for a few minutes at the exit of the Palm Court out of curiosity, and was relieved to see Elsinora actually eating a sandwich with enjoyment. She was relieved that Elsinora's hunger strike was over.

Without being aware of it, she had drifted back to the Tiffany windows.

"Well, lookee here! A refugee from the wilds of Connecticut, peering into those windows just like Holly Golightly," Geraldo's voice rang out.

"Holly-go-who?"

"From *Breakfast at Tiffany's.* Oh, never mind. She's fictional, you're real," he said, giving her a hug.

"Come with us for some tea. Our treat," invited Robbie. "Midtown Manhattan is such a small town. All our show-biz friends are wandering around here with nothing much to do with themselves until curtain time. We all bump into each other, just like in a village square, but today we have surprisingly chanced upon a genuine out-of-towner."

The two men happily squeezed her from either side and marched her into Bergdorf Goodman, assuring her that the currant scones were even better than those served at the Plaza.

SATISFIED BY THEIR repast, Elsinora and Doris left the Plaza and made their way across the street to sit upon the stone benches at the southern end of Central Park. The summer sun was mild and they lifted their worn faces to the welcome rays as they let the teacakes settle.

It was a busy spot with tourists and dog walkers to be watched and then commented upon. They were amused as the driver of a horse-drawn carriage placed a bucket of oats before his resting horse. A dozen pigeons instantly jumped into the bucket with a wild flapping of wings, followed by the wild flapping of the driver's arms and a scattering of the birds. The patient horse ate his oats.

"I'd better tell Hesper where we are," said Elsinora, and she sent a text to Hesper informing her as to their present location.

Hesper's text back informed them that she had bumped into old friends. Elsinora guessed it was Robbie and Geraldo who were always trolling around Midtown on the lookout for interesting people. It was time to forgive them for their snoopiness, she thought. She had more than forgiven Hesper, had she not? The situation that had threatened her privacy had been defused. No more tales would be carried to Barton Ford.

"Take your time. Take another hour," she replied.

In a return text Hesper had ritually protested, saying Elsinora would tire herself out, and her friend as well. Elsinora, as usual, prevailed.

"What a great baby Hesper is," she pronounced, snapping off the device. "But she means well."

"She seems a treasure," replied her friend.

"I'm still on the hunt for year thirteen, Doris. Will you tell me now, if you can, what you can recall of that year? If you have the energy after those honey cakes."

"I'm older than you, *Kemosabe,* but I can keep up," declared Doris, straightening her shoulders and letting her eyes follow a pair of courting pigeons as they jerkily circled each other around the pavement, the male cooing urgently.

Doris took a breath. "Let me lead up to it. My mother went to school with yours, as you know. Mom told me that Greta had always been shy and frightened of everything. I always thought of her as—oh, dear, this will sound insulting."

"Go ahead, please."

"Pathetic."

"She was a weak woman," Elsinora agreed. "And I was a burden to her. I tried not to be a bother, but I always was, or so it seemed."

"Then after your Uncle Conroy returned from Europe with that limp and you all moved in together there was quite a scandal as they weren't married, and because they evicted your granny. Took her home right out from under her."

"I always wondered if they did that. So they lied to me about it being her choice to go."

"Yes. My mom was particularly outraged about it. She felt your Grandma Bessie should have been cared for in her own home, where she had lived her whole life, and raised her two boys."

"Care was not a word that held much meaning at the Homestead."

"You told me about how your Grandma stopped speaking in the retirement home."

Elsinora nodded. She felt sadness permeate her being like water rising up in a container. She needed to compose herself and held up a hand.

"No. Wait, Doris. You were right to be concerned. The sad memories are coming too fast for me. Let's talk about you. Tell me more about how your life has gone."

Doris smiled. Her eyes narrowed. "I am a good enough

psychoanalyst to recognize a resistance when I hear one, and that deflection was a bit clumsy. You have been crouching in wait all through this afternoon, ready to pounce on my recollections, and now as I begin to share them, you suddenly want to hear about *me?* I don't blame you. It was pretty bleak back in the day, but you have long ago lived through it all. Why not let me go on, now that we have started, and get these smelly old memories out in the fresh air where they can evaporate. We can talk about my life another day."

Elsinora nodded, as she had done when, as a child, Doris had taken charge.

"You say your thirteenth year is missing in your memory? I think up until that time we went along as you recall, playing at heroes and heroines although I began to outgrow those games before you did. We stayed away from your home as much as possible, hanging out on my porch reading or playing board games. We were still just children, but you were more and more stricken by the behavior of the adults in your life, and I was aware of that. I liked offering you a refuge."

"I remember your screened-in porch well enough. There were comic books. Great stacks of them. Boxes of them. Oh, Doris, what am I hiding from myself?"

"Humiliation, I suspect. Greta and Conroy became an embarrassing duo. He had yanked her out of her grief and, at least for a few years, out of her fear. They drank and chain smoked and drove around in that ridiculous, pink convertible of his. And there were those romantic displays in public places."

"It's all coming back as you speak."

"It was, pretty embarrassing even for adults to witness, and as kids we were mortified. Then, just as you were becoming a teenager, Conroy started catting around and there were jealous rages, loud fights…in the diner, on the street, once in front of the Baptist church. Perhaps it was the drink. In a big city they wouldn't have been noticed so much, but in Warrensville? They were an ongoing scandal."

Elsinora felt a shiver go up her spine in spite of the warm spot in which they sat.

Doris continued. "The awful thing, at least to me, was how they acted around you, that frightening mix of ignoring you completely except to issue those constant warnings about dying. Watch out for this…watch out for that. It would drive anyone inwards."

"She always did that. From the time I can remember. I could be buried in snow and frozen solid, or choke to death on the dust from under my bed, or the tree branches would poke out my eyes."

Doris sighed. "In the midst of all that insanity you had to fix most of your own meals, and sometimes your clothes were outgrown. You would tell me about your nightmares because your mom wouldn't take the time to listen. How could you not have had nightmares? I've heard many stories of neglect in my professional life, but your situation is one which I witnessed firsthand. And it hurt me because I liked you so much. When Greta would go into the hospital, you were left alone in the Homestead with that crazy man."

Elsinora startled. "Hospital? Mom in a hospital?"

"She was in and out of the Crestone Mental Hospital for all those years and beyond. Surely, you remember that."

"No. I do not."

"Shall I stop?"

Elsinora was pale. "Go on," she whispered.

"Everyone thought that if the baby—"

"Baby? What baby?" Elsinora interrupted. "There was no baby. My mother miscarried."

Doris paused. "Exactly what did they tell you?"

"That Mom went to the hospital to have the baby but it was too early and she miscarried there. A still birth is what they called it. I remember that I was heartbroken. I thought a sister or brother would have been wonderful. Someone in my family I could love. Who would love me."

"I remember how sad you were."

"So what are you saying exactly?"

Doris reached across the short distance between them and took Elsinora's hand.

"We may be at the heart of the matter." Doris said.

Elsinora realized she was feeling a little sick, but said nothing. She felt she must hear what Doris was able to tell her.

"You remember my father was an attorney. He took care of most of the legal matters in the town, and they were *very* small town matters for the most part; leases, wills, that sort of thing, but one evening he came home looking unusually troubled. Being curious I hung around out of sight in order to overhear my parents' conversation. I soon realized they were talking about *your* family. A baby had been born. A healthy baby. A little girl. They named her Emma. Everyone at first had seemed joyful, all smiles and hugs in the delivery room. Your mom was especially happy."

"Alive? I had a sister? Have a sister? Emma?"

"Perhaps you do. Then, after all the show they made of her at her birth, they abruptly announced they wanted to immediately, and secretly, put her up for adoption."

"Adoption? What for?"

"They didn't want her."

"They didn't want—" Elsinora's voice trailed off.

"Although they presented a united front it was my father's belief that your mom cherished the infant, and that Conroy didn't. Dad felt your mother had been bullied into signing those papers, but there was no proof of that. Greta maintained she was willing. You remember how emotionally dependent on Conroy your mom was, in that terrible clutching way. He must have threatened to leave her if she kept the baby. Right after the adoption your mom's mental health deteriorated dramatically. That's when the breakdowns started, and the hospitalizations began."

Elsinora felt frozen. Too stunned to move.

Doris continued: "It is likely you found out the truth, Elsie. Children usually know everything that goes on in a home, one way or another. You might have heard an argument between your mom and Conroy. I don't know. I didn't tell you, that's for sure. That was my cowardice. I was old enough to understand what privileged information was, and would have gotten into terrible trouble if I had told anyone what I overheard my father say that night, but I think you knew, and couldn't bear it, and that is why you've blocked the memory."

Elsinora forced herself to speak. She needed to say the words out loud: "The baby was born alive and healthy. Conroy threatened my mother, and gave my baby sister away. Between them they fashioned a lie and told me that she was born dead."

"Yes. That lie is what they told everyone. Only the medical staff and my parents knew the truth, and they remained silent because of the professional confidentiality laws. Conroy and Greta received a lot of sympathy from people who thought they had lost a child to death."

The present drained away from Elsinora as did the blood from her face.

"O horrible, o horrible, most horrible."

She jerked to her feet and began pacing awkwardly in a small circle, much like the pigeons that surrounded them.

Doris watched her distress, trying to determine what she should do. Certainly, she thought, Elsinora was entitled to the truth she had asked for, so long hidden from herself.

Elsinora could see the whole year now with its madness and grief; hear the raised voices behind closed doors; the sounds of Grandma Bessie's sobs before she went silent forever. She could see her younger self withdrawing from all the pain into a gray, lifeless existence from which she might never have emerged had it not been for the arrival of Fletcher. Had she told him? She thought not. The horror of that act was already buried too deep inside herself by the time he arrived.

She would tell him now!

She stopped pacing and looked around. Fletcher was gone, but her friend Doris was here, sitting on a grey stone bench. She looked like an old lady. This must be a nightmare.

Now Emma was there, tucked into her mind's eye. Sweet, tiny, beautiful, happily alive Emma whom she had never seen, but as she must have looked, like any other healthy newborn. Of course she had aways been there. One does not forget a sister; but at the same time she had *not* been there, her mind refusing these many years to travel to the deception, and its hideous aftermath. And where was Emma now?

Old Doris was still here, looking concerned.

Pigeons were here.

Hesper was here. And Elsinora collapsed into her outstretched arms.

ELSINORA AWOKE TO the clatter of a hospital emergency room. Not a hospital of memory, not the one Uncle Conroy had died in, or the one she had been in for so long following her plummet from the stage, but a hospital of the present moment, glaring and bustling. Oh hell, she thought. She had wanted a quick over-and-out from life, not one bedridden in a medical institution.

"There you are," said Hesper bending close, "back among the living! You fainted. The EMS guys insisted, because of your age, that we had to bring you here for observation."

"And where exactly am I being observed?"

"Bellevue. We were given this nice little curtained cubicle off the main ER."

"If I was still a movie star I would be in a private suite."

She is her feisty self, thought Hesper. A good sign.

"The first doctor checked you over and said that if you came around soon and your numbers were okay you wouldn't have to be admitted, and here you are!"

Elsinora saw that Hesper's relief was real. Nice, she thought. She stands to have the house when I die, but is delighted to see me alive. I got that right.

She looked around her. There was Doris Graves sitting calmly nearby, her expression a mixture of concern and curiosity.

"What was it, Doris? The sun? The brandy? Something we ate?" asked Elsinora.

"Something I said," replied Doris, watching her carefully.

Their conversation came back to Elsinora in tiny jolts, in small pieces that she could face, as the images slowly congregated around the words: Emma, adoption, lies, breakdowns, Crestone Psychiatric.

"I thought I was more resilient," she said. "I am, it seems, more fragile than I knew."

A nurse with a red face and a pinched expression hurried in and began to do what felt like a cursory examination.

"Dehydration," she announced, and handed Elsinora a plastic bottle of water, then rushed out abruptly.

"Must have bigger fish to fry," murmured Elsinora.

Again her mind moved towards the images, but once more she was interrupted before she could speak, this time by an attractive young doctor who told her to sit up and then stuck a stethoscope onto her chest. God, he was young! He looked like a child playing doctor. After listening to her heart he looked at her chart.

It was the young people's turn to be important, she knew, but this generation had not sat at the knee of those who were older and wiser to learn the ways of being human. They had been raised by soulless computers and they often poked at others, expecting instant answers as if they were keyboards or touch screens.

Perhaps it is better to be raised by machines, she thought. You don't expect devices to have a heart, so you are not disappointed.

"You might make a good doctor when you grow up," said Elsinora, hoping to puncture his self-importance, realizing how annoyed she was at the current crop of young adults who now seemed to run everything, though not particularly well.

The intern did not appear to hear her remark. Doctors don't listen to people anymore, she thought, not like *my* doctor. Not like Maurice. She felt like crying, but did not. Why upset everyone when tears of the present were of no avail in the past.

"She will be better off at home, than in here," he announced to Hesper and Doris, as if Elsinora were not in the room. With this decision she was in full agreement, and they began to busy themselves with leaving.

It was not until they were settled in the car and heading out of the city that Elsinora felt ready to speak.

"Thank you, Doris. I can go back there now."

"To the places of the blank year?"

"I see now that it was never really blank, only shrouded. The shapes were always there but I wouldn't look."

"And you can look now?"

"I think so. I can see my mother's breakdowns following what I thought was the baby's death, and how hard I tried not to accept the truth of what they had done when I overheard it. I've captured images of two junior high teachers trying to be kind. You and your mom were there for me, of course. Mrs. Kellogg offered me the job in the library. Mrs. Richie comes and goes, but, oh, the sadness of it all. It really was too much for any child to bear."

Surprising herself, she did begin to weep.

Hesper, somewhat taken aback, for she had never seen Elsinora cry before, efficiently supplied a pack of tissues and gave Doris a questioning look.

"It's a long story," said Doris.

Elsinora's face, wet with tears, jerked up. She spoke with energy, a fierceness replacing her look of sorrow.

"Yet many children have borne so much more than I! Whatever was going on in my home, I was growing up in relative safety, not torn from my parents' arms in a war, or shoved into ghettos to starve, or tortured in concentration camps, or bombed with an atom bomb. As awful as my childhood was, given what was happening in the world at the time, and for that matter ever since, I had it easy."

"You can think that as an adult," said Doris, "but to a child, suffering is suffering. Comparisons are irrelevant. You simply had to bear your own, and if there is a good side, bearing it has made you resilient."

"Do you think I could find her? Emma?"

"Adoptions at the time were strictly confidential, and the records sealed. Her name would have been changed to that of the adoptive parents, and most likely changed again if she ever married. It is a long shot, but you could try."

"It wouldn't be right. Whoever took her wanted her. What age would she be now...seventy-something? Why burden her with the knowledge of parents as grotesque as Greta and Conroy?"

"But how about with a kindly older sister, Elsinora Dean?"

"I have much to consider."

Hesper, clueless during this interchange was looking at Doris for enlightenment.

"Hesper, let's get Elsinora home," said Doris with resolve. "And let's get *me* home."

"Yes," said Elsinora, mopping at her tear-stained face, with a disintegrating tissue.

"She looks done in," said Hesper.

"I can speak for myself now, Hesper. I am quite all right."

"So it appears," said Hesper, glad to hear the sharpness in Elsinora's voice as it indicated she was truly recovering from her frightening collapse.

Elsinora seemed to withdraw into herself then, still clutching the shreds of Kleenex. Doris Graves sighed and sank back into the soft upholstery of the sedan.

The afternoon has been too much for these ancient friends, thought Hesper, as the two women nodded off into exhausted slumber.

XXVII. Their adoption tried.

THE FOLLOWING WEEK, on a day that was fresh and clear, Robbie and Geraldo stood nervously on the doorstep of Elsinora's manor house, each holding an enormous bouquet composed of all her favorite flowers. Robbie had opted for yellow roses with babies' breath, Geraldo was almost unseen behind tall blue irises and sweet smelling daylilies.

They had been sent for. It was Hesper who had phoned them, but she conveyed Elsinora's wish to meet with them.

The men knew they had disgraced themselves in Elsinora's eyes when they went poking about in her house. Why then, they wondered, were they being summoned here today? Another dressing down seemed unlikely. She had been thorough the first time. Could they hope for forgiveness?

They both felt wobbly. Geraldo's chubby cheeks were flushing red making them look chubbier, whereas the color had drained from Robbie's thin face making him appear even more gaunt than usual. They were eager to apologize, for they so adored Elsinora and wished only to return to her good graces.

Hesper let them in with a smile. A good sign, perhaps? They were ushered through the massive entrance hall and through the elegant living room into the dining room where Elsinora received them with an inscrutable expression and a wave of the hand towards the chairs.

She was already seated at the polished mahogany table which was set with four exquisite china place settings next to crystal flutes already sparkling with champagne. Large silver bowls filled with salads, fruits, olives, and nuts adorned the table alongside cutting boards of freshly baked breads and artisanal cheeses, jars of spreads, and confits. This reception was certainly not what they had anticipated.

After gifting her with the bouquets and awkwardly kissing her hand they had taken their seats.

"Try some of this blue cheese," said Elsinora, as she handed the cones of flowers off to Hesper who took them in the direction of the kitchen.

"Thank you so much," said Robbie at the same moment that Geraldo began speaking contritely, "We are both most apologetic and—"

Elsinora again waved a hand, this time at their jumble of words as if she was swatting away flies.

"Oh don't waste my time," she commanded, "I have little enough of it left. You were naughty boys, you've been properly spanked, you're rightly sorry, I'm a forgiving woman. I have a proposition to make to you, but first have something to eat. I don't eat cheese myself, but have no objection to others enjoying it. Nothing has to die for cheeses to be made, and European cows are particularly well cared for, unlike our own. If you don't like Roquefort try the Beaufort Chalet d'Alpage. The herds must be taken up high into Alpine meadows in summertime to graze. I am told one can taste the meadows."

Two sets of gray eyebrows rose and fell as Robbie and Geraldo looked at one another with both relief and puzzlement. Although none of this was making much sense to them, their normal coloration began to return, and their shoulders began to lower as they dared to relax.

What kind of proposition? They wondered, but had simply to wait as both knew that Elsinora could never be rushed. They must live with their ignorance until she was ready to enlighten them. Obediently they surveyed the array of excellent food with pleasant anticipation, in spite of their disquiet.

Elsinora nibbled at grapes and watched as the two men went about filling their plates. Hesper returned with the flowers beautifully arranged in large Oriental vases which she put in their ordained places on nearby side tables. With unexpected casualness she sat down alongside them.

This, too, puzzled the men. Hesper had always kept a servant's distance from Elsinora during meals in years past, hovering nearby in case she should require something, but now she simply joined the party helping herself to figs and brie.

"Perhaps some music, Hesper," suggested Elsinora and Hesper rose again to turn a discreet dial in the wall. Gentle classical music filtered into the room. They all recognized Vivaldi's *Four Seasons*.

"The melon slices would go well with the figs," Elsinora directed, and Hesper, who had returned to her seat, followed her suggestion adding the delicate green and pink slices to her plate.

The mysterious meal continued for some time without conversation as it was clear Elsinora was listening to the music, her eyes half closed. They all knew she was thinking of Fletcher. He had brought glorious music into all their lives; choral arrangements so harmonious that at times one wept and entertained thoughts of heaven. They had envied Fletcher for his closeness to Elsinora and her obvious love for him. Their envy seemed a meaningless expense of spirit to them now that he was gone. How death threw a harsh light onto one's petty jealousies!

At the conclusion of the music Elsinora, instantly alert,

surveyed the table. The men had finished eating, appeared satisfied, and were sipping at their second glasses of champagne in anticipation of whatever it was she might say. Hesper rose with the intention of clearing the plates, but Elsinora indicated that she should remain, so she resumed her seat.

Elsinora spoke at last.

"As you all know, Hesper's ex-husband, Barton Ford, is writing an unauthorized biography of me to be published after I die. You all knew of this before I did, of course, and were imprudently involved from its inception."

She paused and peered at each of them in turn. There was no escaping the dismay in her look. Blood rushed up and down in their respective countenances once again.

"It is my understanding that this book is to be an unsavory piece of work, dwelling on aspects of my past that I would sooner not have disinterred; my unhappy childhood, personal medical issues, and in particular the tragic death of my husband, Oliver-Paul Harding. I understand that even my relationship with Fletcher Mulcaster is not to be spared, sacred as it was to me, and who knows what blasphemies this man may choose to make up, as he seems a person deficient in honor. Hesper, since leaving him, has been completely forthcoming about his plans, his interests, and his thinking, if you can call the incoherent thrashings of a mind such as his thinking."

Hesper was unhappily silent. Barton had once been thought a good writer. Elsinora could certainly be harsh when she was angry.

"I don't believe there is any way I can prevent this book from being written or published. I have many talents and resources, but they end at the grave. I have no offspring to bring libel suits, request injunctions, and otherwise interfere with the profits this scoundrel plans to pocket."

She paused and took a sip of her own wine, watching them over the rim of the glass. No one spoke.

Elsinora continued.

"Hesper and I have discussed the situation and have decided on a plan. She has agreed with my desires and has been assured it will not impact the legacy I have already given her, or certain aspects of my will regarding the house."

Hesper nodded.

Robbie and Geraldo sat mesmerized waiting to hear what this unpredictable woman would next say. They were barely breathing. This was the first they had heard of any legacy. Hesper had not said a word of any such thing to them during their tea at Bergdorf's, although they now recalled that when they had met up with her she was peering into the Tiffany window displays with unusual interest.

"I believe you two gentlemen would agree that you owe me a small favor in balance of your previous indiscretions?" Elsinora asked it as a question, but it had the weight of a declaration.

They glanced at one another, then nodded in agreement, and in trepidation.

"Then I propose to adopt you. Do you agree?"

XXVIII. The beaten way of friendship.

As it was said in her profession, Doris Graves was processing her experience. She was seated in a garden chair on the flagstone terrace just outside the door of her studio apartment at Halcyon Circle. She was contemplating her recent reunion with Elsinora, trying to combine the serious child of her youth, the glamorous actress of stage and screen, and the plainspoken old woman of the present day into one homogenized person.

What I need is my knitting, she thought, and reached into her nearby bag. The occupation of her fingers had always facilitated the workings of her mind. She had knitted through a thousand psychoanalytic sessions. Most of her patients had found the steady click of the needles soothing, but occasionally one would complain, accuse her of not being completely attentive. When this occurred she would put down her wool and gently ask them who had failed to give them proper attention as a child. This usually led to a fruitful session.

She knew she shouldn't analyze her friends, but her mind was her mind and went its own way, and so what was she to make of the Elsinora of today?

She had sent the initial note of invitation to her old companion, picturing a quiet conversation, smiling together over tea, and laughing at the remembrances of their youthful adventures.

She thought it might be an antidote to the forlorn feeling she experienced at times in this new place, this *facility*.

It had certainly been a strange encounter. She could not have imagined the excursion to New York City with visits to The Palm Court, Central Park, and the Bellevue Hospital Emergency Room, complete with the jarring return of repressed memories and a fainting spell, all of an afternoon. A week later and here she was still exhausted! Eighty-seven is not the new sixty-seventy, she mused as her needles clicked on.

Over the years she had worked with several amnesiac patients in the hospital to which she had been affiliated in Albany, but she had never worked with such a person in private practice. All the cases of profound memory loss she had dealt with had followed traumatic head injuries, and so she had little doubt that Elsinora's fall contributed to her friend's difficulties, combined with the fact that she had purposely, consciously, suppressed her traumatic childhood, until recently when she felt it was important to recall all the dramas of her past.

Doris thought it was peculiar, this need of Elsinora's to put her memories into order before she died, writing down her life as if it was a play or a movie script.

Could her friend be on the autism spectrum? Hyperlexia, the ability to read very early, was common among highly functioning children with an autistic diagnosis. She remembered that Elsinora had always been extremely meticulous with her belongings. She had been a demon in their hometown library where she had worked during her high school years, insuring every book was in its proper place, reading every one she had time for. She had never told a lie so far as Doris could recall, and could not abide deception in others. High functioning autism was not a well-known diagnosis in the 1950s, but it would be suspected today of any child exhibiting Elsinora's characteristics.

There had also been Elsinora's marked distress upon seeing the crowded, noisy dining room here at Halcyon Circle whereas others might have seen it simply as cheerful. She had peculiar food issues, too, and there was that distressingly jerky pacing in circles just before she fainted. So was Elsinora a person with what used to be called Asperger's Syndrome, but was now called Autistic Spectrum Disorder Level One…the new category in the diagnostic manual that was surely invented by someone with Autistic Spectrum Disorder Level One.

Maybe so.

And oh, that ferocious need to control what people knew and said about her. How unpleasant the years of her celebrity must have been!

Doris rested her hands on the soft, powder-blue wool in her lap. Of course traumas alone might be enough to account for Elsinora's strangeness; the early loss of her father, the crazy mother, the addition of that bizarre Uncle Conroy to the Homestead, Grandma Bessie's strange withdrawal into silence, the heartless discarding of the little sister. It could make anyone depressed, or brittle, or haughty, or private, or perhaps in the end desperate to make sense of it all. In novels there is a plot. Everything that transpires has a point, what happens to all the characters makes logical sense, and the loose ends are all tied up in the last chapter or the epilogue. Sadly, Doris knew, life was not like a novel or a play or a movie, as much as Elsinora might wish it were so.

Doris knew it was her own emotional reaction to their meeting which carried the strongest diagnostic clue. The woman elicited a feeling in her she remembered clearly from their shared childhood; a desire to protect her, though it was not asked for, and might even be repelled by the present-day Elsinora; yet she had felt it from the moment of their reunion. She did not feel all warm and fuzzy at the reacquaintance with an old school chum as one might imagine. As *she* had imagined. Quite the opposite. It had been a bumpy ride.

Did she want to be involved with such a complicated person at this age when wisdom indicated it was best to simplify one's life?

"Friends disappoint," the Buddha reportedly said, and Doris had never forgotten that truth since coming across it early in her college years. She had always deeply loved her friends, but had tried not to expect or demand too much from them, fearing that she would be disappointed or that she would disappoint them. She had kept boundaries and distance at the expense of intimacy. The result had been a life filled with untroubled relationships, with many unexpected expressions of kindness or generosity from friends, and she hoped she gave as good as she got.

So many of her friends were gone now and the worlds they had built and shared together with her vanished along with them.

Doris heaved a mighty sigh.

She had developed and shared parts of herself with different friends, depending on their personalities, their age and interests. As they died, those parts were now all alone, huddled inside her being, with no one to talk to. She plunged her fingers into her knitting and was soothed by the softness of the wool.

Elsinora. Except for Hesper, she was rattling around all alone in her castle by the water, clearly in as much need of genuine friendship as she was herself.

It really made no difference what her diagnosis was.

Doris would be kind. Elsinora would be who she was. They would bump along.

XXIX. Of accidental judgments.

ELSINORA FELT AS if she were hiding under a waterfall. She sat in her conservatory, a bubble-domed glass greenhouse, which she had insisted on adding to the garden room when she purchased the manor. She had wanted a place to sit inside in any weather, with a feeling of being outside. She particularly liked resting here when rivulets of rain spilled over the glass ceiling and ran down the structure's sides.

Today she had parked herself deep within the foliage enjoying the daylight filtering greenly through the ferns and palm fronds. Trapped light it was called. Trapped light was a good description of her spirit, living as best it could inside her ancient body. She had been a star. She smiled inwardly. The star had fallen. The star was fading. She must avoid becoming a black hole now that she was allowing her mind to move among the grim memories made available after the lifting of her amnesia.

Foremost was the loss of Emma. She had fallen in love with the idea of a baby sister or brother when the pregnancy had been announced. She knew that the tiny human-to-be was a product not of her own imagination, but of her mother's union with her uncle. Something good to come out of it.

With searing accuracy she now recalled the unused cradle, her mother collapsed on the nursery floor, her mind shattering; her grandmother's deterioration, and she herself, like a sleepwalker, going through the requirements of living while her emotions shriveled. Conroy had felled them; all the mothers and daughters of the family.

Hesper entered the conservatory. She peered through the foliage and seeing her employer lost in thought, she spoke as softly as she could so as not to startle her, but still to be heard. "Mrs. Harding?"

"Present and accounted for, Hesper," came the reply, seemingly from a large rubber tree.

"There is a man announcing himself as Detective Inspector Milo Griffith, Retired, at the door. He apologizes for arriving without an appointment, but asks if he might see you."

"Milo? After all these years?"

"He is shaking in his boots and says you may not remember him," Hesper added.

"Yet again," grumbled Elsinora, yanked from one era of her life into another as she registered Hesper's words. "Do they just assume I am gaga? I remember him clear as day." She shook her head slowly from side to side in apparent dismay.

"Shall I send him away?"

"You can show him in here, Hesper. Bring some beer, too. He drinks beer. Tell him he can't smoke."

Milo was disoriented and short of breath, having been led by Hesper through the mammoth entrance hall with the forbidding suit of armor, the drawing room with its oil portraits of Elsinora in her prime, the dining room lined with glass-fronted cabinets displaying several sets of plates, two corridors of contrasting colors, a sitting room thick with overstuffed furniture, past a library with floor to ceiling volumes, into a garden room with its airy mid-century modern furnishings, its walls covered in springtime murals, and finally into the conservatory where Elsinora, having emerged from the foliage, was sitting under a palm tree sipping one of the two cold beers already in place on a wrought iron table.

At a wave of Elsinora's hand Hesper withdrew reluctantly, her face a large question mark.

"Hello, Milo," greeted Elsinora, allowing both warmth and amusement into her voice. She indicated a seat, and he sat down awkwardly after first extending his hand, hesitating, withdrawing it, and letting it fall to his side.

"I hope you are not carrying a pistol," she said as she handed him a beer, which he took gratefully, still breathless.

"My dear Detective Inspector Griffith, look how mature you have become in only half a century. I am curious as to how I can be of service to you after this many a day?"

"Please excuse my unexpected visit, Mrs. Harding," he managed to say after a cold swallow of what turned out to be an excellent brew. "I had the idea to come and just did it. Spur of the moment, you might say. If I had stopped to think about it, or call ahead, I would have lost my nerve most likely."

"I don't bite."

"I know." He managed a smile. "You were always so polite and respectful back in the day, during the investigation."

"But not warm."

"You were in shock."

"I was in a great many things, shock among them; but also anger, sadness, fear, and worry. And, although I did not know it then, relief."

"Relief?"

"Oliver-Paul was not an easy man to live with."

"Ah, yes. There were such rumors, but they could just have been the pulp that the movie magazines printed out. I never put much stock in them."

"Perhaps you should have."

"It is about the investigation that I have come to see you."

"Well, it does seem unlikely you would be having a spur of the moment desire to be tutored in Shakespeare."

"Here is the thing." He paused and took a big swallow of beer. "There is this writer fellow, Barton Ford, his name is. He came poking around recently, down in the police archives even, saying he was going to write a book about you, and wanted to know the details of the Oliver-Paul Harding investigation."

"Yes?" She drew out the syllable slowly, with an upturn of her chin. Her eyes narrowed.

"Well, it didn't strike me right. You being a famous movie star and all. Back in the day. I figured he was just looking for a way to make some money off your fame by rucking up that terrible time in your past."

"No doubt."

"And he made insinuations. Insinuations we put to rest during the investigations."

"So?"

He reached into his bag and pulled out a worn file.

"So I thought you should have this." He handed her the investigative file and her eyes darted over its cover.

"But this is police property."

"Yes, ma'am, it is. And no one knows but me and you where it is at present. The police today don't care about a file that's fifty years out of date with no crime inside it, and that writer guy may guess that I took it if he dares to look for it again, but so much for him." He extended the folder.

"You are giving this to me?"

"Just so."

"If you didn't want it to fall into other hands, why didn't you simply destroy it?"

"It's a piece of history, ma'am. Yours and mine. You were an innocent woman. I did an honest job. It's a record of two good people behaving well under difficult circumstances. Up to you if you wish to keep it or destroy it, but I couldn't take it on to do that myself." He put down his empty glass.

"Just a moment, Sergeant."

Elsinora reached for a nearby bell, pushed it, and in a moment Hesper reappeared. "Will you bring Sergeant Griffith another beer, Hesper? Thank you. And I'll have another myself."

Hesper's eyebrows raised in dismay, but she left to fetch the beer.

Elsinora placed the file on a nearby table, and studied the man before her. He was not the neat, handsome cop of his youth, all regulation and trimness and determination, but an old man, slightly overweight, with a worn out look to his clothes and his face. Life had written hard lessons on him.

He began to fidget under her steady gaze. The beer arrived and the mere sight of it had a settling effect upon him.

Elsinora continued to watch the detective impassively as he drank. At last she spoke. "Now tell me, Sergeant. Did you always believe in my innocence?"

The former detective, startled by the question, looked for a moment like a guilty creature caught in the beam of a flashlight. He pursed his lips and frowned, glanced down at his shoes, then back up to meet Elsinora's eyes. "No, ma'am," he said at last. "No, I did not. The people you were with at Sardi's that night said you had left in a fury with Mr. Harding. The stories of your epic fights were legendary and might actually have been true. And why would a man in a bathtub reach for an electric fan?"

"And yet?"

"After we had talked the first time in the apartment, then more formally at the precinct, then in a friendlier way that time we met by chance in Character's Bar, and finally after you gave evidence at the inquest…well…I became convinced you were telling the truth. Your story of the unhappy night never varied, you seemed to hide nothing; not his bad behavior, or your anger; or your horror at finding him as you did."

"And that was enough for you?"

"I interviewed a lot of people, Mrs. Harding; your fellow actors, friends, landlord. Forgive me, but although you were tremendously admired, you were not particularly well-liked. People said you were standoffish, but no one thought you capable of murder. And Fletcher Mulcaster, the conductor, he was adamant, saying he had known you since childhood and it was not in your character. That, and the lack of any evidence to the contrary…" His voice trailed off. He shrugged. She saw that his mind's eye was deep in remembrance; a place she knew well.

He suddenly straightened, drank down the last of the beer, and spoke with an energy drawn from his youth. "You were so beautiful! Such a marvelous actress. Always so lovely to me. No one so beautiful, so kind, could kill a man. I knew it. I knew it all the way to my toes."

"Why, Sergeant, I see it now. You were a little in love with me."

Milo's eyes darted around the conservatory as if looking for the right potted palm behind which he could hide. Charmingly, he blushed, his old face looking younger and younger, the pinker he became.

"Yes, yes. I was, but—"

"—but it did not blind you to the possibility that I was *acting?*"

He was silent a long time. His flushed face now held a look of deep unhappiness.

She waited, while he found his courage.

"Were you…were you acting?"

She held him in uncomfortable suspense just a moment

longer. "No. I did not murder Oliver-Paul. My husband was drunk and must have been flailing about, and in so doing knocked that stupid fan right into his stupid bathwater, the stupid, stupid man."

She saw relief pass through him, relief that began to relax his features.

"As you always said."

"As I always said; but you were wrong about one conclusion, Detective Inspector Sergeant."

His eyes darted to the file, then to Elsinora. "What? What was I wrong about?"

"Although I did not murder my husband, I am quite capable of killing a man. Another beer, Detective?"

XXX. Who does me this?

BARTON STEPPED OFF the bathroom scale, picked it up and flung it out the open window onto the cement enclosure behind the apartment building where it crashed next to a broken exercise bicycle, a disused radiator, a pair of torn corduroy pants, and other unwanted junk thrown down from the tenants above.

His physical makeover was not going as planned, nor was his book. Nor, for that matter, was his life. Here he was at fifty when he should be at the crest of his life, but the world of his expectations had become distorted and narrowed in unforeseen ways.

Top of the list was the end of his marriage. It hadn't seemed very important to him to be married when he was young, but it was what was expected of a man; to have a pretty woman at his side, keeping his house, cooking his meals, smiling at his guests, at least that is what his father had told him, and his dad had been a successful man, possessed of this pleasing attribute himself. Until she left them. First his mother and then his wife, gone for good.

He was also told he must have a career. He had chosen writing because there was an aura of romance to it. Back in the day Hemingway was romantic. Fitzgerald was romantic. James Joyce was romantic. "I'm a writer" was a more alluring overture to a young woman than "I sell insurance."

He had some talent for putting words together and a nose for what sold. He had always been careful to pick popular subjects to write about, nothing deep. He found an agent who liked selling books more than reading them, and was swiftly on his way. He hadn't produced an actual blockbuster, but he had made a living at it, and believed that it was just a matter of time for fame to arrive.

He had deluded himself with the belief that Hesper had been the perfect wife for him. Circumspect, tidy, supportive, pleased when he had a success. Life had then seemed well-arranged. Unfortunately, the income from his books had been less than was required, and Hesper's paycheck as a live-in housekeeper for Elsinora would be significantly better than as a day maid. The pandemic sealed the deal. She moved in permanently with Elsinora, the damnable witch.

Thinking back, the pandemic had been a perfect time in a way. Lots of freedom suddenly. Sometimes he had a call girl in.

He had not planned on divorce. Had she guessed about the call girls? "Living well is the best revenge," F. Scott Fitzgerald had famously written, and Barton had intended to do exactly that; but he hadn't known how to go about living well in this new world where white men were no longer valued by virtue of their whiteness and their maleness, and a fortunate birth required apology.

At every upscale bar he had entered, having pried a pretty woman away from her smartphone with offers of a drink, he had spoken of his writing to a blank face, and worse: "Elsinora who? That's a funny name. Oliver-Paul Harding? Never heard of them. *When* did you say this happened? Who cares about *then*? Sorry, guy. Thanks for the beer. I have to answer this text."

Barton Ford had been dismissed. He was replaced by the algorithms of a modern life he no longer understood. Someday he would die and no one would care. His books would molder unread on the library shelves of obscure towns and finally be sold at dollar-a-dozen sales.

He looked into the bathroom mirror and saw a tired man in a stained undershirt disappearing over a hill.

Barton shuffled to the kitchen and took a ham sandwich from the fridge. He opened a bag of potato chips and popped a beer.

He knew that food would not relieve the unpleasant feeling churning just below his breastbone. A hunger for something he could not name. A dark, demanding wanting that nothing satisfied and that left him feeling as he had when, as an abandoned child, he had been about to cry.

He whimpered, but no tears came.

He needed a new idea.

He needed a new woman.

He needed a new body.

He needed a new life.

He needed.

XXXI. Remembrances of yours.

WITH A FLOURISH, Hesper drew out a carefully folded black velvet cape from the trunk. Elsinora had worn it in the stage production of *Hamlet* in which she had triumphed, not as Ophelia, not as Gertrude, but as the moody and murderous Prince himself. Robbie and Geraldo will like this, she thought and into their box it went.

As Elsinora rested in the library, Hesper was busy sorting photos, scrapbooks, magazines, reviews, and Playbills from the days of Elsinora's fame, along with stray props and costumes that had been carried forward in the stream of time. Much was to be disposed of. Elsinora called it Swedish death cleaning. Anything touching on Elsinora's personal life was consigned to flames, but professional accolades, flattering photos, and fine reviews were allowed to survive. These would all go to Robbie and Geraldo.

Hesper felt closer to the two men since Elsinora's surprise luncheon. Their destinies were now intertwined. After their jaws dropped into their dessert bowls they had readily agreed to the proposed adoption and had accepted Elsinora's conditions as, of course, there were conditions.

They were to use every strategy within their power, as legal family members and estate executors, to thwart Barton's attempt to publish his book; to sue for any slanders therein should it manage to see the light of day and, in short, to make his life as difficult as possible in the matter of his attempted exposé. Hesper laughed aloud.

The adoption papers were accordingly drawn up and signed. The terms specifically forbade them from challenging Hesper's own legacy or her ownership of Arden Manor. Robbie and Geraldo Fitz-Marco-Harding, as they were now known, would receive a princely sum for their troubles, and would inherit all the celebrity keepsakes which Hesper would soon have sorted and stored for them. These items could be displayed or auctioned at their will, but they too were forbidden to publish. In the event that others came forward with biographies they were to be as diligent in providing legal obstacles to those authors as they were to Barton. The lady certainly preferred her privacy.

As she worked, Hesper wondered what had taken place during the meeting with the detective, as there had been no spare palm tree for her to hide behind and overhear what was being discussed. Elsinora was close-lipped on the matter. However, Hesper had seen her place a file onto a hearth fire after his departure. More mystery.

Hesper wondered if there was any mystery in her own life? Had she any secrets? She knew of none. She wasn't the type. She was as uncomplicated as rice pudding, which, she thought might be nice for dessert tonight.

XXXII. Strict in his arrest.

DETECTIVE SERGEANT MILO Griffin was feeling cheerful. It was a feeling he had forgotten was possible. He no longer wanted to hide away in musty bars and die in his sleep. He had contacted the police academy inquiring if he might teach some courses. He joined a gym and the result of the regular workouts was rewarding as he watched his soft muscles began to harden and take shape again. He looked at travel advertisements on his new iPad and was beginning to explore the world as it was offered up to him online.

This evening he would select one of Elsinora Dean's old movies, and with popcorn and a soda feel young again as he watched her do her dazzling thing. And to think he knew her personally! She had remembered him. He had been welcomed into her elegant home. They had sat together in that beautiful glass room full of trees, and they had enjoyed one another's company.

She liked him! He had helped her! He had revealed his love for her and she had accepted it with grace. And he had been right about her all along. She had not killed her husband.

His chest was full of pride. His heart with love. And sitting comfortably, his brain brimming with happiness, wide awake, and smiling, he died.

XXXIII. That which passeth show.

ROBBIE AND GERALDO sat in the darkened auditorium deep in the bowels of The Museum of Modern Art. They were brimming with anxious expectation for they were about to view the restored film version of *Hamlet,* starring Elsinora at the height of her fame. It had not been shown for decades so they had, until now, only been sustained by their memories of how magnificent she had been.

"I'm frightened," said Geraldo.

"What about?" queried his partner.

"What if…? I mean it's unlikely…but what if…she isn't as good as we recall?"

"That's not possible!" declared Robbie. "Remember when we were writing our reviews? Sometimes one or the other of us was wildly enthusiastic about a performance, and the other, not so much. But both our reviews were in agreement regarding this performance. It was the *Hamlet* for all time, for all souls."

"But it's the film version. Her greatest triumphs were always on the stage."

The lights began to dim. The audience settled as the first chords of the overture were heard, the hushed and brooding melody composed and conducted by Fletcher Mulcaster.

"Oh my God…here it comes. I can hardly bear it."

The music gave way to the drums and brass of the opening

credits, followed by a shortened scene on the battlements where the ghost of Hamlet's father's first appears to the frightened watchmen. There followed a quick cut to the beginning of the palace scene introducing the workings of the court, the happiness of the newly married king and queen.

Then slowly the camera panned to a solitary figure dressed in midnight black, wrapped in the traditional inky cloak; a figure unmoving, watching the proceedings of the court from within a deeply shadowed corner.

And yet, and yet…her countenance lit up the screen before she moved, before her first words as the tragic Prince were spoken. It was her stillness that was mesmerizing, a mortal coil about to spring into the actions of grief, fear, wonderment, horror, doubt, revenge, love, and every emotion a human might ever feel. There she was, a Hamlet for the ages, a little more than kin and less than kind.

Robbie sighed in awe and appreciation. He clutched Geraldo's hand, who squeezed it to show he felt the same.

In unison, they murmured, "Mother."

XXXIV. Unseen good old man

"WE NEED TO visit the Veterans' Domiciliary in New Haven," announced Elsinora over breakfast.

"The *what?*" asked Hesper.

"The VA Hospital in New Haven, the nomenclature of which has been changed for reasons that passeth understanding." Elsinora was studying a note that had arrived with the morning mail. Hesper noticed a slight undercurrent of agitation in her voice.

"When are we to make this visit?"

"As soon as humanly possible. There can be no delay."

"I'll go see about a car."

"Yes, do. And lay out my navy blue suit."

"May I ask— "

"—dying friend."

"Oh, my. Oh, dear. I'm sorry," Hesper murmured, and hurried out.

Elsinora reread the note which had come by special delivery.

Dear Mrs. Harding,

I am writing at the request of Colonel Arthur Osborne, a patient here, as he can no longer write himself.

Colonel Osborne tells me he is dying, and as he has always been very sharp about matters regarding his health I think he may be correct. I've worked with elderly patients for a long time (though never one so old as the Colonel at one hundred and three) and I have learned to trust their instincts in this regard.

I asked him if he had any wish I could grant before he passed and he said he would like to see you once again and he gave me your particulars. I think you are the kind lady who never forgets him on the Fourth of July, and to whom he always sends a thank you note in reply.

I see that your address is quite nearby and so it might indeed be possible for you to visit him, although I know nothing of you or of your circumstances.

My number is on the back of this card. Please let me know if you can, perhaps, come by.

With many thanks,

Sara Benoit, R.N. for Colonel Arthur Osborne

Elsinora sent a text to Nurse Benoit informing her that she was on her way and, leaving her bowl of granola unfinished, she hastened to her bedroom to dress.

A half hour later she and Hesper were in the limousine and Elsinora was silently reliving her one and only encounter with the Colonel, now almost fifty years in the past.

There, in her mind's eye, she saw the army officer, all spit and polish, as it used to be said, standing nervously in her dressing room, unknown and unannounced, both shy and polite.

He had courteously introduced himself, showing her his identification, putting her at her ease and at the same time arousing her curiosity. Standing almost at attention, as he did throughout their meeting, he begged a few moments of her time, explaining that he had known her father.

"My father? My father was killed in World War II."

"Yes. I met him on a battlefield in France."

"But you look too young to have been in that war."

"I was an English upper schoolboy who ran away from home, lied about my age, and got taken into service in the early days of the war. At that time of panic everyone was in a mad rush to get men into uniform and into the fight, so no one made a fuss about my age."

She had heard of such things happening at the time.

"I was placed into an infantry division, and treated almost as a mascot when the other men realized how young I actually was. I think I fought as bravely as the others but as everyone knows we would have lost the war, and lost it badly, if the Americans had not, at last, come in.

"During what was to become known as the Arden Front we were part of a small contingent of British soldiers under the command of Field Marshall Montgomery, and as we moved south towards Paris, or perhaps west towards Belgium (we seldom knew where we were), I became separated from my unit. I wandered around for days trying just to stay alive and thankfully I stumbled upon a well dug-in American regiment.

"That is where I met Master Sergeant Kingsley Dean, your father, and his brother, your Uncle Conroy. I've never met a kinder soul than your father. He took me immediately under his wing and after feeding me up and letting me rest he tried to figure out where my unit was fighting so I could rejoin them, to no avail. So I stuck with him as we painstakingly advanced against the Germans.

"The fighting was brutal and often disorganized. It was muddy and miserable. I was a seasoned soldier by then, but still young and, I am not too proud to say it, very frightened. I knew the word die was in right there in the word soldier. He watched out for me, your father, and more than once kept me from harm's way. Doubtless I owe him my life.

"At quiet times when we were camped, he would talk about your mom, and you, and his mom back in America. He longed to be home; often talking about returning and taking over a place he called the Homestead, a family farm, I guess, and his plans to make it profitable.

"Your Uncle Conroy, a Corporal, stuck close to him, too, but I had a different feeling about Corporal Dean. He never joined in the talk of how good it would be to go home, but seemed to brood whenever the subject came up. He never spoke of his own plans, and oddly seemed jealous of the warm way I was treated by your father, which was uncalled for as Sergeant Dean related to your uncle with the same kindness and protection he extended to me.

"There came a night when we were dug in near the base of some hedgerows and found ourselves under a strong attack. An order came to advance regardless, which would expose us to the worst of the German fire. Reluctantly we crept out of our shelter and crawled through the fields.

"Our comrades were falling on either side of us, but following orders we pressed on towards the enemy line. I will spare you the barbarous details. That's when your Uncle Conroy was injured, taking a bullet through the flesh of his lower leg. Your father and I did our best to staunch the bleeding and I was sent back towards our previous encampment to try and find a medic, which I was able to do. The medic asked me to retrace my steps to where Conroy and the others lay injured, and we started back, but the medic fell to gunfire and was killed almost right away. There was chaos on every side, and I thought only of returning to your father, my friend, my protector. The moon came out from behind the clouds, made its way through the fog of war and helped me to find my way.

"As I approached the hollow where your uncle lay wounded,

I saw him raise his gun. How brave, I thought, for him to go on fighting in his injured condition. But, using the clear light of the moon, he aimed the gun directly at your father's back and shot him dead. I screamed and he turned the rifle towards me. I felt one bullet graze my leg, then another my skull and I fell unconscious.

"I awoke in a Red Cross station behind the lines. I was shipped home and never saw either your father's body or your uncle again. Attempts by a semiconscious boy to report the crime went unheeded, and bloody history with its tens of thousands of dead men rolled over the incident.

"You can see by my present uniform that after the war I immigrated to America and I have served in the United States Army ever since. It has been my tribute to Master Sergeant Kingsley Dean."

"My father," was all she had managed to utter.

"I thought you would want to know. I am sorry to so deeply distress you."

Elsinora had seen in the mirror how she had blanched. Her hands had trembled. She remembered that he had poured her a glass of water from the pitcher on her dressing table.

"Thank you," she had murmured, as she sipped at the water, attempting to regain her composure.

"This is a true account? You would swear to it?"

"On my honor as a soldier, and on my life."

"Does anyone else know of this?"

"No other soul, now living. I did write to your grandmother, may she rest in peace, and asked if she wanted to know how her son had died. She urged me to write again and tell her whatever I knew. She replied that she had feared this might be so, for Conroy had always been jealous of Kingsley and had often been violent towards his brother in ways he had learned from his father. It was her deepest grief. Some fault in his brain, she thought. Nevertheless, she had loved them both."

They had looked at each other for long moments, their eyes conversing in the silence.

"Promise me you will not speak of it further."

She had felt that all the soldier had said was true, and she had made him swear to secrecy.

She had understood for the first time her Uncle Conroy's vagueness about the war, saw the falsehood in his account of somehow losing sight of her father behind a hedgerow. How do you lose your brother? Now she knew. He had so eagerly taken over the Homestead on his return. It was what he had coveted, his brother's land. And his brother's wife. He had won Greta over quickly enough. At least he had given her a year or two of happiness before he began his cruel adulteries.

Perhaps Conroy had lusted for her mother all along, through all the early card games and the joy rides in the Cadillac. Perhaps they had even been involved before the war, but a tiny child could not have known that, even the precocious little girl Elsinora had been. Nevertheless, she had sensed there was something wrong all along. Now she was certain that the revelation of the fratricide had struck her grandmother dumb.

She understood, at long last, the note she had been handed. She knew what the missing words had been, the words that were lost from grandmother's handwritten message when she had hastily torn it from her note pad with shaking hands:

"(Your father's) death is not what it seems."

As THE CAR pulled into the parking lot of the hospital Elsinora very much hoped she had arrived before the Colonel's demise.

"I think I shall go in alone, Hesper."

"Are you sure?"

"When have I ever not been?"

She allowed Hesper to help her out of the limousine, then walked steadily across the gravel and into the starkly modern building. It took only a few moments for Nurse Benoit to appear, nod, and show her a short distance down a tiled corridor and into a private room.

The Colonel was propped up slightly on some comfortable-looking pillows. He opened his eyes at the sound of footsteps and smiled at Elsinora.

"You came."

"Yes."

"Nurse Benoit, may we have a few moments alone?"

The kind nurse, although curious, nodded respectfully and slipped outside, gently closing the door behind her, leaving them in privacy.

"Pull the plug, if you don't mind, Ms. Dean," requested the Colonel, then laughed weakly at her startled expression. "Not *that* plug," he said.

He then indicated an electrical outlet in the wall by the bed. "There is a camera up there," he pointed jerkily to the device in a corner near the ceiling. "We don't want that on, now do we?"

"No, indeed," she agreed. She pulled the camera's plug from the socket, and checked with habitual thoroughness to be sure that the green light had clicked off. She sat down in the chair closest to the bed.

"Now we are alone," he said with a quivering voice. "I will not live to see the sunrise." He paused for a moment. "Tell me?"

"No. But I will tell you I acted as I thought right."

"Was I acting rightly then, to inform you?"

"Yes. You did the honorable thing."

"I thought as much judging from the cards you always sent, but I am glad to hear you say it. It has been nice to be remembered by Kingsley's daughter all these years. I thank you for that."

Elsinora took his fragile hand. It was icy cold. She wanted to warm it and so she placed her second hand on top, making a cradle of her palms. "It is I who must say thank you. It has sustained me to know we always shared an unspoken understanding."

"Was there anyone else?"

"My dear cousin, Fletcher Mulcaster, knew. Corporal Conroy Dean was thought to be his father, although that was probably a convenient lie on his mother's part. There was no love lost between them. It was right that he should know…before…and after. He raised no objection. He is no longer with us."

"I know of Fletcher Mulcaster's death from the newspaper. I didn't know Conroy had a famous and successful son."

"Conroy did not deserve Fletcher. He was not a father you would wish on your worst enemy. Fortunately, he pretty much ignored us both."

"You will be all alone with the memory now."

"Yes."

"I am glad you took action, that you were brave and delivered some justice in this sorry world," he managed to murmur.

"I've never been certain of that. It has troubled my conscience."

He seemed not to hear her remark. "Will there be justice after death? Or something else?" he asked. "Perhaps I should be frightened?"

"I think there is nothing to fear."

He sunk deeper into the pillows then, satisfied. A wish he had long cherished had been granted. He was sure Elsinora had not failed. His face grew still, peaceful.

She stood to go.

His eyes flickered, but did not manage to open. He appeared to have used up the last of his energy.

She bent and kissed him on the forehead. A faint smile wavered across his lips. Then, suddenly, a jolt seemed to go through his entire body. His eyes flew open in surprise. His face seemed to lose its age, and his smile broadened. The Colonel's arm reached up and pulled her close with unexpected strength so that she could hear his last whispered words, followed by his last, long exhalation.

"Death is not what it seems."

XXXV. Excellent good friends.

DORIS WAS WALKING alone in the cemetery. She did not particularly enjoy this stoney landscape but it was one of the few places to which the sidewalk from Halcyon Circle actually led. The level pathway was all a little too convenient, she judged.

In the opposite direction from the senior housing the pavement ended abruptly at a scrubby woods which, as a child, she would have happily explored but at eighty-seven might well be an act of suicide. So she marched around the gravestones on the well-kept paths, enjoyed the occasional flowers left at the newer interments, listened to the conversational birds who were clearly happy here, and enjoyed the peaceful nature of the place, albeit with the somewhat sobering awareness that she would soon be a permanent resident.

Today her eye was caught by a vibrant cluster of golden-yellow roses. They were planted upon a recent, still slightly mounded, grave. She went closer and read the chiseled inscription on the gravestone, and was surprised to see it was the resting place of Fletcher Mulcaster. My goodness, she thought, whatever is he doing here?

Her mind reeled back to the obituary, which had been quite prominent in *The Times*. The funeral had taken place in the cathedral where he had reigned for decades, but the burial had been designated as private.

So here he was, resting close to the home of his beloved Elsinora. Had she planted the roses? Most likely, she thought. Their color summoned the eye, lifted the spirit, and although they were moving only modestly in the light breeze of the afternoon, they evoked a desire to sway along with them, and perhaps to sing. She hummed a few bars of *Thank You for the Music,* and then laughed. Dear Fletcher.

She and Fletcher and Elsinora would all rest near to one another in this place so far from their childhood hometown. Life was a continuity of surprises, even as it drew towards a close.

There were footsteps behind her on the path and she turned to see Elsinora walking methodically in her direction, doubtless coming for a visit with Fletcher. For a moment she thought of moving away to give Elsinora solitude at the graveside, then decided the meeting was fortuitous, so she turned to greet her old friend as she drew closer. Elsinora gave a slight wave as she recognized Doris and she appeared pleased to see her.

"I've been admiring the roses," said Doris.

"It was our custom. Yellow roses on opening night performances, his and mine. These are closing night roses."

"I didn't know he was here."

"Where else was he to go? Certainly, not back to that wretched Ohio town, or to England. I'm glad this is where he chose to go to ground. I think of him vividly when I visit. There is a bench just over there. Let us sit."

They made their way to the bench in the comforting shadow of an ancient oak and in clear sight of the grave.

"What do you remember most about him?" asked Doris.

"Fletcher was set to music. He had a rotten childhood in Liverpool as the bastard child of an alcoholic mother, Conroy as a supposed father; but Fletcher's brain had been dunked in a bath of melodies before birth. Sometimes he was hearing the great classics, or he was composing his own music. There was a harmony playing inside of him whatever else was going on in our lives. His was a gift I did not share, but one I marveled at throughout my life. And you? What do you recall?"

Doris was silent for a few moments as her mind moved back and back, bumping into some childhood jealousy with an unpleasant thud. "I remember he took you away from me, just at adolescence, yet I couldn't resent him because he was so good to you and always polite and kind to me, to everyone. Where do you think he got that from, everything considered?"

"I think he looked at the traits of all the adults that surrounded us and said, 'not that, not that, not that', and when all their failings and bad habits were discarded, when all the sour notes rejected, what was left was a way to compose a life as a successful human being; add his musical genius and you arrive at a Fletcher."

"What a remarkable idea. An elimination diet for the soul. Did you wish he could have been your husband? Did you wish he was not a gay man?"

"Perhaps initially, but it became merely incidental as we went onwards. In all but the physical he was my life's partner."

"So not Oliver-Paul."

Elsinora laughed so loudly and unexpectedly that Doris jumped.

"Oliver-Paul was his own life's partner, short as it was. He was in love with his own celebrity, and the mannequin he made of me. He never understood, as I did, that fame is a chimera. It is just the fantasy life of a bunch of strangers that gets pasted onto you, but he wanted to be famous, worshipped even. His audiences, his followers, fans, sycophants, public…that's what mattered to him. He hadn't noticed that the word *die* sits in the very middle of the word audience. I served only as a conveyor belt for more admirers."

"Yet knowing all this, you married him."

"The heart believes in what it wants to believe in, but the heart and the loins can get very confused with one another sometimes. He was a force of nature, like Fletch, but in a very dark and different way. And what could I have known about real love? Lust was enough for Oliver-Paul but, as it turned out, not for me. And although I knew my fame was a fiction it allowed me a life that was unexpected, and for a time, alluring."

"He died an awful death. Were you devastated?"

"Yes."

"So then you did love him."

"It was the shock of his death, so to speak, that was devastating. And all the awfulness of the inquiry and speculation that followed."

"Yet your mind did not dodge away from all that, like it did from the loss of baby Emma?"

"Perhaps because I was in possession of an adult's brain by the time his death occurred. The scene is as clear as a movie clip."

"Will you tell me?"

"Yes, you, I will tell. It followed a terrible evening out, fighting in the taxi on the way home, both of us drunk, just like my Mom and Conroy writ large.

"I went to my suite first, he to his, and I started to prepare for bed. Then for some reason I thought I couldn't live without dental floss, and I marched into his bathroom to get some. He was sloshing around in his tub, howling about what a prude and a stick I was, how I was nothing without him, how he had engineered all my fame.

"There was truth in what he said, and I was jealous of a pretty ingenue he had set his sights upon, embarrassed for the way he had acted in front of our friends, yet I didn't say a word in reply to his ravings. I yanked open the door to the medicine cabinet with full force. The door hit the fan on the bathroom counter and knocked it into the tub. It was truly an accident, but *my* accident, not his. And it was horrible. It has not been an easy memory to live with, though Fletcher saw the irony in it."

Doris placed her hand on Elsinora's. "The irony?"

"Killed by a fan."

The two ladies were quiet for a moment, and then the girls they had once been began to laugh together softly.

"Friends are God's apology for family, aren't they?" said Doris.

"That is true."

"What happened then? What did you do?"

"I didn't know what to do. There was grief. There was guilt. I can tell you, Doris, one feels just as guilty about killing someone accidentally as killing them on purpose. More so in a way, as there is nothing to confess to, no way to relieve one's conscience. The guilt may be unwarranted, but one feels it all the same."

"A useless emotion, guilt."

"Do you think so? I believe Uncle Conroy could have done with some guilt."

"I meant guilt is useless when one is innocent, as you were in this case, when the harm was accidental."

"Perhaps."

"You carried on bravely."

"I had already been booked to play Gertrude on Broadway. Hamlet's mother is a thankless part if ever there was one. Probably I wasn't thinking clearly, but immersing myself in a role had always been the foolproof method for escaping from my own feelings. We had sold out houses, the audiences now

eager for the sight of a tragic celebrity. It was at an early preview
that the stage set jolted and threw me into the orchestra pit. To
me it was a sign; the scales of justice leveling out by providing
me with an accident just as awful as the one I had provided for
Oliver-Paul."

"Do you believe that even now?"

"A little. It finished a chapter of my life, the movie star, the
lavish lifestyle, all of it had to go."

"And you never told anyone about your part in the death of
Oliver-Paul?"

"Only him." Elsinora nodded at Fletcher's grave. "He knew all
my secrets. They won't be easily unearthed."

"And then?"

"After my physical recovery I started life anew in the voca-
tion for which I was always destined. Teaching would immerse
me in the literature I loved, and the work I loved. I only took
the occasional onstage role. I have tried to pass on my love of
great writing, great acting, particularly of Shakespeare, to new
generations of actors. Teaching is my way to hope for a better
world."

"And it's been the right choice for you?"

"Can I get on my high horse?"

"Hi-yo, Silver! Away."

"For forty years I've watched this country decline, and its
decay began right in my own profession. Once we actors 'held
the mirror up to nature' and the scripts, and the screenplays
were, for the most part, reflective of the best in human nature;
intelligent people, decent family life, romance, heroism, adven-
ture, the classics. Sure there was conflict, crime, war, fear...there
has to be in order to structure a dramatic plot...but actors were
kept busy showing Americans what they could attain at their
best. Television arrived soon after the war and generated plenty

of wholesome work initially, remember our heroes? The good guys always won."

Doris smiled.

"But a need for more and more entertainment has produced, year after year, scripts and screenplays of lesser and lesser quality, and I dare to say it, more and more unsavory material. Soon American minds were filling up with dysfunctional families, drug addiction, flagrant immorality, the corruption of police, political crimes, serial killers, pedophiles, and ever-escalating violence. The arrival of reality TV shows, based purely on the humiliation of others and viewed as entertainment, signaled the beginning of the end. I am not one for conspiracy theories, I think it is all quite openly driven by profit-making, but the content has normalized the worst of us for the most of us. And look at the result."

"You mean the dreadful state of the society we find ourselves in nowadays."

"Yes. And what I once saw as a noble profession, the conveyance of art and beauty and intelligent thought is now in ruins. I saw an episode of a television series not long ago, for I do keep in touch with what's out there, Doris. I watched a brilliant actress, one who could do justice to Rosamund or Ophelia, to Nora or Laura; one possessed of incredible depth of talent and impossibly fine skills reduced to playing a neurotic, drug-addled detective living in a derelict neighborhood, drinking herself to death. I wept, not for her character, but for her. I was right to step away when I did."

They were silent then. Doris knew what Elsinora said was true, and it saddened her.

Elsinora broke the silence. "But let me not turn the day gloomy, Doris. Perhaps it is time for you to speak of your life at last."

Doris sighed. "Just as you kept your innermost self hidden by becoming an actress, so I kept myself veiled as a psychoanalyst. I'm not sure if, at this late date, I even remember how to reveal myself."

"Psychoanalysts have to remain anonymous, neutral, don't they?"

"Yes. The treatment doesn't work unless the patient can transfer their problems onto the analyst, like a film image is projected onto a blank screen. Then the problem is animate in the room, and can be addressed and often resolved."

"Genius, Freud. Wasn't he? To figure all that out?"

"People don't think so anymore. He has been thoroughly trashed in the interests of a pill and a pat on the head. I've outlived my profession, sadly, as you have outlived yours."

"Well, there is no going back, is there, Doris?"

"No, only onwards."

"What is the thing you wanted most in your life that you failed to attain?"

It was a surprising question and Doris knew she was under no obligation to answer it truthfully or at all. She could choose any number of her life's disappointments which would satisfy her friend's curiosity, but the Elsinora of childhood and the Doris of childhood had once shared everything. This current Elsinora was different in so many ways, but she was still, in some essential way, Elsie. Her interest felt genuine to Doris, so she opted for the truth.

"Masculinity." She watched as the self-assured Elsinora was taken aback.

"Truly? You wanted to be a boy, a man?"

"Yes. As far back as I can remember, but we lived in simpler times, didn't we? We were what we were in those days, and whatever our longings may have been, we were little girls, and as much as we played at Lone Ranger and Tonto, we were destined to be Little Women."

"Young people today have options we didn't even dream of, if they are brave."

"What I worried about all through adolescence was whether I was a lesbian. It was you who told me what a lesbian was. You had found out about it in one of your books."

"I remember. Radclyffe Hall's *The Well of Loneliness*."

"It turned out that I wasn't a lesbian. I was quite satisfied in my marriage. I am a creature Freud would describe as suffering from penis envy, though it wasn't the penis I coveted. I wanted the powers and the freedoms of being male. You remember how the differences between the sexes were so rigidly drawn back then. I didn't want to be a housewife. I didn't want children. We were strange creatures, you and I, wishing for so much more from life than our mothers had aspired to, or that our bodies told us we could have.

"Using my brain was the only way to escape a traditional life," continued Doris. "Like you, I managed a scholarship. Just think, Elsinora! What might we have become had we been born into families that valued education for women; had we been schooled as a preparation for a profession. You helped yourself to all that was great in literature, and I practically lived in the science laboratory at school, but no one encouraged you to write a Pulitzer Prize-winning novel, or suggested to me that I might win the Nobel for medical research."

"But we made good lives for ourselves," replied Elsinora, acknowledging the truth of Doris' remarks.

"Yes, yes. We did what we could. Fletcher, even though he was gay, had the white male edge on us, but I'm glad that he succeeded."

Elsinora was pensive. "I never wanted to be a boy. I knew about war. I read a lot about war, and it was what men did. I thought it was stupid, to risk the only real currency we have…life…in fighting. It had cost me my father. All I wanted was to get out of Warrensville and never look back."

"I did go back to Warrensville once for a high school reunion," said Doris with a shake of her head. "Most of our schoolmates were still in place, married, divorced, kids, dismal dead end jobs, no one it seemed was either happy or unhappy with their lives. I don't think they thought about the currency of life, as you put it. They simply lived it. Perhaps it is easier to be the sort of person who just accepts the lot they are given in the wasteland they are born into."

"I remember when you left for college. Fletcher and I were brimming with envy. Western Reserve University."

"It was only forty miles away, but college had its rewards. I discovered I liked sex with men for one thing, though in my fantasies I shapeshifted back and forth between male and female. I thought for a while I might be crazy. Thank God for coming of age in the sixties! At least we could experiment, even if we couldn't just declare new genders.

"Of course the country was in a terrible crisis then…all those young men in Vietnam, dying for no good cause, year after year. Becoming a psychoanalyst helped me sort myself out, keep my balance, not fall victim to drugs like so many of my angry and confused friends. In time I accepted who I was. A woman with varied longings, but sane. There. I've never told anyone but my own analyst about all that. Satisfied?"

"Do you still think about sex?"

"I dream about it."

"So do I. Only with the good lovers though."

"Plural?"

"You said it yourself. It was the sixties for a whole decade."

"So all the world knows about Oliver-Paul, but I sense there's another. There is, isn't there?"

"After Oliver-Paul's death and my fall from the stage there was a doctor who cared for me during my long recuperation. Maurice Schadad. A quiet, determined man, focused on the healing of every person he touched. He was a brilliant doctor."

"And a brilliant lover?"

"Only in dreams. It was not to be. He was married to another, a boundary we didn't cross, but he did love me. I know he did. It was magnificent to be loved, just as I was, broken and lost. It felt like he entered not my body, but my soul. He mended a shattered spirit. I still love him, the memory of him."

"How swiftly can the most important events in our lives be summarized," said Doris, shaking her head.

The friends rose then, each giving a small groan as their knees unbent. They smiled ruefully again, remembering the lithe bodies of their girlhood, the tumbles they had taken without complaint, the lightning-fast healing of their youthful bruises and scrapes. Now every movement required consideration.

"Gravity is very persistent," said Elsinora, and supporting one another along the level path, they left the place to which they would soon return.

XXXVI. Now I am alone.

D R. MAURICE SCHADAD paced the sandy boardwalk. The sun seemed to be concentrating on the top of his head, making his self-imposed daily exercise uncomfortable. He knew it was important to keep moving, for health, for his treacherous state of mind.

Since Fletcher had died he had been grieving. He had often grieved when a patient died, but this death carried an added loss. Fletcher Mulcaster had been his lifeline to Elsinora. His only way of discreetly knowing how she was faring. He had sworn Fletcher to silence about his inquiries and knew that Fletcher had honored his request for they did no harm.

He stopped to catch his breath and leaned against the metal railing which was hot to the touch. There before him was an expanse of well-oiled bodies crowding together on the Coney Island beach, their colorful umbrellas and towels giving the scene the appearance of a carnival. He saw smiles, and laughter which pleased him, but knew that all those healthy Coney Island revelers would sustain injuries, develop illnesses, undergo operations, in short, they would all need doctors soon. It was in the nature of bodies to age, get sick, and die. People seldom noticed that the word *bodies* ended with the word *dies*.

He felt less like a doctor and more like the Captain of the Titanic standing there, his hands clutching the railing, overlooking the people enjoying themselves below, the expanse of sea beyond. He was happy for the sunbathers with their present pleasures, "but we will all go down with the ship," he murmured, "sooner than we expect."

What dreary musings! He must pull himself up. He shook his head, squared his shoulders and continued with his march. We are all given the gift of a mind wrapped in a package of time, he thought. It wouldn't do to waste his gift being melancholy. What had he so often advised his depressed patients? Exercise, of course. Well, he was doing that. And to develop a new interest. Having once been told that he had some artistic talent, he had tried sketching, laying down his pencils and sketchpad within a matter of days, as the flowers and birds that he drew failed to show any signs of life.

It was also important to connect with those whom one loves, he would advise, but that was easier said than done. His children and grandchildren were all excessively busy. Three of his children were professionals, and the two who were not were both artists with less time to spare than the doctor, lawyer, and engineer he had spawned.

Most of his tried and true friends had vanished into death or dementia or senior housing in the South where the tornados born of climate change threatened to carry them off like Dorothy in *The Wizard of Oz*. He was the sole holdout of his intimate group of New York City colleagues.

It seemed that his advice to others was not working so well for himself, so Maurice turned around, heading back to the subway entrance for the long ride back to Manhattan.

Once seated, and ensconced behind a newspaper he peered over its edge and began to watch people, a form of amusement he enjoyed on subways. He was determined to imagine a happy future for each person who caught his attention: the black man also holding a newspaper would do well in his new business; the mother with one child too many to keep under her control would find the perfect nanny; the children swinging around the poles would grow up healthy and happy and get into Harvard; the exceptionally thin, pretty woman with dark hair and blue eyes nervously watching everyone on the car would find success in her dancing career. Their eyes met. Hers darted away. He smiled, knowing his paper would hide the smile, which might cause her more nervousness. No, he thought, I am too old and frail to strike fear into the hearts of young women, though inside this ridiculous body, I am young and full of feeling.

Perhaps he should try sketching people, not flowers. Happy, healthy people.

The subway car rattled and jolted. *He* rattled and jolted.

He looked back at the woman, closing his eyes halfway, blurring his vision and softening her image, and he imagined the woman of long ago.

What are you doing now? What future can I imagine for you, my dear one?

XXXVII. Seek not thy noble father in the dust.

Elsinora was ensconced in her red chair. The lake was as blue as the sky. Nearby a male cardinal, red as blood, was singing its heart out in the green of the old oak hoping no doubt to win the affection of the orange female bird that was so studiously ignoring him.

Elsinora had had a good night's sleep and eaten a healthy breakfast.

She opened the book in her lap. The new author she was reading was too young, describing a personal world as yet unclouded by grief. She had no desire to read fantasy. She dropped the book onto the grass. For inspiration she needed Shakespeare.

"I have of late, though I know not wherefore, lost all my mirth," she quoted.

But she *did* know wherefore. Once at a dinner party she had been seated next to a prominent psychoanalyst. She had, as an amusement, asked him to explain the process of psychoanalysis in one sentence.

Laughing, he had replied. "I don't need a full sentence, only four words." He had paused for effect, then said: "My mother, my father."

Mine is a variation. She wrote:

My mother. No father.

Though sometimes I was frightened by my mother's calamitous warnings, I tried my best to ignore them, even make fun of them behind her back, giggling with Doris at one of her ridiculously imagined catastrophes. Sadly, the day has come when I sometimes think Mother was right. The world is always preparing for its next Pearl Harbor, its next surprise attack.

Hesper, always vigilant, called to her from the doorway, "Mrs. Harding, do you need anything out there?"

"Religion," she replied.

"What did you say? A *pigeon?*"

"I don't require anything, Hesper. Not a smidgeon."

Elsinora chuckled. Dear Hesper was inside busily scanning the computer, efficiently planning a trip to Bermuda paid for with money from her legacy. Why should Hesper not have some pleasure, some dreams, interspersed with the hard realities of her life like everyone else? Elsinora was pleased she could provide them for Hesper. She admired the easy-going soul in her companion, not given, as she was herself, to endless rumination about life and death, as Hamlet was, or like dear Pierre in *War and Peace,* or sad Uncle Vanya. Those were her soulmates, her imaginary companions in real life, and there was now no cheerful, melodious Fletcher to balance them all out; but Hesper was, well, for lack of a better word, nice.

Elsinora knew, of course, that the religions of the world offered solace for the misfortunes of existence, and she was glad for the people, not herself but others, who could find comfort in their beliefs of divine interventions and heavenly rewards to come; of angels and dakinis and elephant gods. There were no fairies at the bottom of Elsinora's garden. Only the patient white bird, the heron hoping for a morsel of satisfaction as he stood in the mud up to his impossibly backward knees.

The time when she might have found religion had been during that year of her recuperation after the fall. She was as vulnerable then, as open as she had ever allowed herself to be, but instead of God it was Maurice who appeared, a source of pure kindness, and she had let herself love and be loved, like the tiny child she had once been on her grandmother's lap, or in her father's arms. It had been enough. So poor, dear God had missed his chance with her.

There was pain in her knuckles and she felt her breath working its way in and out of her chest in short, unsatisfying gasps. Nevertheless, she was determined to come to a final understanding of herself. Her time alone with her uncle must now be remembered in every detail, sparing herself nothing. Grimacing, she again took up the pen.

Conroy's evil was unimaginative: greed, everyday jealousy, and the coveting of his brother's wife. Sins long ago forbidden and chronicled in The Old Testament.

I know he must have been brought up as a well-loved son. My grandmother was capable of nothing less. Perhaps the early death of his harsh father is what warped him in some way modern psychology might be able to explain. Or was it the disfigurement of his cauliflower ear? More likely, it was the blow that had caused it. Who would do such damage to a little boy, even in the era of "spare the rod and spoil the child?" How humanity always gets things backwards!

Or perhaps he was one of those genetically malformed creatures born without conscience, destined by some twist of DNA to be labeled sociopathic, with no ability to feel

anything for anyone but themselves? I'm sure my grand-
mother came to think so and the belief destroyed her.

I suppose the monsters of fairy tales take their inspiration
from such creatures. There seems to be no lack of them in the
world, hiding behind bushes, hiding behind assault rifles,
disguised in government offices, shielding themselves with
misshapen ideologies: Boko Haram, Taliban, Isis, Proud
Boys, Hamas, Ku Klux Klan, Mafia...endlessly preying on
others, on the weak, on women, on the disenfranchised.

She sighed, shook out her writing hand and continued.

Conroy broke all of the rules by which decent men live
one with another. I was merely collateral damage, an
unimportant bystander. He never hit me, never assaulted
me. I was too insignificant for him to bother noticing. He
destroyed my family before my child's eyes, so self-assured in
his performance that he did not care if I saw him or not. He
almost broke my belief in the goodness of mankind.

And yet, for life relishes its ironies, Conroy was the father
of Fletcher. Conroy, the man who poisoned my life unknow-
ingly provided me with the antidote. His accidental act of
goodness did not save him in the end.

She smiled, leaned back and rested her eyes and her pen.

Decades before, shortly after Colonel Osbourne had come
to the backstage dressing room, Elsinora had told Fletcher
the soldier's story of her father's murder. Having made it into
adulthood she and Fletch considered themselves toughened up
by life, but it had still been difficult to tell him. Fletcher had
listened carefully as she spoke of the man said to be his father.

"Do you think it is true?" he asked solemnly.

"I felt that what he said was genuine."

"Perhaps his account could be verified in some way?"

"How? My father's body was never found. And it's been over thirty years."

"It does seem rather hopeless."

"We could ask Conroy, I suppose," she ventured. "Watch how he reacts?"

"You know he is a bone-deep liar, it would be hopeless to try to get the truth out of him. He barely knew me when I saw him last. Of course, he never did know me. He didn't want to," he said, a mixture of sadness and revulsion shadowing his features.

"You're right, of course," she agreed. "No matter how he might react, no matter what he might say, I wouldn't believe him. I did trust Colonel Osbourne though. I think his story is true."

"Bloody hell! Then my father murdered your father."

How stark and shocking it sounded.

"How ugly the world can be. How tragic." He continued dropping his head, shaking it slowly from side to side and staring at the floor for a long time.

Suddenly he fell to his knees. Wrapping his arms around her legs, and holding her tightly, he had pleaded through a rush of tears, "Please, please don't let this come between us. I love you as my sister. A sister who has always been loving and good to me. One who has given me a family. Don't let my father's crime infect our relationship. I couldn't bear it."

She pulled him up, took his head between her hands, placed her forehead against his own and looked deeply into his brimming eyes, his weeping soul. "Never will anything come between us," she vowed. "Evil, even the devil's own pitchfork, could not scratch the surface of our bond."

And what she said had proved to be true.

It was several years later, shortly after her release from the hospital, when Fletcher again approached the subject of Kingsley's murder.

"Let's go together to France," he suggested one afternoon when they were sipping martinis together in Sardi's. It was a quiet Monday afternoon when most theaters were dark and they had the end of polished bar to themselves. From time to time a stray tourist wandered in to gawk at the celebrity drawings and hope to spot one alive. Elsinora, her hair pulled back in an unflattering ponytail, without makeup, and wearing a flannel shirt looked about as uncelebrity as was possible. Thankfully, they went unnoticed.

"France? Lovely. Why France?" The idea of foreign travel had an immediate appeal.

"You're at sixes and sevens about what to do next with your life, and I have a half-dozen guest-conducting engagements at St. Eustache in Paris and the cathedrals in Caen, and Rouen. Come with me. While we are in the region we can inquire about the war years, perhaps learn why so many men went missing and were unrecovered, make our own judgement about the possibility of Conroy getting away with murder during a battle."

The suggestion was a jolt. She had tried, unsuccessfully during her convalescence to push the knowledge of her father's death far from her consciousness, but the images of the murder crept into her dreams, and sometimes into her waking life as well, urging her to respond, pushing her towards impossible thoughts of revenge.

She realized that Fletcher's suggestion for the journey arose from injured feelings somewhere within Fletcher, although he had disguised it with a casual air. Elsinora knew he loathed Conroy, and a cloistered part of his psyche ached at the idea of being the offspring of a cold blooded killer. Gentle, melodious Fletcher. And, whereas she had heard the ring of truth in the Colonel's voice as he told his sorry tale, Fletcher had received it only second-hand. He must, she thought, harbor a modicum of disbelief inside himself, some hope that it was not so.

And so Elsinora, out of love for Fletcher, agreed to the journey, though her own heart had not, at first, been in it.

> We went from town to town in France, talking to mayors, and priests, and local farmers, old men and women, and the sons and daughters of the townspeople who had lived through the bloody horrors of World War Two, as it was fought inside their forests, on their village streets, over their farmlands, and in their backyard gardens. My French was, as Fetcher put it, nothing to speak of, but he was fluent and his broad smiles and hearty laugh opened doors wherever we found ourselves. Everyone, it seemed, had stories about the fighting, about the American troops who had, alongside the British, liberated them; but none of the stories were of fratricide.
>
> I think I was reluctant, feeling frightened, but was soon caught up in the investigation. These were the last places where my father had been alive, the places in which he had fought, the people he had been trying to save from the invasion and oppression by the hateful Nazis.
>
> We learned all the reasons that bodies went missing, especially in areas where fighting had gone back and forth over the same ground many times by the opposing combatants. Artillery shells and bombs could blow a soldier to fragments; Germans often ditched and burned enemy bodies to get them out of their way; and sometimes they had stolen their identifying dog tags as souvenirs.
>
> In between these macabre inquiries were the glorious choral concerts conducted by Fletcher in the cathedrals of the Norman cities, the late nights of fine wine and French cuisine, the morning awakenings to birdsong, and the

*laughter of children on their way to school when they stayed
in the small, countryside villages.*

*Fletcher sometimes prowled the night, and would arrive
at our luncheon table with a self-satisfied expression. Good
for him, I thought, although I was not yet ready to think
about physical love. Memories of Oliver-Paul were still too
raw. Memories of Maurice were still too sadly tender. And
my body ached from the fall in ways I knew would always
be with me.*

*"You might talk to old Henri," said the patron of an
airless bar, sitting over a tankard of cider in the village of
Caumont. "He finds things sometimes in his fields where the
fighting was the heaviest between the hedgerows."*

"Hedgerows? Things?"

"Things from the soldiers in the war, both sides."

*We had seen such artifacts in other villages, plowed up by
the farmers, proudly shown off to us, the curious Americans:
a wedding ring, an old combat boot, a pocket knife, even
some bleached, white bones which made me shudder; but
Caumont was one of the villages closest to where we had
determined my father's unit had been fighting at the time he
went missing. The mention of hedgerows ignited my imagination. "I lost him between the hedgerows," Conroy had
once said, long, long ago.*

*Old Henri, who looked like he had been alive forever
with a wrinkled sun-browned face and a crooked stance,
eyed us suspiciously when we showed up unannounced at
his ancient farmhouse door; but when Fletcher flashed an
excellent bottle of brandy and I held out a basket of sausages,
fresh bread, butter, and cheese he agreed to talk with us over
the unexpected repast.*

He told us about his farm, owned for many generations

by his family, how it had been ravaged in the fighting, how his child was killed by a bomb. He cried.

We told him about the Homestead, how it had become a wasteland during the war, about my father, how he had died somewhere near this place, perhaps on his land. I cried.

With some effort Old Henri then got down a wooden box from a high shelf and from inside he pulled out a metal dog tag, its letters stamped out to reveal a soldier's identity and next of kin. It read:

KINGSLEY DEAN

4389457   T42

GRETA DEAN

1962 PAISLEY WAY

WARRENSVILLE, OHIO

Old Henri handed the dog tag to me unhesitatingly. He was a man who knew about loss.

"I sent this to the address when I found it, but it came back."

I had no words. It rested in my open palm, glinting in the dusty stream of sunlight from the open window. It felt more precious to me than any jewel.

He told us that it had surfaced not long ago from a spot he had cleared near a damaged hedgerow. He had seen no sign of a body. He assumed the heavy bombing had destroyed the soldier's remains, and the many years since had disintegrated whatever was left deep into the French earth.

I was clasping the dog tag tightly, as we walked out to the spot where its silvery gleam had caught the farmer's eye. The two men left me there and returned to the farmhouse, and I sat for a long time trying to see what my father might have seen in his last moments. It was late afternoon. There was no gunfire in the darkness, no screams of injured men, no explosions or flares from enemy fire. It was tranquil there now, not beautiful, but pleasant ordinary countryside rolling out before me, with rows of corn grown knee high and green. I took a handful of the earth, slipped it into my trouser's pocket and began the long journey home.

Our expedition had provided no confirmation of the Colonel's story, nor would there ever be one, but my father was no longer missing in action. He was, I was sure, resting in peace deep in Old Henri's field.

Elsinora, however, was not at peace. Not yet.

She put down her pen and closed her eyes. She reached up to touch the dog tag held on a beaded chain around her neck. She had never taken it off, from that day in France to this, and she never would.

Opening her eyes again, she looked around at reality's present offering. The lake was still blue, as was the sky. The cardinal in the tree had flown, but a fat robin worked its way in tiny jumps across the lawn. An acorn fell from the oak and a chipmunk scurried to own it. The white heron stood unmoving, but for its watchful eyes.

XXXVIII. Fretted with golden fire.

HESPER WAS ENJOYING the Bermuda sunshine. She loved walking on the warm sand. She was delighted to find the exquisite shells that dazzled at the water's edge, and oh, the air! It was so different from any air she had known in her Connecticut life, or in the New York City apartment of the past.

She was sitting on a large striped beach towel provided by the waterside resort. She adjusted the huge umbrella, sipped at her potent drink with its tiny pink umbrella, and was happy as the big blue sky.

It was true that bubbles of regret sometimes drifted through her happiness, thought bubbles which asked her why it had taken so long to discover this kind of enjoyment, but she blew them away.

She was certainly not an adventurous person. Being a free woman, enjoying life's simple pleasures was sufficient. She asked for nothing more. She had no need for romance, sex, complication, anger, disappointment, shame, loss, and guilt, having experienced all of these with Barton in that descending order.

Hesper looked around at the other sunbathers sprawling contentedly nearby, walking along the water's edge, sipping their own umbrella drinks on the patio. It was all so simple and peaceful. Exactly what she desired.

A suntanned child with a purple kite ran by kicking sand

onto her blanket and she moved to brush it off. She squared the edges of the towel and slipped four small hot stones onto its corners. There. Perfect, she judged approvingly.

It was then that she noticed a remarkably pretty woman who was watching her from the terrace with an interested smile. She was younger than herself by twenty years, Hesper thought. She had a beautifully curved body, most of it observable given the microscopic size of her red bikini. Her arms rested casually on the deck chair. Having caught Hesper's eye, the woman raised one hand slowly into the air. She was holding a glass of champagne and, with her other hand, she gently waved to Hesper.

Hesper felt something stir inside herself, a response to this woman that was new and startling. No, not new, she now remembered. Old. A long forgotten feeling from her youth when she was first drawn to the men she had dated, and to the young Barton before he became the old Barton.

Attraction.

Self-consciousness rose up like a tidal wave inside her chest, throat, cheeks, temples. She remembered this, too, from even younger years. It was the kind of anguish she had felt when a boy had seen her at a school dance and pried her out of the wallpaper she was trying so hard to merge into.

She hadn't concerned herself with her own attractiveness in decades, only with being healthy and clean and properly dressed, a tactic that had kept Barton at a distance which, of course, had been the point.

Hesper tried to ignore the woman in the lounge chair and sipped again at her drink. She edged more of herself under the umbrella's shade and dared to look down at her own white woman's body, so discreet, wearing a navy blue one-piece suit in contrast to the lovely black woman's red bikini.

Eating healthy food and doing daily housework has kept me

in reasonable shape, she thought. I'm neither over or under-weight for my age, and my muscles are toned. I've gotten a light tan over this past week and the sun has lightened my hair a bit. I'm okay. I'm just fine.

Hesper was pleased at her self-assessment, and surprised herself in the process.

Out of the corner of her eye she saw the woman on the terrace now pick up a bottle of suntan oil and hold it aloft, looking in her direction with a questioning expression.

Could she?

Hesper allowed herself to imagine what it would it be like to oil this stranger's dark, alluring body in the warmth of this heavenly sunshine. Her hand tingled slightly at the thought. Other parts tingled. She moved to touch the religious medal still clinging like a limpet to her throat.

A woman? she thought with amazement. A *woman?*

Hesper reached up again and unhooked the chain from around her neck and laid the crucifix gently on a smooth grey stone for a beachcomber to discover, or a wave to swallow.

Then she rose and crossed what seemed a desert of sand towards the terrace. Mesmerized, she walked towards the oppo-site of peacefulness.

XXXIX. Thus conscience doth make cowards of us all.

WITH HESPER AWAY on her vacation, and Robbie and Geraldo dispatched cheerfully to a Broadway opening and its afterparty, Elsinora roamed the silent house looking for the exact place to revisit the most concerning moment of her past. She carried the cigar box of mementos with her, hugging it close to her chest. She wanted to feel as close as possible to her father; and also to Fletcher, so she decided to place herself in the living room where the grand piano, though standing mute since his death, had once been his to command.

She put on one of his recordings, the Saint-Saëns Organ Symphony. He had guest conducted the piece at the Berliner Philharmonie, his protégé performing upon the organ with its sixty-five hundred pipes. It had been judged magnificent.

As the music began to move into her she poured herself a hefty Scotch from the supply Fletcher had left her and settled into a corner of the overstuffed sofa where she saw, in her mind's eye, those happier times there; the evenings when Fletcher lived. Oh, happiness!

Now insulated by this memory she at last allowed her mind to enter the harrowing time soon after their return from France, and as the great blasts of air pushed the music from the organ's pipes she opened her journal. Conroy would be dealt with at last.

The months passed by slowly. Fletcher was busy with new musical challenges and a new lover.

I began teaching at the prestigious Thespian Atelier while rehearsing an off-Broadway production of Romeo and Juliet, in which I had taken the small role of Lady Capulet who, nevertheless, I found challenging as the character's controlling nature reminded me of Oliver-Paul. My hope was that in returning to the classical theater, where I had once done my best work, I might do even better. Whether I accomplished this or not, I would be immersed in the imagined worlds of genius in which I was happiest. I needed to work at something that mattered in the world, and this determination, coupled with the teaching, began to look like a life I could fully inhabit.

The first course I taught was, of course, Shakespeare. I noticed that as I stood before a class of eager young actors, my determination to confront Uncle Conroy strengthened or weakened depending on the play under study. When I was teaching the revenge tragedies, Macbeth, Othello, especially Hamlet, it was strong, and I imagined how satisfying it would be to kill him though I knew I would not be wielding a dagger anytime soon.

When the comedies or histories were on the syllabus, the belief that Fate would deal with my uncle's vicious nature seemed satisfying enough, and that it would be healthier for me to think less about Conroy and get on with my new endeavors. He was, as far as I knew, alone, poor, estranged from Fletcher, sick, and possibly in the beginning stages of dementia.

Yet, in my melancholy moments I could not help wondering what my life would have been like if instead of Conroy, my father had returned from the war, hearty and happy, allowing Grandma to continue living at the Homestead where she had been so content. Perhaps he would have loved my mother enough to bring out the best in her, soothing away her anxieties, strengthening her fragile soul. And with his approval and encouragement my own little girl self might have been nourished into a happy adulthood. Maybe he would have provided me with sisters and brothers who would have thrived; who would be my companions now. Conroy had deprived me of all those possibilities when he had taken my father's life.

Soon enough Fletcher left on another conducting tour, and it was while he was away that a call came in from a hospital in Ohio, informing me that Conroy was dying. Pneumonia, they said, asking if I could come soon.

"Why me?" I protested silently. But with my mother gone, and Fletcher abroad, I was the only available next of kin.

I was hoping for a second call, one saying he was dead, but after three days I canceled my classes and flew to Cleveland. I had to deal with what would surely be a nightmare. At least, I consoled myself, it would be a favor to Fletcher, having this unsavory matter attended to while he was away, hopefully concluded by the time he returned.

Elsinora realized she was squeezing the pen too tightly, enough to cause pain in her fingers and she released the pressure and shook out her hand; then willed herself onwards.

When I entered the hospital the nurses were eager to speak with me. I had dressed in an old black pantsuit and wore huge sunglasses, a costume of woe. Fortunately, Conroy had listed me by my childhood name, Nora Ellen, not Elsinora, on his list of contacts so I wasn't recognized.

The nurses assured me of the excellent medical attention he had been receiving. As if I cared! But they, of course, didn't know I was other than the worried relative of a confused old man in dire health. They had no way to guess what kind of man he had been, what he had done, how he was loathed.

"You will be so relieved to know he is making an unexpected recovery," they informed me with smiles.

My heart sank.

"I thought you said he was dying."

"We didn't think he would survive the pneumonia, not with those lungs, but he has rallied. He is still critically ill. The doctor says, even with the best of care, it is a matter of weeks, months at the most. I'm sorry."

"Well, I'm here now. Can I see him?"

"Yes. He is in a private room."

"How does he rate that?"

"He gets into terrible panics at night, and scares the other patients. Before, when he had more strength, he used to run around the ward screaming that he couldn't breathe. We would put him back to bed, tranquilize him, hook his oxygen back up. Now he is too weak to leave his bed, but he raves on about hell and damnation. He is afraid he is going to go to hell. It is not an uncommon fear for patients with mild dementia and a Catholic faith."

I remained silent. My uncle had never shown the least sign of any faith, Catholic or otherwise, but his fear of hell was justified.

"This way, please," said a nurse, ushering me towards his room. The door was ajar. I remember hesitating. I had not laid eyes on Conroy in years.

The lighting was dim, but even under stage lights I would not have recognized the man, except for the dreadful cauliflower ear. His face and form were half the size I remembered, his cheeks had caved in, the cannula in his nostrils revolted me. His boney arms lay bare on the sheets, the ancient skin snakelike, rough, darkened, weathered.

He turned his head slowly to see who had come in. Those alarming mismatched brown eyes squinted in my direction.

I approached the bed. "So, Uncle, there you are."

"What took you so long?" he retorted.

"I've been getting reports of your bad behavior from the nurses. You were disrupting the ward at night, running about in your hospital gown yelling your head off. Not a pretty sight, I imagine."

"Fuck the damn ward." He gasped. It was taking him great effort to speak. "This place is a prison. At night they cut off my air and I can't breathe! They don't give me enough oxygen."

"You have smoked yourself into emphysema, Uncle dear, so you actually don't have enough oxygen, but these kind and diligent nurses are providing you with all that you need, not that you deserve it."

He turned to look at me directly for the first time. "What the hell d'ya mean by that?" he croaked. "Who the hell are you anyway?"

"You know exactly who I am, and what I mean."

He said nothing more, his eyes slide off my face as if unwilling to see me any longer.

"I need more air. The bitches are killing me. They want me to know what hell is going to be like." This rant left him breathless.

Did I smile? Yes.

"What can I do?" he whined suddenly, his voice was pitiable.

"Lie still. Just as you have been told. See, here? Here is the line sending oxygen right into the cannula and up your nose."

I held the tube aloft between my thumb and forefinger for a moment where he could see it. I could feel the faint pressure of air passing within. It was working properly.

"Just lie still and breathe in little breaths. There will be enough air if you lie very, very still, and take tiny, tiny breaths. You will soon relax and be able to sleep."

I said this as if I knew what I was talking about. He lay quietly for a moment, the oxygen giving him strength.

"Who are you anyway? I know. You're Nora Ellen. Kingsley's brat. Kingsley. Handsome Kingsley. Older Kingsley. Smarter Kingsley. Dead Kingsley." His eyes narrowed. "You got old Nora Ellen. Where's my brat? Where's Emma? Oh, she's dead. No, that's a lie, just outta the way. Good riddance. Who needs kids? Where's Fletcher?"

"Slovenia."

"Who's Slovenia? Some woman? Fletcher only likes men. Disgusting faggot son. He's a faggot, right?"

"How about if you just shut up and breathe."

It was then that I arose, went to the door, and looked out into the corridor. All was quiet. I shut the door and came back to the bedside.

I heard him murmur. "Holy Mary, Mother of God."

"Oh, no you don't! We'll have no last minute purging of your damned soul! You will go to your account with all your imperfections on your head." I think I kicked the bed.

He stopped praying abruptly and seemed to lose consciousness, then awoke with a start. "Nazis!" he choked out. He looked around wildly.

"No one here but your next of kin. It is fate, I believe, that brings us together at such a moment."

He peered at me, confused. "Fate?"

"Yours and mine. Now let's see what it will be."

He continued to stare. Did he understand?

I held the tubing loosely in my hand. My palm was dry. My own breathing felt normal, and I could hear my heart, temperately keeping time.

"I'll sit right here until you drift off," I said in my gentlest of stage voices. Did he catch the irony in my tone?

I watched as he calmed down and his shallow breath became slower. I knew I didn't have to do a thing. He would die of his own accord soon enough, and not easily. I could, if I wished, for life must have its ironies, be kind only to be cruel.

Looking again at the flexible tubing, so thin, so fragile, delivering his wisps of oxygen, I knew it was the only thing this greedy man had left to crave in life. I picked it up again, letting it rest in my palm. The lifeline felt smooth and warm.

Suddenly his eyes flew open and he stared directly at me, panic seizing his features. Yes! He understood. He knew that I, Nora Ellen Dean, Kingsley's brat, held his life in my hand.

"This is for my father whom you murdered without mercy," I said calmly, pinching the tubing, cutting off the oxygen flow.

Conroy tried to reach for me, but was too weak and fell back, his wide, frightened eyes stared at my face.

"I'm right, aren't I?"

He said nothing, but he jerked his eyes away from mine, providing the guilty confession I required.

I released the pressure, allowing the oxygen to flow again, then held up the life-giving cord where he could see it clearly and pinched it again between my thumb and trigger finger.

"And this is for my sister, tiny Emma, who you told me had died; and this is for my mother whom you drove into madness and an early death; and this for my grandmother, your own mother, whose heart you broke into pieces with your actions and your lies."

I kept squeezing the oxygen supply off momentarily, over and over, as I pronounced each of his crimes.

There it was! The look of pure terror I had wished to see.

I pressed my free hand down upon his chest, quelling his weak movements. His eyes flashed with outrage. And then, something else. Something perverse. His lip curled and in that horrifying expression I recognized pleasure. He had brought forth pure evil from my soul and he was enjoying the sight of it, my wish to kill him; reducing me to someone no better than himself.

He stared at me in satisfaction, then the eyelids jerked, narrowed, and closed. His breath became hoarse, uneven, then seemed to stop.

Had I done it?

His eyes flashed open and I stared into the abyss of pure evil that he was now seeing reflected in my own eyes, and its force seemed to slap me down into the bedside chair.

He was gasping audibly now and his hand again flailed in my direction as I allowed the oxygen to flow freely.

He sucked in a breath, and another, but then he seemed to collapse inwardly, as if all the fight had gone out of him. Still he stared. He was waiting. Daring me.

It required only one more closure of my finger to my thumb.

I dropped the tubing. He sneered, and his exhausted breaths evened out as oxygen filled his ruined lungs, *becoming shallow and far apart. His eyes again closed. I knew the struggle had rendered him unconscious.*

I sat staring at the still, almost dead man, one who had in life so mercilessly destroyed my family. He was now just a helpless, yellowing, bag of decay.

Though it might be minutes, or hours, or even days, before he took a final breath, it would not have been the natural, gentle passing that it would seem to others. Nor would it be murder.

I had stepped back from the horror of deliberately taking another's life, and had issued him a reprieve, to make of it what he would; giving him a last few gasps of his miserable life.

I called for the solicitous nurses, and on their arrival I performed a scene of great distress, producing the requisite number of sighs and utterances at such a sad spectacle of a dying man. Weeping actor's tears, I left the hospital. I said I would be back the next day to manage bills and paperwork. I lied.

Outside, I sat for a while in a nearby park shaking from feelings that were all too real, and returned on the first flight I could get to New York.

The next morning I received another call. Uncle Conroy had died in the night. The nurse who delivered the news, assuming I would grieve, and not knowing what had transpired in that oh-so-private room, assured me that he had passed peacefully.

I can see myself then, standing in my apartment holding the dead phone long after the nurse had rung off. I felt no guilt, no remorse, no joy, no relief, no accomplishment, but I burst into unexpected tears and wept violently.

And now, with my own life drawing to a close, what

self-judgment should I render? I made this evil man face what he had done and briefly suffer for his actions. He had felt the fear of death from my hand, then asked for death, knowing it would blacken my soul.

Should not the love I felt for my murdered father require me to revenge him at any cost? Yet in that moment when I had only to press my finger and thumb together for one moment longer, I had not done so.

Why had I not? Was I a coward?

The answer that comes to me now is simple. I was the child of a fine and loving man. I was my father's daughter. I was Kingsley's brat. I had chosen to honor his memory by not doing murder. Conroy has been left singular in his depravity.

Elsinora had not noticed when the music of the recorded symphony had ended. Her mind rang only with Hamlet's words:

"Thus conscience does make cowards of us all,
And thus the native hue of resolution
Is sicklied o'er with the pale cast of thought,
And enterprises of great pitch and moment
With this regard their currents turn awry
And lose the name of action."

Thankfully.

Exhausted now, Elsinora walked towards her bed, pausing before the mirror in the dimly lit hallway. There, beside her own image a ghostly figure seemed to sway within the reflection. "Who's there?" she whispered.

It was her father's image. Gently he floated away into the mirror's depths leaving behind a slowly dissolving smile.

XL. Time out of joint.

"IT IS TIME for me to make an exit. We must attend to this immediately," Elsinora announced this as if she needed to catch a train. "By the way, the vegetable fritters were excellent tonight."

Hesper and Elsinora had just finished a light dinner together.

Have I forgotten some event? wondered Hesper. Lately her mind had been all awhirl, remembering her luxurious second week in Bermuda, thinking of Rosetta, of things said, and touched, and felt. She had not yet told Elsinora of her love affair, but maybe, in spite of her discretion, some change in her demeanor was apparent to her employer, for Elsinora had smiled knowingly at her return. Did she know? Surely not. Did it matter?

"I believe all *my* affairs are now in order," said Elsinora, "and yours, if I am not mistaken, are in happy disorder. Am I right?"

"How did you know?"

"You glow." Elsinora paused and smiled. "And now you blush. It becomes you."

Hesper could feel the heat in her face. I'm like a schoolgirl with her first crush, she silently chided herself. "It's true. I met someone," she admitted. "Her name is Rosetta, and she is a lovely person. You would like her."

"Maybe, maybe not. What is important is that you like her. Her. Interesting. I truly wish you well."

"Thank you." Hesper managed, relieved that her news had been met with acceptance.

"Now, as I was saying, my affairs are in order, my possessions well disposed, Fletcher is dead, as are many of my old and dear friends. Those that remain are content, and you, dear Hesper, have even managed to slip a wedge of happiness onto the grim plate that is life, which pleases me."

She smiled again, a somewhat wistful smile, and continued.

"I have reviewed my life and I have made peace with the past. Yes, I have regrets. Who does not? But I believe I have acted justly in an inherently unjust world, been of some small benefit to others, and can now depart with a clear conscience."

"Depart?"

"I have decided it is time for me to die."

Hesper startled. She blinked in disbelief, but there was a tone in her employer's voice; a tone she knew well and it indicated that Elsinora meant business.

"No one just decides to die," she countered.

"What other people do or don't do has not been of much interest to me for a very long time, as you, of all people, certainly know. I have nothing I particularly wish to experience in life anymore, the country I grew up in has gone to the wolves, and I don't want to live long enough to become incapacitated or to suffer from some malicious disease. So I will now take a bow and leave the stage."

Hesper's mind was reeling. "What can you be thinking of? Suicide? No way!"

"There. There. Tomorrow evening perhaps you will create for me one of your particularly delicious dinners, and we will have it with the best wine from the cellar. You can invite the boys over for this last meal if you wish, but you will not say a word to them of my decision. I don't want to deal with the ruckus they would make."

"Last meal? My food is not lethal."

"Your food is always excellent, dear, but I plan to stop eating, just as I did as a child after my father went missing, and as I did for a brief time after Fletcher died. After your lovely meal, I will neither eat nor drink ever again. I'm going to go to bed and start rereading my favorite novels and plays. In a few days I will grow too weak to hold a book. Perhaps you will read to me then, as I drift in and out of sleep? There will be periods of unconsciousness that will last longer and longer. Then I will die. I suggest you call a nurse in to tend to my most intimate needs. The whole business will be over within a couple of weeks. And it is perfectly legal. The government cannot yet force-feed someone. You run no risk of prosecution for being in attendance. I have seen to all the legalities."

"But why would you want to die? You are in good health, you have all your wits, and you are more than comfortably well off. You still enjoy reading and finding new authors to support, and have people who care for you. It doesn't make any sense."

Elsinora was thoughtful for a while. She held up a book. "Hesper, have you ever been reading a book, a good one which you are enjoying and then, for no particular reason, you suddenly have had enough of the thing? You put a bookmark into place, and set the book aside."

"Yes. It has happened sometimes."

"Well, I have grown tired of life in the same way. I just want to put it down."

"But you can't come back to life the way you can come back to a book, later on, in a different mood."

"That I have considered. Some books go unfinished. It's not a tragedy. Now will you be kind and cooperative in this?"

"If I refuse?"

"Oh, Hesper," Elsinora chided. "Do we not know each other better than that by now? It is the kind of death you would wish for me, is it not? To die peacefully in my own bed with the sound of literature in my ears. I know it seems one of my particularly unusual choices, and that you have to ritually protest, but in the long run you won't deny me your kind attention. You've never denied me anything important that I can think of. Now you go and sort out what you would like to cook, and I'll get the right books down from the shelves."

"No."

"No?" Elsinora's eyebrows raised.

"No."

"You mean that?"

"I mean it."

"Oh dear. Then I suppose I will have to shoot myself. But this is curious. You better tell me more about this…what's her name? Rosetta?"

"Rosetta? Rosetta has nothing to do with this."

"Of course she does, dear Hesper. We have often sparred with each other, you and I, but you have never refused a directive outright. This is a sudden change in you, from a compliant and trustworthy companion to a full-blooded rebel. Why, look at your hands. You have clenched your fists. Rosetta has changed you."

"I have changed *myself*."

"You're right to correct me, but she has surely been the catalyst. This is the kind of transformation that only love can bring about. Rosetta must love you, and you her."

"Yes. I believe she does. I do. We do." It felt strange to be saying such a private feeling aloud.

"Magnificent. I had almost forgotten how love can take one by force, and mold one into the very finest version of oneself."

To Hesper's astonishment, Elsinora began to laugh.

"I don't see what's so funny! And I don't like being laughed at."

"I am not laughing at you, Hesper. I am laughing at how amazing life can sometimes be. I am remembering how a healing touch, an empowering love, once transformed me from a self-centered and rather unpleasant human being into a tolerably acceptable one. His love healed me when I was broken and lost, and it helped me to find myself, my best self, to go on into a life that has made sense for me. Sadly, this new improved self had to live life without him. He was pledged to another. Life sometimes deals out heartbreak with its blessings."

"Who was he?"

Elsinora paused, judging Hesper. She seldom spoke of Maurice. He was a precious memory that needed to be placed into caring hands, as she had done when she had told Doris about him.

"Maurice was a doctor, a healer, and a gentleman. It has been over forty years since I last saw him, but my love has not lessened in all that time. Love, the particular kind of which I speak, is a force woven into the fabric of the universe. It arises and seizes us without our consent, enfolds us, infuses us. This force has found me twice. Once in my father's arms as he lifted me up in farewell, and once in the hands of Maurice as he restored me to health. I've loved in many other ways, as I did Fletcher or Oliver-Paul, or Shakespeare or the night sky, and though every love nourishes us and teaches us how best to be human, *this* love, this power of which I now speak, is of a different nature from all the others.

"Think of it, Hesper. Everything in our lives is in motion, in ceaseless, unrelenting change, but this stays constant. In time we realize that, by an act of grace, we have been united, not with a man, nor woman either, but with the one power in all of existence that is unchanging and eternal.

"It is this silent enduring force that has been my strength, and now, dear Hesper, if I am right, it has seized you and Rosetta. *This* love gives you its strength. Am I right? It's a rather grand thing, don't you think?"

"I can believe what you say is true, Mrs. Harding. I mean all this about the power of love. And I do feel stronger somehow. But I wonder if it occurs to you, that I might simply hold an affection for you that would prevent me from allowing you to harm yourself, Rosetta or no Rosetta?"

"Forgive me. It has never been easy for me to acknowledge unearned good will. There was a neighbor once…and a librarian—" Her voice trailed off.

How much the past is with her, thought Hesper, while I think only of the future.

"Well, both of us will have to make some adjustments then, won't we?" declared Elsinora at last.

Hesper saw her lips tighten and relax, her head turn a little to the left, then the right, as though trying to put her thoughts in order.

"You know that I care for you in return, although I am not graceful in saying such things unless, of course, they are part of a script that has been written by someone else." She was able to smile once the words were out. "So that is quite enough of awkward affection. I am enormously pleased for you, and for Rosetta."

"All of what you have just told me came in response to my 'no'?"

"Yes. And now I am very tired and must sleep. We will talk no more of suicide tonight. Goodnight, Hesper."

Elsinora stood and left the room with slow but steady steps.

Hesper, so swiftly dismissed after such an emotion-filled conversation, felt equal measures of distress and relief as she made her way to her own room. She believed a crisis had been averted, but for how long? Since Fletcher's death Elsinora had become increasingly erratic, difficult to anticipate, sometimes showing her characteristic steel, at other moments seemingly as fragile as ribbon candy.

As Hesper fretted over her employer's state of mind, Elsinora was walking through her house quietly. She took time to notice the many things within it that she had curated and cherished over the years... small original paintings and bronze sculptures, fine furnishings, China vases, Japanese prints... they were only things, but beautiful things that belonged to a world from which she was soon scheduled to depart. She felt a satisfaction in knowing that Hesper would care for them well. She went to her library and opened the locked box with her cigar box of mementos, her journal, and Uncle Conroy's gun.

A few moments later Hesper passed the closed library door, and was surprised to hear Elsinora moving about inside. Why had she gone to her books and not to her bed? She had looked ancient and sounded exhausted.

The evening light that had made its way into the hallway was fading fast and Hesper was tired, but she hesitated. Standing still, outside the library door, she allowed the words of their conversation to play again through her mind: *depart, time to die, tired of life, leave the stage, no more talk, close the book*— and suddenly she knew what she must do.

She hurried to her room and made two telephone calls in quick succession. Those accomplished she found she was too agitated for sleep. Rather than prepare for bed she sat at her desk and called Rosetta, but on reaching her was unable to convey with any precision what had just occurred; how a discussion of suicide had morphed into a speech on the healing power of love, but left her, nevertheless deeply unsettled, both sure and unsure about the phone calls she had just placed.

Outside her windows, the darkness had completed its fall.

The doorbell rang, its chimes interrupting their conversation.

Hesper made her way quickly to the front door. Looking through the glass she saw an attractive, elderly man standing in the circle of yellow porch light. He was wearing a well-cut suit, and was holding a hat. He appeared perfectly harmless.

Well, I'll be damned, she thought. I'm really good at this, and with a sure hand she pulled open the door without delay.

It had taken only the two swift telephone calls. The first call was to Doris Graves, whom she had guessed correctly, knew his full name, and said if he was still alive he was probably in New York City and that she could perhaps find a listing for him on the internet. The second was to his number where she left a detailed message on his answering machine.

And now here he stood with his eyes so filled with the anticipation of seeing Elsinora that Hesper felt like she had become invisible. She stepped aside and, just as a pistol shot was heard, Dr. Maurice Schadad entered Arden Manor to be reunited with the woman he loved.

There was no time for introductions.

"The library!" Hesper shouted and ran. Maurice followed, though his old bones refused to run.

A second shot rang out. It must mean that the first shot has not killed her, thought Hesper. Was she wounded? Trying a second time? She was almost at the library door.

Another shot. Maurice, his heart pounding was a room behind Hester's frantic progress through the house. He felt his whole body jolt with each concussion.

Hesper grasped the handle to the library, thanking God as it turned, that it was not locked. She pushed open the heavy door.

Elsinora sat unmoving in the big winged armchair, the gun in one hand, her journal in the other, both resting in her lap. Her eyes were closed and her expression seemed one of contentment.

"Oh my God!" cried Hesper.

Elsinora raised her head. Their eyes met. Elsinora raised the pistol and pointed it across the room indicating the opposite wall where flames burned low in the fireplace grate. Hesper's eyes followed the aim.

On the mantelpiece over the fireplace, the three Oscar statuettes had each been shot to pieces.

"Annie Oakley," said Elsinora, with a bemused smile, blowing on the end of the pistol. "Forgive me, Hesper. It was impulsive of me. The statuettes always represented capitulation to me, not accomplishment."

Astonished, Hesper watched as, with a steady hand, Elsinora removed the remaining bullets from the revolver and placed them on the end table. Then she tossed the gun into the flames. "My uncle's gun will not kill again."

Next she held up the journal and then flung it into the fire where it landed on top of the sizzling pistol.

"And so Uncle, there you are!" Elsinora exclaimed, as the flames flared, illuminating her fierce look of satisfaction.

Hesper stood astounded. Elsinora was burning a book! What in God's name could have been written on the now blackening pages?

Then, as Elsinora registered a second figure arriving in the doorway, her expression rearranged itself into one of perplexity.

"Who's there? she whispered. Her eyes were still as blue ice. She stared at the breathless man who stood in the shadows beside Hesper, as if she might be seeing an actual ghost.

Maurice's expression was one of relief as he saw that Elsinora was alive, and recovering both his breath and his composure he stepped further into the room, into a circle of lamplight.

He spoke with a tenderness that seemed to place time somewhere outside the room. "Remember me?"

Elsinora stood up from the armchair with a grace that defied her age, and turned slowly to fully face Maurice.

Hesper and the library faded into backdrop. Elsinora stepped slowly forward into the shared light, as if onto the center of a stage.

"Remember thee? Yea, from the table of my memory I'll wipe away all trivial, fond records,

All saws of books, all forms, all pressures past,

That youth and observation copied there,

And thy commandment all alone shall live

Within the book and volume of my brain,

Unmixed with baser matter."

And she merged into his awaiting arms.

XLI. High on a stage, be placed to a view.

IT WAS NOT long after their reunion when Elsinora found herself sitting alone backstage in the green room of a Hollywood theater watching, on a large monitor, the shenanigans taking place onstage. There was Lance Brilliante raving about her talent and how he adored her. She stifled a guffaw. The last time she had walked onto a Broadway stage or stood before a Hollywood movie camera he hadn't been born. Nor, perhaps had his father.

Behind him, on a giant backdrop, flashes of her work began to appear and disappear, clips from all of her films. She *was* pretty. Oliver-Paul had never allowed a shot in her movies that didn't become her, sometimes reshooting whole scenes under more flattering lights to enhance her beauty.

There she was as Anna Karenina, Mary Queen of Scots, Anne Boleyn. My, she did lose her head a lot. Now they were showing a scene from *Joan of Arc,* the film that failed. She was burned at the stake in that one. What had Oliver-Paul been trying to tell her? What had all the male playwrights and screenwriters been saying about women? There she was as Cleopatra with her deadly asps, as mad Ophelia, about to commit suicide, and there as Desdemona soon to be murdered by her husband. Why, she had died in every film, and lived to tell the tale.

Now Brilliante was enumerating her stage credits. Oh, don't bore them with that, she thought, but on he went, her life truly flashing before her eyes as she listened to the list. The audience was quiet. Could they really be attentive? Or were they bored? She knew how to read an audience. She listened. They were rapt. And now he was speaking of her years at The Thespian Atelier, how she inspired generations of young actors to attempt and succeed at Shakespeare; how she had volunteered in underserved schools to teach the classics. Her lifetime achievements. She had only immersed herself in what she truly loved, and as she had aged she had shared those things with others.

A production assistant, who was young enough to be a great grandchild, reached out a helping hand.

"Ms. Dean?"

"Mrs. Harding," she corrected.

"Sorry. Mrs. Harding. It's time for you to go on stage."

Elsinora smiled, and stood up without taking the girl's hand. "All right, Mr. DeMille. I'm ready for my closeup," she said.

"Huh?"

She was escorted by this virtual child from the green room to the wings of the stage. She noticed that she felt no fright at all. She had agreed to participate in this event on the condition that no speech would be required of her, so there was nothing to fear.

A grinning Lance Brilliante opened his arms wide in her direction, and Elsinora stepped firmly onto the stage wearing a perfect smile, one she had crafted carefully for this occasion, composed of equal parts happiness and humility. The audience applauded loudly.

She stood before them all in a stunning blue and silver kimono of flowered silk which complimented her features, her silver hair, her pale complexion. It enhanced her slight but still curvaceous figure, its hem just brushing the floor, concealing the medium-heeled pumps she had chosen which allowed for a steady gait but also a bit of feminine lift and allure. Her eyes were caught in the gleam of the lights. Those famously sky-blue eyes.

She knew exactly where he was in the sea of faces, and her smile changed to one of deepest affection as her eyes caught his. Those loving, steel-gray eyes.

Maurice was seated with Hesper and Rosetta, Robbie and Geraldo, all grinning like Cheshire cats. Doris was alongside them wearing her calm approval face. The whole audience was standing up now. The applause continued and Elsinora slowly began to realize that she was enjoying herself. She had finally agreed to making this appearance, not because she cared about the achievement award. Her life was its own achievement. She was here because she wanted these few people who knew her, yet loved her, to enjoy this experience.

Now she was allowing the smiles and the applause to reach her, perhaps for the first time in her life. How lovely it felt to be cheered, not as Cleopatra or Rosalind, or even Hamlet, but as Elsinora Dean Harding.

How would Mrs. Richie or Mrs. Kellogg or Grandma Bessie feel if they could be here to see this? Her mother would warn her not to get too close to the edge of the stage. The thought made her laugh out loud, and at the sight the crowd laughed with her in delight. How pleased Fletcher would have been to see her shine. Perhaps Emma, her sometime sister, was watching on a television set far away, not knowing of their kinship, protected by Elsinora's discretion from the cruel knowledge of her natural parents. She wished her well. What would her father think of her? She hoped it would be pride.

And what did *she* feel?

As her movie images cartwheeled across the gigantic screens behind her, Elsinora stepped, unexpectedly, to the podium.

She looked at the applauding audience for a long, long time, allowing herself to take in and be warmed by their genuine appreciation. When the theater quieted at last in response to her stillness, she spoke.

"When first I heard of this award I had no wish to accept it," she said, in a voice trained to reach the back of the house. "Perhaps, I was o'er hasty?"

She smiled and the audience laughed again.

"You have remembered me. Thank you."

She received her Oscar and held it slightly aloft.

"This one I will cherish."

Elsinora Dean Harding then gave the audience a perfect bow, and left the stage forever.

Acknowledgments

It takes a team to bring a novel into being and I am blessed with extraordinary good fortune in that regard, beginning with my wonderful publishers, Mary Bahr and Ulrich Baer at Warbler Press, and their "proofreading goddess." Thank you.

> "Those friends thou hast, and their adoption tried,
> Grapple them unto thy soul with hoops of steel."

So thank you to my friends Michael, Meredith and Daniel Bergmann who support my life and work in every possible way; to Ann Davies, Hatti Figge, and Milton Deemer who have been invaluable supporters of this novel from the beginning to the very last line.

And, of course, to William.